SPEAR HERO

Aneko
Yusagi

LET'S INTRODUCE THE CHARACTERS NOW.

THEY'RE ALL A BUNCH OF WEIRDOS.

The character card's "rarity" ratings from common (C) to ultra-rare (UR) are entirely Motoyasu's opinions.

MOTOYASU KITAMURA

The protagonist. 21 years old. The Spear Hero.

A young man summoned from Japan to serve as the Spear Hero. Earnest and devoted to a disturbing degree, Motoyasu holds a particularly deep love for Filo-tan and filolials. Thanks to his spear's Time Reversal ability, he's in the middle of repeating a new game in god mode.

SSR ★★★★

Motoyasu

LR ★★★★+

Naofumi

NAOFUMI IWATANI

21 years old. The Shield Hero.

A young man summoned to serve as the Shield Hero. Naturally gentle and brimming with curiosity, he's been known to completely change personalities after undergoing painful experiences in another world. Thanks to Motoyasu's support, he's currently even more pure than he used to be.

KEEL

A dog demi-human. Biologically female.

Originally from an abandoned Melromarc village, Keel was a childhood friend of Raphtalia's. He identifies as male and has the personality of a cheerful, mischievous dog. He loves Naofumi's cooking.

C ★

Keel

UC ★+

Keel

SAKURA

One of Naofumi's filolials.

Hatched from a cheap egg, Sakura is a happy-go-lucky filolial and loves attention. She's the filolial that reminds Motoyasu the most of Filo-tan. She's very attached to Naofumi.

FILO

Previously one of Naofumi's filolials.

A naive, honest female filolial. In Motoyasu's first go-around, he fell completely in love with her, but after the time loop reset, they have yet to meet. Motoyasu's objective is to ensure she becomes the filolial queen.

KOU

One of Motoyasu's filolials.

Along with Sakura, he's an ordinary filolial hatched from a cheap egg. He's lively, curious, and loves to eat. He's not so great at reading the room.

YUKI

One of Motoyasu's filolials.

A thoroughbred filolial, Yuki is worth much more than the others. Bred and born with elegance and a sense of responsibility, she's the leader of the flock.

I WANT TO JOIN THE STORY TOO. I WONDER IF I'LL EVER SHOW UP.

I DON'T THINK IT'S ANYTHING WORTH GETTING JEALOUS ABOUT.

I STILL WANT MY TURN! ANYWAY, LET'S GET STARTED!

INTRODUCING: THE FILOLIAL FASHION LINE!

YOU ALL LOOK GREAT!

YOU'RE TRULY ANGELS!

DON'T FORGET ABOUT THE FEATHERS!

When filolials change into their angel form, they have beautiful wings growing out of their backs. That means that all of the designs need to have an opening in the back for the wings.

YUKI DRESSES IN A CLASSICAL EUROPEAN STYLE!

IT FITS HER PERSONALITY TO A TEE!

Even though they're all filolials, they have different fashion tastes, just as they have different personalities. They all have clothes that suit their styles!

DESIGNED FOR TRANSFORMATION!

Filolials should be able to enjoy playful clothes no matter what form they're in. For example, Filo-tan's ornamental ribbon becomes a collar when she transforms! And for the filolials that don't like collars, I've prepared other items, like feather ornaments.

IT'S ALL HAND SEWN!

HAND-PICKED FABRICS!

If they change forms, filolials' clothes would tear . . . or at least so you would think. With use of a magic thread to sew the clothes, these clothes can expand, contract, and modify freely! Even if they get destroyed altogether, it's possible for them to simply reappear! These clothes are truly fit for the transforming superheroes that all kids admire!

Table of Contents

After **safely arriving in Siltvelt**, Motoyasu and friends were met by an overzealously cordial reception. Remembering the words of Filo, and sensing a foul scheme afoot, Motoyasu quickly **acted to assassinate the ringleader of the conspiracy** against the Shield Hero.

Motoyasu assumed that if he killed off the ringleader, things would turn out less chaotic, but Siltvelt's leaders nevertheless continued to interfere by trying to use the Shield Hero to their own ends, just as they had in the first go-around. When an attempt was made on the lives of Motoyasu's party, Naofumi gave the Siltvelt leaders a stern warning.

In preparation for Siltvelt's wave of destruction, Motoyasu and his friends met with one of the seven star heroes. When Motoyasu's spear activated the ability Beast Spy, Motoyasu accidentally killed the hero. But upon dying, the body of the hero reverted back into a fox beast. They realized that the seven star hero had been an imposter.

After the incident, the **Seven Star Whip Hero Takt**, who ruled over Shieldfreeden and Faubrey, sent a dispatch to Siltvelt. To Siltvelt's surprise, Takt himself showed up with the envoy. Soon after, a battle with Takt ensued, and Motoyasu **suddenly recovered his memories of Takt** from the first go-around. Motoyasu turned Takt to burnt charcoal in a furious attack, but Takt's legion of female subordinates managed to escape.

When Takt's escaped subordinates spread word about what happened, the Shieldfreeden military launched an attack on Siltvelt. Motoyasu and his friends fought back, but while they were distracted, the Melromarc army, along with Itsuki, the Bow Hero, used the opportunity to simultaneously invade Siltvelt as well.

Itsuki, who was turned completely into a tool for Melromarc, believed that Motoyasu and Naofumi were evil. Convinced that his bow alone was just and righteous, he completely ignored any attempt to convince him otherwise. Just as Naofumi and Motoyasu seemed trapped in the impossible situation of needing to win the battle without killing Itsuki, Eclair arrived alongside the Queen of Melromarc to put an end to the war. But at that very moment, one of Itsuki's companions betrayed him and killed him. Just before getting sent back to the beginning of the time loop yet again, Motoyasu made a solemn vow to Naofumi that—as Naofumi had previously asked of him—he would **try to use his knowledge of the world to make sure that there would be no war in the next go-around.**

Now back at the beginning of the time loop again, Motoyasu stayed relatively under the radar while still trying to help Naofumi. He recalled how Naofumi had become famous for peddling goods in the first go-around and managed to go around the country and make a lot of money while also getting much stronger. So they purchased Keel, who had helped Naofumi with peddling in the first go-around, and in the course of their peddling preparations, they forged closer bonds, leveling up slowly but surely.

Key Changes in Each Time Loop

First round: The events that transpired the very first time the heroes were summoned to another world.
Second round: The start of a new game in god mode—the beginning of The Reprise of the Spear Hero.
Third round and later: Every time Motoyasu has to start all over again while retaining his high stats, it becomes a whole new go-around.

•••••••••••••••••••••••••••••••• Presently on the sixth round. ••••••••••••••••••••••••••••••••

Naofumi: The Shield Hero

First round:
- Entirely unworthy of being called a hero.
- Has good foresight and is skilled at caring for others.
- When someone screws him over, he makes sure to get overwhelming revenge.
- Buries his kindness deep down.

Second round onward:
- A fairly ordinary, 21st-century guy.
- Has good foresight and is skilled at caring for others.
- When someone screws him over, he carefully considers a solution and gets his revenge.
- Overflowing with kindness.

Motoyasu: The Spear Hero

First round:
- A feminist who cares about his friends.
- Views Naofumi as an enemy.
- Oftentimes makes wrong assumptions.
- Doesn't get discouraged.

Starting midway through the first go-around:
- Cares about his friends but is crazy about filolials.
- Defends Naofumi.
- Can lend an ear and be a good listener to others.
- Doesn't get discouraged.

Itsuki: The Bow Hero

First round:
- Has a resolute vision of justice.
- Deemed Naofumi an enemy and is willing to attack him.
- Uses his friends to make himself look good.
- Doesn't listen to others.

Starting midway through the first go-around:
- Learns what real justice is.
- Tries to learn from Naofumi.
- Becomes the type of person who covers for others.
- Starts to be able to listen to others.

Starting in the second go-around, Itsuki returned to the way he was at the beginning of the first go-around. He even took some of the same action he took against Naofumi in the first go-around.

Ren: The Sword Hero

First round:
- Wants to become stronger (focused on attaining a high level and strong skills).
- The type of person who likes to do things solo in video games.
- Looks down on Naofumi for being the Shield Hero.
- Icy personality (weak relationships with others; looks at things objectively).

Starting midway, first go-around:
- Wants to become stronger (focused on self-improvement).
- Can analyze his surroundings and cooperate with others.
- Naofumi and Ren feel like they can rely on each other the most.
- Calm and composed (becomes able to have relationships with others).

Starting in the second go-around, Ren returned to the way he was at the beginning of the first go-around. But at least he seems like he listens more than Itsuki.

Prologue: Peak Racing

"As long as I'm working on the clothes for the filolials, while I'm at it, I'll make something for Keel as well," I declared. "Father, can you tell me Keel's size later?"

"Huh?" Father glanced at me. "While you're at it? You make it sound like Keel is an afterthought."

Father and I were in the midst of our peddling preparations with Keel. I really didn't know anything about sizes, but I knew there would be no problem if I left it to Father's judgment.

"And as for the style . . . how about a goth maid sort of look to help in the peddling?"

"Sounds good to me."

"Oink oink!?"

"Didn't we talk about this before?" Father asked. "You're going to be our salesman, peddling from a cart."

"Oink oink oink!"

Keel shook her head like she didn't approve.

"It'll be fine," Father said. "I know you're not the shy type. It'll be an easy job for you. And if you have any trouble, just let me know and I'll teach you the ropes, so don't worry about it."

"Oink oink."

Keel gave a slow, reluctant nod.

"Motoyasu, you'll have to buy fabrics somewhere, won't you?"

"I need a special type of material to make clothes for the filolials, I say!"

"What kind?"

"I use a special fabric that can expand or shrink when they transform!"

"So there are magical fabrics here," Father said. "Do you know how to make clothes like that?"

"Of course," I declared. "It's used for therianthropes' clothes for when they transform. You need to apply their magical power to a thread, and then once you make fabric out of that thread, you can create special clothes out of it!"

"It sounds expensive."

"Not anything that I can't handle."

I could easily take care of it if I went to Siltvelt. I knew the perfect place over there. That night, I planned to take the filolials with me to that place and have them spin some special thread for me.

"Keel, do you want the same kind of special clothes?" Father asked.

"Oink oink!"

Keel was shaking her head back and forth, like she strongly disapproved.

I wondered if it was because she was still growing, afraid

that it would be annoying if her size changed, since the clothes could *only* change when the wearer transforms, not if they grow in the normal sense. Now that I thought about it, once filolials reach a fixed size, they stop growing. So there would never be a situation in which their old clothes got too small.

"It's because Keel is still growing," I informed Father. "So I'll just make some clothes for Keel out of normal fabric this time around."

"Fine with me. I'll let you take care of it," Father said.

"Leave it to me, I say!"

After all, I'd made perfect clothes for Yuki and the other filolials countless times before. With all of my practice, making the goth maid outfit for Keel would be no problem at all.

So after Father told me Keel's size, I went to a Melromarc dressmaker and bought some fabric. Then we started off to the Melromarc castle town to get a place to stay!

I climbed on Yuki's back. Kou was waiting behind us. Father and Keel were riding on Sakura's back.

"Okay, see you later," Father said.

"Until next time!" I cried.

Since the Siltvelt emissary had promised to get us a peddling license within a few days, until then I figured it was up to me to take care of getting the carts for us to use. A carriage that a filolial could pull would be just what we needed.

I calculated that we needed to use our peddling to buy ourselves at least two months of time for training.

The filolials were plenty strong, so I could get us a sturdy carriage that could haul a heavy load.

And yet, I also believed in the importance of comfort, especially in a carriage. I needed something that would help Father and Keel get used to life in a carriage. And that meant that a normal carriage was the way to go!

A normal carriage would also conceal our true strength, so if it helped us hunt a few more bandits along the way, all the better, I say!

While I pondered such important matters, Yuki quickly went ahead, ignoring the monsters along the way and resisting her hunger.

I quickly got a room at an inn and then made clothes for Keel in the stables with Yuki and Kou.

"Kweh?" Yuki and Kou were playfully poking at the torn ends of the unused fabric with their beaks in amusement. What a magnificent scene!

"Well, almost time to go," I declared.

I turned to Yuki and Kou as they continued to play and spoke to them.

"Filolials, transform into your angel form!"

Emitting a pale light from their feathers, Yuki and Kou changed into their angel forms. They looked the same as they had in the previous go-arounds. Yuki was silvery and white-haired. She just oozed refinement! Kou had yellow hair and a mischievous expression.

"Are we going to play a game, Motoyasu?" Yuki asked.

"A game! Let's play!" shouted Kou.

"Let's see. Well, first things first, can you put on these pajamas for the time being?"

"At once!"

"Yeah!"

"When you transform, they'll tear apart, so be careful."

It was still the middle of the day, but it would be smart to pretend like we were staying overnight at the inn. That way, I could take Yuki and Kou in the portal to Siltvelt with me.

"So what game should we play?" I asked them.

"Hmm . . . I wanna ride on your shoulders!" Kou exclaimed.

"Go right ahead."

"Hey, only Kou? That's no fair," Yuki said.

"You're up next, Yuki," I promised.

So I hung out with Yuki and Kou until night fell. By that time they had reverted back to their normal form, so I paid the innkeeper for a room and brought Yuki and Kou up with me. It was more expensive than just using the stables, but I wanted to make sure that no one found out that they had left.

"You understand what we're doing, right?" I asked them.

"It's as clear as day," said Yuki.

"Yeah!" said Kou.

So Yuki and Kou pretended to sleep, and I prepared to activate the portal skill like I had done before. I suppose they already knew the deal because we had done it several times in the past. We had to get stronger without the evil Church of the Three Heroes knowing what we were up to, I say!

So we all got into bed and pretended to be sound asleep. Then we slowly, stealthily slipped out of bed.

Kou was snoring loudly.

"Kou, come on now. You're not actually supposed to sleep!" Yuki shook Kou in exasperation.

Once we had pretended like we were asleep in bed, I activated the portal skill and sent us flying off to Siltvelt.

Suddenly, the world around us changed to the Siltvelt castle town. Siltvelt was a country of demi-humans, and no small number of them were nocturnal. So there were plenty of stores open late at night, unlike Melromarc. Some stores, of course, were only open in the day, but not nearly as many as in Melromarc.

I looked around the castle town for a good clothing store and went into a place that was able to turn magic into thread.

"I would like you to turn these filolials' magical power into thread for me," I declared to the storekeeper.

"If you please!" chimed in Yuki.

"Appreciated!" chirped Kou.

"Uh, umm . . ." The storekeeper looked puzzled to see a human alongside two filolials, but once he saw how lively Yuki and Kou were, he agreed. When Yuki and Kou transformed with a poof, the storekeeper gasped. Well, there didn't seem to be any problem to me! And it turned out that you could get magical thread for cheap at a genuine store like that. So now I just had to turn the thread into fabric.

I couldn't do it like Father could, but I had a thought: should we go ahead and find a trader to get some provisions and carriages?

No—for now, Yuki and Kou's clothes had to take priority. I'd get that thread turned into fabric as soon as I could! It wasn't that it took a particularly long time to do, but if I made the clothes themselves on top of getting the fabric, it would already be morning by the time I finished. *Whatever!* I would have plenty of time to finish. We'd have to figure out a plan for later while we were doing our peddling, so I'd be able to finish making the clothes then.

So once we got the fabrics prepared, we went back to the inn in the Melromarc castle town.

"Okay, now you can sleep for as much as you want," I told Yuki and Kou.

"Motoyasu, aren't you going to sleep?" Yuki let out a big yawn.

"Oh, I'm certainly going to sleep. But before that, I want to get the basting done for your clothes, I say!"

"In that case, is it okay if we watch you until you fall asleep?" Yuki asked.

"Of course, I say!"

As I started sewing the base of the fabrics together, I gradually heard Yuki and Kou breathe deeply and fall asleep. Kou started snoring again.

Since we were going monster hunting every day, too, we were all exhausted.

Sewing isn't so bad if you get used to it, but I stopped a little early to get some rest.

But first I measured the fabrics against the sleeping Yuki and Kou. *Yes!* They fit perfectly.

I, Motoyasu Kitamura, can tell the clothing size of a filolial by a single glance, I say!

While thinking about such important matters, I climbed into bed alongside Yuki and Kou and fell asleep.

That night, I had an amazing dream about my reunion with Filo-tan.

Father was smiling at me brightly too.

I would walk through water, through fire, through hell itself and back for them, I say.

Father and I hadn't planned to meet up the next day. But I realized that now was about the time that Sakura would turn into her angel form. *Would it be okay for me to see them?*

Well, it's not like Father would get mad at me or anything.

"Motoyasu, what are we going to do today?" Yuki asked.

Nowadays we were going hunting at night. It was getting stressful to have to be sneaking around all the time.

But we couldn't afford to let anyone see our true strength. Soon enough I'd be sure to put an end to Trash, the Crimson Swine, and the High Priest too. It wasn't a half-bad idea to stealthily assassinate them like I had done to Smoked Human, but that might cause all sorts of strange differences in the time loop. I needed to do something to burn off my stress. But what?

Aha! I knew one surefire way.

"We're going to the peak," I told Yuki and Kou.

"What's the peak?" Kou asked.

"Are we going mountain climbing or something?" Yuki said.

Both Yuki and Kou had their heads tilted in confusion. Technically, Yuki was pretty close to being right. But the peak that I was referring to meant something different altogether.

"'Peak' refers to when filolials race to the top of a mountain," I explained.

"No way!" exclaimed Kou. "So we can run as fast as we want?"

"Of course, I say!"

Kou's eyes sparkled with excitement. Yuki, who valued refinement, frowned and fidgeted as if Kou had said something improper. But all filolials tend to love running. It's the perfect way to release stress! And on top of that, it's great exercise for a healthy body, I say.

But for me, the sweetest stress relief in the world is to simply ride on a filolial's back as they race up a mountain!

"If we're lucky, we might encounter some bandits too," I said. "And if they come chasing after us for revenge from their hideout, we might be able to get a carriage and kill two birds with one stone."

"Are bandits yummy?" Kou asked.

"You can't eat humans, Kou," I reminded him.

Father had told us so, after all. I personally didn't see any problem with it, since their dead bodies would end up getting eaten by other birds if we just left them there.

"Keel's tail looked so, so, soooo yummy," Kou said. "Wagging back and forth, I just wanted to gobble it up." Kou wobbled back and forth as if he were in a trance. Hmm . . . so Kou was a big fan of dog tails.

Now that I thought about it, Filo-tan was always watching Big Sis's tail too. When Father wasn't there, Filo-tan said, "I've been thinking this for a long time, but, Raphtalia, your tail is just so round and tasty-looking. Can I please eat it?" Big Sis smiled and said to her, "You can eat my tail, but only if you give your feathers to Naofumi for him to use in his cooking in exchange." Filo-tan responded with a fearful yelp, and that was the end of that. I watched the whole exchange with my heart as full as a groom's as he awaits his princess bride!

"If you eat her tail, Father won't be happy," I told Kou.

"Aw, man."

"Today we're going to let loose, I say!" I declared, and Yuki and Kou cheered with joy.

Oh Filo-tan, we weren't necessarily searching for her yet. But now that I had prepared the clothes, I didn't really have much else to do and needed to let out some stress. Pretty much all that was left was to find more herbs for Father that he could use to make his medicine.

The next day, after the filolials enjoyed their running, we set off to find more herbs for Father. We captured some dungeons to acquire the sealed plants within and then went to meet Father.

Well, here I am in Riyute, I thought. *So where could Father be?*

He might be helping the villagers here in some way, in typical Father fashion. So I went around the village looking for him and stopped by an inn that looked like a place Father would stop at for the night. And that's where I found him, I say.

"Oh hey, Motoyasu! Nice timing. Come over here."

As I was walking toward the inn, I heard his voice out the window.

"Whatever may it be?" I asked him.

"Hm, well, we've had an issue. I don't want to say it out loud, so just come inside," Father told me.

"At once!" I declared and rushed inside to Father's room.

"So yesterday, Keel and Sakura and I were going around the area, taking care of some monsters and collecting herbs. Then, when we came back here, I thought Sakura would get lonely, so I got a room for us to stay together."

My heart fluttered. What a wonderful glimpse of Father's loving compassion! He was making Sakura a beloved companion, just as he had in the last go-around.

"But it's what happened next that I want to tell you," Father continued. "I was keeping a close eye on her because you told me about how she would change forms, right?"

"I deeply apologize for the interruption, but is it necessary for you to explain all that to me?" I inquired. From everything that had happened in the past, it was only a matter of time before Sakura changed into her angel form. *So what was the problem?*

"Yes, and that's what happened in the end, but not quite the way you'd think," Father said.

I had no idea what Father was talking about.

"Oink oink!" added Keel, but unfortunately, I could not understand a word she said.

"It's kinda hard to explain," Father continued. "I want you to see Sakura's human form for yourself."

"So she turned into her angel form!" I exclaimed.

"Wait, is that Yuki behind you?" I asked. "I mean, you did

explain it to me before, but . . . she does look like a little child, doesn't she?"

"Like a child, you say?" I asked.

I mean, they were pretty much the same size and height as Filo-tan was. I didn't see any problem there. More than half of the filolials in angel form that I had seen were about that same height. But the way Father was speaking, I wondered if Sakura had turned out different.

"Sakura, can you come over here?" Father called.

"Huh? What's up?"

I looked over in the direction of Sakura's voice.

When I saw her, I noticed the same pink hair and wings growing out of her back . . . but it was in the body of a calm-looking angel who appeared to be around 17 years old. She was wearing the same clothes as the local villagers.

Could Father have told her to become this way?

HERE'S THE RUN-DOWN ON WHAT HAPPENED UP UNTIL NOW, I SAY!

First Go-Around

The story of The Rising of the Shield Hero.

Second Round

The King's Plot
The king plotted a false accusation of Naofumi.
The false accusation did not come to reality.

Treatment of Naofumi and His Personality
Naofumi was chased away from the castle.
Naofumi didn't have many allies.
His personality didn't end up getting all twisted.

The Invitation from Siltvelt
Naofumi was sent alone to Siltvelt and was killed by Melromarc forces waiting at the Siltvelt border.
Ended with the death of the Shield Hero.

The King's Plot
Disclosed shortly after the heroes were summoned to the throne room.
Naofumi escaped the false accusation, but Motoyasu was caught in a trap instead.
The king launched assassination attempts on both Naofumi and Motoyasu. Because no one trusted Naofumi, they decided to escape Melromarc.

Treatment of Naofumi and His Personality
Naofumi was rescued by Motoyasu after being taken by the imposter Siltvelt emissaries.
A pure, unbroken Naofumi.

The Invitation from Siltvelt
Naofumi worked alongside Motoyasu.
For cooperating with the Shield Hero, several countries invaded and attacked Siltvelt. As a result, Itsuki was eventually killed.
Ended with the death of the Bow Hero.

Third Round

Motoyasu launched an attack at Itsuki to test the conditions of the time loop.
Ended with the death of the Bow Hero.

Fourth Round

Motoyasu launched an attack at Ren to test the conditions of the time loop.
Ended with the death of the Sword Hero.

Fifth Round

Sixth Round

The King's Plot   *That's where we are now!*
Fully executed.
They launched a false accusation against Naofumi. However, Motoyasu intervened to help him escape. Melromarc is watching them closely but hasn't done anything yet.

Treatment of Naofumi and His Personality
His personality hasn't changed yet.

The Invitation from Siltvelt
Declined by Motoyasu and Naofumi.
Thanks to the help of the Siltvelt emissary, Motoyasu and Naofumi are getting a peddling permit.

Important! See Filo-tan once again!

The new strategy: Go around selling in Melromarc while leveling up on the side!

Chapter One: Carriage-Crafting

"Sakura?" I looked at her in surprise. That was strange. In the previous round Sakura was pretty much the same height as Yuki.

In terms of her figure, she was like Filo-tan's big sister. *What in the world had happened? How could there be such a big difference between this round and the previous one?* The only familiar thing about her was her hair that stuck up in one place, a cowlick like a flower.

"Sakura, you got so big!" Yuki exclaimed.

"You think so?" Sakura yawned and rubbed her eyes. "Naofumi, what are we doing today? I'm hungry!"

"Uhhhh . . ." Naofumi faltered and turned to me. "Motoyasu! What should we do?"

I have seen one example of a filolial like Sakura before. That is, of course, Chick.

I do recall that when Chick turned into her angel form, she looked more like an adult woman. It was far from a common occurrence.

Perhaps Sakura had become this way to make Father like her even more. That may have made sense. Whatever the true reason, it wasn't like there was no such thing as filolials that became adults in their angel form. Every filolial is different, I say, even when they take their angel form.

Still, I could hardly suppress my surprise. Since Sakura's eye color was also different from the previous go-around, I realized that there could be all sorts of other differences that pop up. And with her pink hair, I almost felt like I was looking at Éclair standing next to Father. They looked to be about the same age and same height.

"Uh, Motoyasu, are you listening to me?"

"Most definitely," I assured Father. "Yes, I too have absolutely no clue what's happening here, I say."

My only guess was that Sakura had become an adult in her angel form because some sort of condition was met.

Well, since there seemed like no reason to be concerned about it, I let it be.

"There's no problem whatsoever!" I announced.

"Huh? No problem?"

"No problem at all! Sakura, you know what you have to do, don't you?"

"Yeah! It's my job to protect Naofumi!"

She still looked sleepy, but I could tell from her voice that she was determined.

"Oh, got it. Thanks," Father said. Sakura came to stand next to Father and he patted her on the head. She closed her eyes and bowed her head happily.

"Anyways, Motoyasu," Father said. "Look at Kou. Why is he looking at Keel like that?"

Kou was staring googly-eyed at Keel from behind. "Keel's tail," Kou whispered.

Keel yelped and rushed to Father's side. Kou trotted after Keel, but Sakura came in between them.

"Don't even think about it," Sakura told Kou. "I'm going to protect Keel. Just like from that thief from yesterday."

"Did something happen with a thief?" I inquired.

"Yeah," Father said. "We were attacked while we were riding Sakura. It was probably a thief or some other criminal."

"Yeah! And in that fight, I protected Naofumi and Keel!" Sakura said proudly.

I couldn't help but notice that Sakura lit up whenever she talked about protecting Father. What a glorious sight! I felt especially happy that she took such pride in it.

Normally, I would be the one protecting Father, but we couldn't be together too often at the moment.

"Whenever he started to speak, you just slapped him around. Is that because he was lying?" Father asked Sakura.

"Yeah! I couldn't speak human language well at the time, so I just slapped him around because he was lying."

"He did have a weird look in his eyes," Father said. "So maybe he was disguised as a thief. Based on what Motoyasu told me, he was probably a follower of the Church of the Three

Heroes. His clothes did look too nice for a thief, so maybe he was purposefully acting like a thief to try to trick us?"

Hmmm. I tried to remember if Father had ever been attacked by a thief at around this point in the story. But I didn't know enough of the details. Perhaps the person claimed to be a thief so that Father wouldn't suspect what he really was. If Father had found out who he was and told Siltvelt, a war might break out between the Church of the Three Heroes, so he was likely being careful to hide his true identity when he attacked.

I figured that they wanted to be able to attack but didn't want to risk us attacking them. It all pretty much made sense.

Keel oinked a few times.

"Keel, I know you don't have any experience, but you'd really be a great salesperson for us," Father said. The topic appeared to have changed back to Keel's clothing. "I get it, you're a boy who looks feminine . . . Where I come from, we'd call you a *bishonen*. But either way, you still have an attractive face."

Keel oinked softly.

"So you don't want to wear the outfit. You might not like it, but I know you can do it. Try it on, persevere through it. Remember, we're doing all this to get revenge on the people who destroyed your village."

Keel oinked and nodded.

"Thank you, Keel. Do your best."

Father patted Keel's head and turned back to Sakura.

"So what should we do about Sakura's clothes? I'm thinking it would be best if you could make some for her soon, but . . ."

"In that case, I would need for her to come with me," I informed Father.

"I want to protect Naofumi!" Sakura said. "I can't leave his side."

"But . . ." Father started.

"Well then, we'll just have to make do with normal clothes for her for the time being," I declared.

"Should we stop by the weapon shop to see if the old guy has any good clothes?"

"I also know that the monster tent should have some as well," I said.

"Do they? Well, let's check out the weapon shop first," Father said.

"Of course!"

And so we went back to the Melromarc castle town. When we got to the weapon shop, the old guy looked curiously at Yuki, Kou, and Sakura.

"Wow, that's incredible. Did your filolials transform into humans because you're heroes?" the old guy asked.

"Motoyasu, is that how it works?"

"Just so," I said. "When heroes raise filolials they achieve exceptional growth, I say!"

"So what can I help you with?" the old guy asked.

"That's right," Father said. "Well, we need some clothes that are made with magical power for Sakura here. I thought it was possible that you might have some. I know that they have those sorts of clothes in countries with a lot of demi-humans."

The old guy shook his head. "I know about those sorts of clothes, ones that can expand or contract and that have exceptional defense. They're out there, but not in my store. Stuff made out of magic is outside my area of expertise."

Sakura was looking around at the swords on the shelves.

"I want to try using a weapon!" Sakura exclaimed.

"Huh? W-why?" Father asked.

"Well, I know there are times that I need to stay in my human form, like in the inn, and I want to be able to protect you even when I'm in my human form!"

"Can't you just turn into a filolial when the time to fight comes?"

"Hmmm." Sakura thought about it. "I don't know!"

"You don't know?"

"Well, a sword might be more effective than talons alone, if you asked me," the old guy chimed in.

"Yeah! I wanna use a sword!"

"It's great that you're interested," the old guy said, turning to Father and me. "So what are you going to do?"

It was certainly true that filolials tended to pick their own weapons, even if it was just a beak or talons. I was a believer in the individuality of each and every filolial. But in this situation, I was concerned about our money. We couldn't just keep spending willy-nilly, I say.

Of course, we planned to make money via peddling sooner or later, and it was always possible to get money by going to Siltvelt as well.

"Regardless, after the attack yesterday, we need some new equipment," Father said. Father glanced at Keel, who took out a spare sword and handed it over to Sakura.

"Do you know how to use it?" Father asked her.

"I learned by watching Keel!" Sakura said.

"Oh really?" Father turned back to the old guy. "So you really don't know anything about clothes made out of magic thread?"

"Unfortunately not," he said. "Maybe if you go to the magic shop you could find something."

"The magic shop?"

"The biggest magic shop around is right in this area," he said. "I thought that you kiddos might have seen it yourself."

"Are you talking about that giant bookstore place?" Father asked.

"Probably the same place," the old guy said.

"Got it. Thanks. We'll try there."

"If you tell them I sent you, you might get a little discount too," the old guy said and handed Father a letter of introduction.

With that, we headed over to the magic shop.

When we got to the magic shop, a middle-aged pig started oinking at us suspiciously. But the pig's expression quickly softened and it started to oink in a friendly tone.

"Ah, hello there," Father said. "We're looking for some magic thread for special clothes. Can you help us with that?"

"Oink!"

"Your magic types are healing and support, Father!" I declared. There was no need for me to see any further since I already knew what Father could do in previous go-arounds. Father had mastered some first-rate protective spells back in the day!

The pig let out a series of oinks and squeals.

"Well, even if you let us take a look, we don't exactly have a lot of money at the moment . . ." Father trailed off.

Yes, that was our problem. In order to make money, we needed to buy a bunch of stuff in order to complete our peddling preparations.

The pig continued to oink for several moments.

"A magical orb? What's that?"

Oh, I remembered that, I say. After the false accusation was successfully launched against Father, Trash took the remaining heroes, including myself, and gave us a jewel that helped us acquire magic abilities. They were especially useful for beginners.

I remember back then when Melromarc would give me anything I wanted. Life was much easier back then.

Still, if you learn magic through a magic jewel, your power won't be as strong as it would be if you had learned through a tome. You'd have much less control and it would probably be impossible to learn a Liberation-class spell with a jewel alone.

Liberation

A special type of magic used exclusively by the heroes. The user combines a series of spells like a puzzle in their head, and the resulting spell depends on the specific combination by the hero. They usually amount to extremely powerful spells.

I explained to Father about the magic jewels.

"So you're saying that they gave it to us back at the castle?"

"They gave out the magic jewels to the heroes after you left, Father," I said.

Father frowned. "They really did try to screw me over every time they could."

"Once we get some money, it will be better to just purchase some tomes, I say!"

The pig oinked at us. Keel was examining some of the crystal balls in the store. Sakura was clinging to Father like an escort. She really looked so different and mature!

"Oink!"

The pig appeared to be willing to show us around the store. After that, I started to look all over the store myself. After a while, I saw something that brought back memories.

It was a device like a spinning wheel. If I wasn't mistaken, you could use it to make thread infused with magical power.

"But how much does it cost, Motoyasu?" Father asked after I pointed it out.

The pig chimed in with a series of oinks and squeals.

"Oh, you'll give it to us for free?" Father asked. "Wow, thanks so much."

It appeared that the old guy had made some arrangements to really help us. I wondered if this was in exchange for how I had given the old guy some free materials before.

"Thank you very much," Father said.

"Do you think you might also be able to throw in a magic tome?" I inquired.

The pig oinked.

"Motoyasu, she wants us to buy that," Father said.

Well, at least I tried.

I did want Father to learn some magic, but getting the hang of it was far from easy. I figured it would be best to take our time learning magic down the road.

The pig started oinking again.

"Okay! Just a moment!" Sakura said.

Then Sakura went into a corner of the store to take off her clothes and transformed into her filolial queen form. Father politely turned around when Sakura was getting changed.

Ahh, so close! It turns out she really did have a different coloring from Filo-tan, after all.

The shop owner looked very surprised for some reason.

Sakura slowly turned the spinning wheel to wind out thread and applied her magical power to it. Sakura was just as calm and relaxed as she had always been, so everyone got bored watching as she slowly spun the thread. Fortunately, she didn't seem to get as sleepy as quickly as she had in previous go-arounds.

"Sakura, you're too slow," Yuki scolded.

"You think so?" Sakura whined.

"Everyone's different, Yuki," Father said. "Be patient."

"But Sakura is . . ."

"Oh yeah," Father interjected. "If you're bored, why don't you go with Motoyasu to get a carriage for us? Sakura will probably be done by the time you get back."

"We should acquire one soon," I agreed. I hadn't forgotten about it, I say! But getting a carriage was bound to be annoying. You couldn't really just buy a carriage without everyone seeing exactly what you were up to. In fact, it would be fastest to just make it yourself.

Even faster than that would be attacking a thief who had already procured a stolen carriage and just stealing theirs, I say! *Hmm. Perhaps we should fix up an ordinary cart as a stopgap measure?*

Ultimately, I decided it wouldn't be too hard to get wood from the forest and make ourselves a carriage!

"We'll build one, I say!" I declared.

"I'll leave it to you," Father said.

"Yes, sir, I say! How big should it be?"

"Well, we all have to fit in it, so it should be pretty big."

"Understood, I say!" I turned to Yuki and Kou. "Let's go!"

"At once!"

"Ooookay!"

Yuki, Kou, and I left the magic store to go about our carriage-crafting.

We set out for the woods in the mountains near Riyute. I cut down some trees with my spear. At my level of power, I can cut through trees like tofu. We quickly set about gathering wood and building a cart.

Filolials are creatures who simply love to pull carriages, I say.

I've made carriages from scratch before, I'll have you know. Making the wheels is probably the most frustrating part. For the time being, a wooden cart should do the trick. If it becomes necessary later, we could always have the old guy at the weapon shop do it up in gold leaf, the type that Filo-tan always adored. I knew that the old guy was a real pro at gilding because he'd made a golden carriage for Filo-tan before, I say. He had skills.

"Let's put on the wheels already!" Kou shouted.

"Kou, you need to shave them down more," I said. "Otherwise, it's going to be too uncomfortable to ride in."

"Got it!"

"Let's make them lustrous!" Yuki called.

Yuki and Kou were making a real effort at carriage-crafting!

So we kept up the work, slowly polishing our creation.

I used magic to start a fire to heat up the wood and cut the pieces, allowing them to bend into a more flexible shape. "Yes, a little heat doesn't hurt, I say!"

Of course, besides racing up mountains, we needed the cart to be able to withstand the bare minimum of being hauled around. We needed the structure to have a bit of bend to it.

At last, we finished making the cart. All we needed was a good canopy to cover it and we'd have ourselves a proper carriage!

"We did it!" Kou shouted.

"Everyone will be so glad," Yuki said with a smile.

"Perfect, I say!" I declared.

It was just an ordinary carriage, but to me, it looked like it was sparkling with light.

I remembered the carriage that I decorated for Filo-tan with all of my passionate love! She kept it hidden away in the village storehouse, so I know that it was precious to Filo-tan.

|| Filo's Decorative Carriage ||

Motoyasu stole Filo's precious carriage and tricked it out, covering it in gold and illustrations of Filo, making it look like one of Japan's famous decoration trucks.

When I glanced up at the sky, I saw that the sun was already starting to go down.

"Let's hurry back to Father," I called.

"Roger!" Kou said.

"I'll go ahead and pull the carriage," Yuki said.

"Hey, I wanna!"

Yuki and Kou scrambled for the reins.

"Yuki's the leader, Kou," I said. "So Yuki's first. Then when we get to the castle town, we'll switch to you!"

"Of course," Yuki said.

"All right!" Kou said.

I boarded the carriage, and we set off to meet up with Father again.

When we got back to the magic shop, we found Father and the others waiting outside.

"Oh, welcome back." Father yawned. "Wow, you really did get a new carriage. Wasn't it expensive?"

"We made it ourselves, I say!"

"W-what? You made that? Amazing!"

"My spear can cut through wood no problem at all," I explained.

"I didn't know you could make carriages. Wow."

Father went over to look at the carriage and placed his hand on it.

"So I guess we can finally get started," he said.

Keel oinked in excitement, racing around the carriage and peering inside it. Sakura looked sleepy, as usual.

"Oh, about the thread," Father said, nodding at Sakura. "We made it—but barely. That device that turns magical power into thread—Sakura kept turning slowly, but eventually the magical jewel that we were using as the pivot shattered! I was surprised."

"Oho? It broke? In that case we ought to acquire another magic jewel to return to the magic shop, to make up for it," I said.

"Yeah, good point," Father said. "Oh, Motoyasu. They turned the magic thread into cloth for us, but what do you do now? We could just ask a tailor to do it."

"I shall make it, I say! Sakura, what sort of design do you like?"

Just to be safe, I wanted to confirm with her. If I went with the same sort of clothing as last time with the current adult Sakura, it would have a very different impression.

"Hmm." Sakura glanced at Kou and Yuki. "Weeeell, I can tell you that I *really* don't like what Yuki's wearing . . ."

"How dare you!" Yuki cried, glaring angrily at Sakura. Sakura hid behind Father.

"Sakura, do you like dresses?" I asked her.

"Weeeell . . . I don't hate them, but I don't like them either, I guess."

Interesting. So her tastes had changed a bit from the previous round.

"So would you rather have something more like Kou?"

Kou was wearing overalls. It was a more boyish, rascally outfit. It was a good look, I say!

"I don't know. I don't really like that either."

Then Sakura suddenly pointed at a passerby on the street. "That! I like that!"

So it was kind of like what Big Sis used to wear under her armor. I tried to imagine it on Sakura.

"Okay, I've got it," I announced. "No problem, Yuki. Now, Father, everyone—it's time to board the carriage!"

"Oh, yeah. We still need to go pick up the peddling permit from the Siltvelt emissary, don't we?"

"But of course," I agreed. "Shall we hurry to receive it, as promised?"

"Yup," Father said. "All right, let's get on with it!"

Following Father's orders, Sakura and Keel got onto the carriage.

"Departure, I say!"

Kou took off with delight at the sound of my voice. Before the sun had even set, we had left the castle town at a galloping pace. I only hoped that Keel wouldn't get carriage sickness or anything and force us to slow down.

Chapter Two: A Lazy Pig

Just as the Siltvelt emissary had promised, he got us a peddling permit. We finally embarked on our peddling journey.

To start, we prepared to sell the medicine that Father had made, with Keel standing out front to try to attract customers. At first Keel was too shy to do much of anything and constantly asked Father for help, but soon enough she got used to it and started selling medicine without any hesitation.

It was gradual, sure, but we slowly started to make some money. We used that money as capital to buy more ingredients for Father's medicine, and Father got better at remembering all the different combinations.

Since the filolials were such an unusual sight, word spread and we started to attract more customers. It was just like they were pulling the carriage of the holy saint of the bird god!

"Yuki, can you pull just a little slower?" Father asked. "The carriage is shaking."

"At once!"

Yuki slowed down according to Father's wishes, and we continued on.

We had established a solid rotation for the filolials: Yuki, Kou, and then Sakura pulled the carriage. When Sakura pulled the carriage, it shook the least. She must've been especially looking out for Father.

I also finished making Sakura's clothes on the day after we set out. It was a plain, unembellished tunic, like the one I saw Big Sis wearing when we first met. Of course, I couldn't make Sakura magic armor myself, so it wasn't the exact same outfit as what Big Sis had, but it still looked cool, like it was made for a dashing swordsman.

I could vaguely remember the sort of outfit that Father had always liked on Big Sis. Was it a shrine priestess outfit? I didn't think that would particularly suit Sakura.

Father called out to me. "Motoyasu, by the way, it seems like you've mastered reading the language here. Should I try to learn it too?"

I thought about it. "I suppose so. You had learned it in the previous go-around."

I made a chart of the Melromarc alphabet and handed it to Father.

"If you memorize this chart whenever you have some spare time, you'll be reading in no time, I say! As a matter of fact, you were the one who taught me how to read the Melromarc language. I'm sure it'll be no trouble for you."

"So there's no skill or something that lets you understand the language?" Father asked.

"I don't believe so," I answered. "I figured there might be

something like that, but I haven't seen it in any of the weapons I've encountered in this world."

Learning the language was no easy task. Actually, it was very hard, but when I thought about how I could teach it back to Father, it felt like it was all worth it, I say!

"Got it. I'll just practice a bit at a time."

Then I heard Keel oink loudly.

We had arrived at the village and Keel was starting to sell medicine.

Father looked outside to confirm and started mixing some ingredients. While he was doing that, we collected some more herbs. We always need more ingredients, I say.

Father had stuck to recording all of our transactions for acquiring herbs from other pharmacies, so we could pay fixed rates. Then, with my spear's ability, we could make the best medicine out there!

I continued to teach new recipes that were recorded in my spear to Father, and I could tell that he had improved his skill at mixing as we went along. I knew Father would be a natural!

Soon enough, we had a respectable assortment of products. Since we were selling below the market price, we had plenty of demand. Almost too much for us to keep up with ingredient-wise.

For herbs and ingredients, we could always get more by defeating monsters, but we thought that a method like that might result in suspicious eyes cast our way. That made it tough to keep up with our demand.

When I got back to the carriage from harvesting herbs, Father beckoned me over.

"Whatever may it be, Father?"

"So . . ." Father trailed off, a troubled expression on his face. "Well, this girl says she wants to join us."

Join us? She was probably a spy for some church or other, so I assumed that Father would simply reject her. Needless to say, it was hard to imagine someone in Melromarc wanting to become allies with the Shield Hero. I may need to eliminate her in secret at some point.

"Oink."

It was an exhausted-looking pig sitting on a stump, waiting.

What was up with that pig, I say?

I examined it with dubious eyes. The pig kept grumbling in a bored voice. It was acting as if it had seen me before, I say.

"Her name's Elena," Father said. "She's a Melromarc noble, and her father told her to help one of the heroes, so she came here."

Elena? The name sounded familiar, somehow.

Who was Elena? It was oh-so vaguely familiar. I had the sense that she was a close friend of the Crimson Swine.

Which means I had to exterminate her as swiftly as possible!

"Oink oink oink oink," it said.

"Well, even if you say so, we can't just believe you," Father said.

"What is the pig saying, Father?" I inquired.

Elena

Originally a member of Motoyasu's party along with Witch, Elena betrayed Motoyasu and tossed him aside when he was no use against the Spirit Tortoise. She managed to keep up a good-natured act in front of Motoyasu, but in reality, she found him tiresome.

"She's saying that she really doesn't want to, but her father commanded her, so she doesn't have any choice."

"Shall I simply exterminate all traces of her from this world, then? I'll make sure it won't hurt at all!"

I gripped my spear and pointed it firmly at the pig, but Father pulled my arm.

"Motoyasu, calm down! There's no need to do anything extreme!"

The pig continued to grumble.

"Now she's saying that she thought that out of the four heroes, we looked like the easiest to help out, so she came here," Father said.

I must say, this pig appeared to be completely bored out of her mind.

If I couldn't kill her, she should return home at once, I say.

I heard more vile, bored oinking fill my eardrums.

"She says that she can be useful to us because her mother

was a merchant. She says she can help out." Father looked at the pig. "But I think Keel is doing just fine for us," he said.

Keel squealed and oinked furiously in response to that, I say. It sounded like she maybe wanted a companion.

"Huh? Well, you're right, it could be hard to expand our sales with only Keel," Father replied. "But still . . . Why did you think it would be easy to join up with us? I mean, as a Melromarc noble, I figured you'd assume that joining us would be the hardest," he asked her.

Squealing and oinking, oinking and squealing. It went on for some time. Father did me the favor of interpreting.

There seemed to be other reasons that the pig had come to us, besides just the command from her father. According to the pig, there had been a lot of discord within Trash's faction, and if they continued to support him, then there was a good chance that they would lose their standing. Of course, Trash had a bad relationship with the Spear Hero in addition to the Shield Hero. And furthermore, according to the so-called Elena, the Sword Hero, Ren, had also turned against Melromarc. Since Elena's family were powerful, well-established merchants, they didn't have to be too afraid of Trash. It seems he wasn't powerful enough to be able to confiscate their fortune or bring their family to complete ruin.

Then, besides the fact that it was strategic to her family, she wanted to join us out of personal preference. She said that the most important thing of all was simply that she thought we would get along. The Bow Hero was busy subjugating corrupt nobles across the land, and the Sword Hero was focused on exterminating monsters. Then she heard that the Spear and Shield Hero had started to sell medicine together.

Apparently, the pig had watched all the heroes for some time. She thought Itsuki was too self-righteous. She thought that Ren wanted to work alone for the most part, but even when he did cooperate with others, he often made them do annoying work in the course of monster-killing. Meanwhile, we were just traveling around in a carriage. It looked by far the easiest.

So this pig really did just want to take the easiest way out.

From this day forward, I shall refer to her as Lazy Pig, I say.

According to Lazy Pig, it was important that not just the Shield Hero, but also the Spear Hero, was involved. She chose us because we were working together, so it seemed.

I supposed if it had been just Father, then it was possible she'd get more criticism for working with the Shield Hero.

If I'm not mistaken, in the first go-around, it had taken Father a little bit longer to start really boosting his reputation with his peddling.

"And Elena also says that when the Queen got back to Melromarc, she said that the Shield and Spear Hero would eventually have the best social status. Well, that's pretty much it. She seems like a good person. What do you think?"

"I think it would be best to immediately exterminate her," I advised.

"What? Motoyasu, were you even listening? Please be reasonable. Aren't we trying to make sure that there's no war?"

"You're right," I agreed. "For that reason, I shall exterminate her in a coolheaded and reasonable manner, I say."

"W-what! Wait!" Father groaned.

Lazy Pig oinked in confusion.

"Listen, we've got a lot to do, and we can't afford to be spied on," Father said to her.

"Oink."

"Huh? You'll become a slave if it helps us trust you? Since a slave wouldn't be able to spy?" Father glanced at me. "In return, she just wants us to put in a good word for her family when the Queen eventually comes out on top. Well, if that's really what you want . . ."

Hmmm. As a slave, she wouldn't be able to betray us, so it reduced the risk on that end. A slave wouldn't be able to reveal any of our secrets, true. But why would she want to join us *that* badly?

"Oink oink oink."

"Well, we have a lot of plans, and it's definitely true that we'll need more help to accomplish them all. If you become a slave, you won't be able to betray us so . . . All right. I still don't really trust you, but if you really want to, you can join us. If we can talk more, from merchant to merchant, I'm sure we'll start to trust you."

She oinked in agreement. So Lazy Pig joined us as a slave.

The biggest problem was that now the inside of the carriage was really starting to turn noxious with the heinous stank of pig.

"Oiiiiiink!"

Lazy Pig—Elena—when we weren't selling anything, spent all of her time on the hammock inside the carriage, dozing off. But in that sublime trembling of the carriage that my noble filolials' rapid pace on the road caused, a bit of dozing off could mean certain death. And yet, somehow, she slept.

Even I couldn't fall asleep while we were on the road. I, Motoyasu Kitamura, admit that I felt envy, I say!

Lazy Pig was taking advantage of Father's kindness! Even though she was supposed to be a slave, she was acting as if we hadn't even activated the slave seal. She was mocking us!

Well, even though we did register Keel as a slave with a seal, I'd never seen the seal itself.

If I were in charge of registering Lazy Pig, I'd kill her as quickly as I could instead.

As I stared angrily at Lazy Pig resting, Father called over to me.

"Oh, Motoyasu, by the way, I heard that you have a secret plan, but what are you thinking?"

"Yes, I do." I thought about it. "It's almost time."

It had been about five days since we started peddling. We were going around Melromarc, selling our wares in different villages and cities. I opened my map of Melromarc and thought about our potential route. I needed to select an area that we could get through in one day.

"I propose that we go about in this area at a distance that we can do a full loop back in a single day," I said to Father, pointing at the map.

"That's fine with me, but why?"

"That's my secret plan, I say!" I declared. "It's a plan to go off and level up while pretending like we're still in the carriage the whole time!"

This was my infallible method! Since the trip would require Portal Spear, we needed to devise some sort of scheme. I supposed that even if there was someone watching us, they simply wouldn't realize that the hero that they were supposed to be watching was no longer there.

"Sounds like that will take a lot of work. So what's the plan?"

"Since we're usually shut up in the carriage for days at a time anyways, I think that will make for the perfect smoke-screen," I explained.

"Pretty much all the time." Father sighed. "Well, we do stop at inns from time to time."

In our five days on the road, we had killed a few monsters that showed up, but besides that, our leveling up had really slowed to a halt. If Father didn't start leveling up more soon, it would be a cause for concern.

"We can just leave it to our sales team and the filolials while we're out, I say!"

"So let Keel handle things? Or Elena?"

I shook my head. "We can't trust Lazy Pig. But we need Keel to level up too."

I heard an oink from the other side of the carriage. Lazy Pig had woken up and was now looking over at me. *Yes, you heard me right, Lazy Pig! I'll never trust you!*

"We never asked the likes of you to join us! Beat it, swine!" I quipped.

Lazy Pig had but a meager oink in response.

"Well, let's not get all riled up," Father said. "I applied the slave seal and everything, so there's nothing to be worried about, Motoyasu. Let's just make sure Yuki keeps a watch on everything. That'll be enough, won't it?"

I nodded. "So for now, Kou will pull the carriage, Lazy Pig will handle the peddling, and Yuki will keep a close eye on her."

"Whatever you command, Motoyasu!" said Yuki.

"Woohoo! More pulling!" shouted Kou.

I didn't know what level Lazy Pig was, but I figured she was strong enough to fight. The only real situation to be worried about would be if thieves attacked and realized that there was no one actually inside the carriage. Actually, since Yuki was keeping an eye on things, even if Lazy Pig tried to poke a hole in her slave seal or something, Yuki would dispose of her swiftly.

"Let's get on our way then, I say! First, I'll use Liberation Fire Mirage to keep us hidden, and then as soon as we create some distance, we'll use Portal Spear."

Yes, our objective here was to keep all enemy eyes on our carriage and our peddling. Filolials have great instincts for sensing hidden enemies, and I can pretty much sense the presence of anyone hiding with magic too. I double-checked that there was no one hiding inside the carriage. That meant that from now on, it should be enough for Yuki to keep an eye on the outside of the carriage. Plus, our carriage was moving so fast that it would be hard for anyone to even get a grasp on what we were doing. Ultimately, I decided that even if there was no one left inside the carriage, outsiders likely wouldn't realize that we had left.

With that, Father and I embarked on our leveling-up mission.

"Wow! That was crazy," Father said.

"Oink," agreed Keel.

We had just arrived in Siltvelt. I supposed that this was Father's first time in the portal in this go-around.

"What would you like to do, Father? Should we head toward the castle?"

Father scratched his head. "If you don't mind, let's focus on leveling up first. I'm also getting a bit worried that I haven't leveled up at all."

"Agreed. So why don't you go do that with Sakura?"

"Sounds good. Keel, you can come too!"

Father leapt up onto Sakura's back and helped Keel up. He looked like he was enjoying himself mightily, I say.

"In the meantime, I'm going to go pick up a few things that I wanted to give to you before," I said. "Be careful!"

"Thanks," Father said. "We'll go level up a ton and see you later."

"Leeeeet's gooooo!" Sakura sang, taking off into a sprint with Father and Keel on her back.

While they were out, I went to get the drop items that I had collected and hidden the last time I had gone to level up with the filolials. I wondered if Father would come back with some good drop items. I figured whatever they were, we could always use them to make more medicine.

That evening, Father came back with a big smile on his face. I had stuffed the ingredients that I had collected that day in a bag.

"Man, that was great," he said. "I leveled up so much I could hardly believe it."

"So what level are you now?" I inquired.

"I'm level 18, Keel's level 19, and Sakura's level 35."

That's all? Maybe it was because Sakura was a relatively low level, but that wouldn't be nearly good enough.

"I'm going out with Sakura tomorrow to level her up, posthaste," I announced. "We need to get her higher."

"Really?"

"I should've leveled her up more before."

I should've recognized that this was the more pressing issue. In order to level up Father faster, Sakura needed to be a higher level. But I had been more concerned with Yuki, so I focused on leveling her up first. I explained what I was thinking to Father.

"You can't take Naofumi away from me," Sakura protested. "I need to protect him."

I burst into tears at the sight of Sakura's heavenly display of devotion. How incomparably noble!

"Sakura, I have no words for your devotion. Only admiration."

"So what are you saying?" Father asked.

"Make Yuki and Kou come with us!" Sakura said.

"It's a good idea," Father said, "but since only Motoyasu can level up Yuki and Kou . . ." He trailed off.

Sakura's devotion was so noble that it was causing us all sorts of problems, I say.

"Well, in that case, I'll go back to the carriage tomorrow," Father said. "We can't be gone two days in a row or it'll be suspicious, and I can keep an eye on Elena instead of Yuki."

Keel nodded with an oink.

"And I'll pull the carriage!" Sakura chirped.

"Exactly," Father said. "Then the carriage won't shake and I'll have no problem learning new compounds for medicine."

"Yeah!"

"That settles things," I said. Leveling up Sakura could happen later. "In that case, Father, I present to you these drop items." I bowed my head.

"Uh . . . okay, thanks. Wow, that's a lot of stuff."

"Not nearly enough to make your shield stronger, dear Father," I said regretfully.

"Yeah, we thought we were making progress today, but I guess it wasn't good enough." Father scratched the back of his head with a grimace.

My current objective was to secretly level up Father as fast as I could.

"It might be an obvious point, but I noticed that the medicine that they have around here is different from Melromarc," Father said. "The monsters are different, so the item drops vary too. There are recipes for making medicine, which helps, but I'm not sure they'll work when I actually try to make it."

"You'll just need to learn by trial and error, I say."

Of course, since I was just making everything with my spear, I had no clue what I was doing. There might be a lot of small differences in the herbs and recipes, but there was no reason we couldn't sell the medicine from Siltvelt. Only a hero with a holy weapon could tell the difference, after all!

As I thought about such important matters, Father put the ingredients that I had given him into his shield. Then Father asked me, as he had done before, about how to go about making his shield stronger. I advised him to use the items we had collected on his shield now, since we could always replenish our item supply later. I also explained to him what types of minerals he needed to strengthen his shield. Regardless, the most important thing was for Father personally to level up.

"I believe it's about time to head back," I said.

"Got it. Thanks, Motoyasu."

"Of course, Father! Portal Spear!"

I prepared to send us flying to the place where we had planned to meet up with Yuki and the rest. As always, before we left there, I was able to vaguely see what was going on. The carriage was waiting for us, just as planned.

The timing was tricky. If I activated a concealment spell before we went, it might be misleading for Yuki and the others. And then there was Father's order to not kill anyone if I didn't have to, which, while being incredibly annoying, was an order from Father.

Things would be so much easier if we could just go and I could kill anyone who spotted us. *Alas.*

So I had no choice but to activate the concealment spell, use Portal Spear, and remove the concealment spell after we boarded the carriage.

Lazy Pig started oinking and squealing in mild surprise as we appeared, as listless and lazy as ever. The pig didn't even stand up to greet us.

I nearly cooked a feast of lazy pig roast right then and there.

"We're back," Father called. "Did anything happen when we were gone?"

"There was no incident," Yuki responded. "*She* didn't do anything peculiar either." Yuki nodded at Lazy Pig. "However . . . I did not feel the slightest hint of energy or enthusiasm from her either."

Lazy Pig oinked some bored retort.

Father chuckled. "That's all for the best. So there were no thieves?"

"None."

"So maybe we didn't need to be so concerned about security? Motoyasu, your plan really worked."

"Thank you, Father, from the very bottom of my heart!"

"So let's keep on secretly leveling up while we do our peddling," Father said. "Then we'll have no problem getting stronger. Of course, we can't be too careful either."

Father was as right as ever. So the next day I decided I would level up Yuki and Kou. Our first objective would be to class up. The problem was that Yuki and Kou were already quite strong. They needed to get special assistance from Fitoria-tan, the filo-lial queen, to class up again. It was going to be difficult for us to meet up with any other filolials in our current circumstances.

Class-Up

A special ceremony for those that have reached their maximum level. Class-ups can only be completed at the dragon hourglass. Not only can you further level up after undergoing a class-up, but you also get considerably stronger overall.

The first time I met Fitoria-tan was when I was peak-racing with Crim. So if we went running in that same area, would we run into her again? I had a feeling that it wouldn't be quite so simple. The other place where it seemed possible to find her was on the way to Siltvelt.

It was all well and good to try to find her, but since we had to return via Portal Spear within a set period of time, it would be quite the endeavor.

Now that I thought about it, I remembered Father telling me in a previous go-around about the time that he met Fitoria-tan. Fitoria-tan was ridiculously strong . . . I think it was back when Father had been a wanted criminal and he was hiding in Melromarc.

But that whole series of events was in another time loop altogether.

So I thought that maybe I should just make our priority getting the class-up bonus . . . Oho?

"I remembered, I say. I remembered!"

Father leapt up in surprise. "Jeez! What are you talking about, Motoyasu?"

"I had completely forgotten, but in the seven star weapons' power-up method, by trading away levels, you can get a weapon core power-up! With that, it's possible to increase your weapon's base status growth, I say!"

I explained the power-up method to Father. That was definitely how it worked with the seven star whip. By trading off levels, you could increase your overall growth rate. As a result, even at an identical level, you could end up much stronger than you would've been otherwise. With this method it wouldn't be impossible to get by with a little smoke and mirrors.

I figured we could rely on this power-up method without having to find Fitoria-tan. Since this kind of core power-up makes you stronger even at a lower level, with our current cap at level 40, we would easily be able to dispose of powerful monsters. It was a strategy well within the realm of possibility.

In the end, our plan to focus on core power-ups advanced smoothly. Father took care of the money we made off of peddling and made sure to only spend it in Melromarc, and in Siltvelt we made money to spend off of drop items from monsters.

Still, we wouldn't be able to use the core power-up method for Keel and Sakura's weapons. Their strength would depend on raw leveling up. We also didn't want to start waving around weapons right here in Melromarc, so we could only use them in Siltvelt.

We spent about a week continuing our medicine peddling and working on Father's shield core power-ups.

For people with grave sicknesses or deep wounds, we covered them up with a robe so they couldn't see how we healed them. Since we could increase the efficacy of the medicine with our heroes' weapons, if we didn't cover the wound, it would look like their injury had miraculously vanished. I also assisted with those procedures, naturally!

It sounded like nowadays we had started to develop a reputation as the miracle-makers from the bird god's carriage. Whenever we arrived at a village, people would come flooding out and bow down to us, begging us to heal their illnesses. Father would smile gently and go about healing as many of them as he could.

Since we had only been traveling for two weeks, it's not like we had covered a massive region yet. We wouldn't have nearly enough time to go all across Melromarc. We had about two months, so I supposed we'd just go as far as we could in that time.

"It's been almost three weeks since we were summoned here, hasn't it?" Father asked me.

"You're right," I said. "That means we have just one week until the first wave of destruction."

"We've already made a decent amount of money, but I think we should consider selling stuff besides medicine too," Father said. "We're not exactly making a big profit."

That's because Father had such a generous heart! We were selling the medicine for cheap, and Father always took the time to heal the patients fully. We had started to see more desperate patients come to us, begging us to save their lives. Father was spending a lot of effort on those patients that couldn't afford to pay, always saying that he had the time.

"I get that in our situation we need to be cutting corners and squeezing cash every chance we have," Father said, sighing. "But I think knowing that we can always get more money in Siltvelt made me take this less seriously. Sorry, Motoyasu."

"Do not worry about it in the slightest!" I insisted.

In the first go-around, Father became known as the saint of the bird god. I felt good that this time we were on a similar track.

When we started chasing after Father in the first go-around, lots of villagers helped him escape, which I could tell now was because of how he had helped so many people in his travels. Running short on money seemed like a cheap price to pay for that sort of reputation.

"Our real problem is classing up, I say."

"Good point." Father scratched his head. "The trade-off method is working so far, but I think we should try to actually class up if we can."

Keel oinked in agreement.

"Exactly! Keel should be able to transform into a therianthrope soon. I think we should try to class her up."

"Oink!" Keel looked genuinely excited and jolly, I say. So she wanted to class up that badly?

"I've also been thinking that I want to go talk to some people in Siltvelt, so why don't we head there?" Father suggested. "Elena, what will you do?"

"Oiiiiiink."

"Huh? It sounds annoying, so you'll just wait in the carriage."

Lazy Pig's head suddenly dropped as she dozed off. Her laziness was truly unlike anything I had ever seen before.

Whatever, I thought. But either way, we still needed to get to Siltvelt without anyone realizing.

I wondered if the disguised thieves sent by the Church of the Three Heroes had given up on surprise attacks now that Father had developed a good reputation. Instead, they seemed to have been spreading rumors about the appearance of a criminal known as the Shield Hero.

I remembered hearing those rumors in the first go-around

shortly before the first wave of destruction. But their lies didn't matter, not this time. Father wasn't famous as the Shield Hero, but as the legendary saint of the bird god.

Even if the Church of the Three Heroes disguised themselves to attack us, that wouldn't change the fact that we have the filolials to stop them. If they tried to get Itsuki and Ren to help them, even they would be suspicious about attacking a saint of the bird god. And if everyone found out that the saint of the bird god was the Shield Hero, then that would just turn the people against the Church of the Three Heroes instead. If they told everyone we were only pretending to be good, people would hardly believe it. People tend to draw simple conclusions based on what they see, after all.

In the first go-around, just before the first wave of destruction hit, I went with the Crimson Swine over to Zeltoble to strengthen their defenses.

Before that, Filo-tan kicked me so, so many times. If only I could see her again.

Filo-tan . . .

Nowadays, during our breaks, I was passing time by drawing pictures of Filo-tan. We had a lot of spare time while waiting for the carriage to move from place to place.

"Are you drawing another picture, Motoyasu?" Father asked me.

"I am, I say! Did you finish preparing?"

Father nodded, glancing at the picture I drew of Filo-tan.

"Not bad," Father said. "Is that the girl you like?"

"It most certainly is."

"She looks a lot like Sakura. Her coloring is just different."

"That is precisely correct. She isn't too different from Sakura, I say."

Sakura came over and looked at the drawing as well.

"Huh? What's wrong, Sakura?"

"Motoyasu says the girl he likes looks similar to you," Father explained.

"Really?"

"This is her angel form," I said.

"She looks like a video game character," Father said. "She looks like a cute, honest girl."

Oh, my Filo-tan . . . my beloved, wherever could you possibly be?

Sakura tilted her head as she took a closer look.

"Motoyasu says that I was this girl's master," Father said to Sakura.

"Do you wish I looked more like this?" Sakura asked Father.

Watching them interact was always a treat for the eyes.

"No, not at all," Father said. "You're just as beautiful, Sakura."

"Do you like girls, Naofumi?"

"Well, sure, just as much as any other guy. But right now I'm more focused on other things."

"Do you think I'm cute?" Sakura asked.

"Of course you are!"

Keel oinked something in response.

"Yeah, Sakura is beautiful," Father responded. "But you're a close match, Keel."

Keel snorted and squealed.

"Yes, sorry, I know you're a boy."

As Father and the others engaged in such trifling chitchat, Yuki was looking at my drawing as well. It was only natural. *Filo-tan makes for a striking figure!*

"Is this your future sweetheart, Motoyasu?" Yuki asked.

"That's right," Father said, and with a coy smile, "You aren't jealous, are you, Yuki?"

"I am not jealous!" Yuki said, shaking her head vigorously.

Father watched her, grinning. "You sure?"

"I simply want to do all that I can to help Motoyasu," Yuki said firmly.

"Really? I really thought that you had feelings for Motoyasu," Father said and glanced over at me for some reason or other.

His gaze reminded me of my middle school friends back in the day. They were guys who knew everything there was to know about pigs. For some reason we got along and used to hang out a lot. I had almost no guy friends, other than those few. They often tried to push pigs in my direction, I recall. They knew about the pigs' hobbies, behavior, and even carried around photos of pigs.

But then I went to a different high school and never saw them again. Thinking back, they were such mysterious boys. If you wanted pigs that badly, would you really try to talk to them using all of that information? I don't get them anymore, even though I didn't think anything of it back when I used to know them. They were the very definition of fastidious. They knew so much about pigs, but it felt like they were gathering so much information not to go after the pigs themselves but to try to push pigs in my direction.

"I respect Motoyasu very much, but we don't have that sort of relationship!" said Yuki firmly. She seemed a bit stiff.

I laughed. What an adorable response, I say! I rubbed her head.

"I believe I mentioned this before, but Father is amazing at telling jokes," I explained. I turned to Father. "Filolials are like my children, you see."

"Your children?"

"Yes—and all children are adorable, I say! Obviously, you would never even think about romance or marriage with your children! The only one I desire is Filo-tan!"

"Uhhh, right," Father said, nodding. "Well, do your best, Yuki."

"I told you I don't feel that way about him!"

Yuki kept yelling at Father, who tried his best to calm her down.

Chapter Three: A Hidden Passage

"Hey, hey, Kitamura! Look!"

Kou pointed at the nearest mountain range.

"I can smell something super delicious coming from over there!"

Father had been trying to calm down Yuki. But he glanced over in the direction Kou was pointing.

"Huh? What's over there?" he asked.

I referenced my map. It appeared to be somewhere in the south-southeastern corner of Melromarc, not too far from the border. I think that even if you crossed the mountain you would still be in Melromarc.

Sure, we could head there. Why not? I thought to myself.

Oho? When I looked closely, I thought I saw the outline of a person flickering through the trees.

"If Kou smells something, there must be something over there, right?" Father asked.

"Yeah! There's definitely something," Kou said, drool hanging from his beak. "And it's not too far, right?"

"Let's go check it out," Father said. "It looks like we don't need to go too deep into the mountain."

"Woohoo!"

So Kou started pulling us toward the mountain. The carriage clattered and rattled at his intense speed. The road faded farther and farther away, and we followed something like a game trail deep into the mountain.

Father opened up the map again.

"Could it be someone's campsite?"

"Found it!" called Kou.

Kou detached from the carriage and raced off. Father peeked outside and looked around carefully.

"Some kind of animal? Monsters?"

Then we heard a loud, sustained scream coming from Kou's direction. But not Kou's voice.

"Kou! Wait—wait, don't do anything!" Father shouted, taking care to check his surroundings and then jumping out of the carriage. I followed Father's lead and glanced around suspiciously.

"What in the—?"

Like a hunter holding his triumphantly captured game, Kou held something by his feet.

"H-help me!"

It was begging for its life. It was a . . . a mole. A talking mole.

Now that I thought about it, there had been a talking mole back in Father's village, I say.

"Kou, let him go! That's not a monster!" Father shouted.

"We need to confirm what it is first," I suggested.

"Aw, man," Kou said and reluctantly took his talons off of the mole.

"Sorry about that," Father said, rushing from the carriage up to where Kou and the mole were. "That must've frightened you. Please forgive us."

"Oh, t-thank you so much," the mole said. "D-don't w-worry about a thing. I was following the mountain road and could hardly see, and that's what happens when you get lost in the mountains."

The mole stood up. Father checked to make sure it didn't have any injuries, and then, bowing his head, he sincerely apologized.

"You need to say you're sorry, Kou," Father said.

"Come on," groaned Kou. He bowed his head.

It wasn't quite an apology, but Father seemed more focused on talking to the mole than forcing Kou to say sorry.

"It's nice to meet you," Father said. "Are you a therianthrope? What are you doing here?"

In Melromarc, demi-humans and therianthropes were at the very bottom of the social ladder. When you think about how all human societies work with an upper and lower class, it's not all that unusual.

"Ah, yes. I am a lumo. You see . . ."

Even if he was a brigand or a thief, he didn't appear to have any weapons and looked like an ordinary villager from Siltvelt. And not a merchant or a salesperson, but more like a lumberjack or woodsman. Or maybe a palanquin bearer.

Still, I couldn't help but sense that he was hiding something from us.

Then, from a slight distance, we heard the sound of clashing metal. The mole instantly tensed up at the sound.

"What's that?" Father asked, looking toward the sound. The mole suddenly raced off in the same direction.

"Wait!" Father called. "Seems like there's a lot going on here. Let's find out."

"Are you sure, Father?"

If we got involved in a troublesome situation, it could end up drawing attention to us and prove our very downfall, I say.

"Well, we can't just leave here like we didn't see anything," he said.

"You are quite right, Father. So let's get going already!"

I didn't have a great feeling about all this, but Kou went back to the carriage and sent us chasing after the mole as fast as he could.

The sound of clashing metal turned out to be a battle.

"Hehehe . . . Don't try and resist anymore! You're just causing us trouble!"

"What is going on?"

Father looked outside the carriage again to observe the

situation. A large group of people was rushing to attack a cave, with a number of moles defending it.

Keel let out a series of oinks at the sight of the battle before racing to climb down out of the carriage. Meanwhile, the mole that we had talked to previously was wildly swinging an axe, charging into the fight.

"Wait, Keel!" Father said. "It's too dangerous to go alone!"

Father climbed down from the carriage after Keel and grabbed the mole by the shoulders, preventing him from entering the fray.

"Let me go!" he shouted, struggling to enter the battle, but Father, as the Shield Hero with impressive defensive capabilities, didn't even blink.

"Please, let me go!" the mole cried. "I don't mind if I get caught myself!"

Keel oinked angrily.

"Wait a second," Father said in a quiet, threatening tone. He glared at Keel and the mole before speaking calmly. "Keel, this doesn't have anything to do with us. We just need to figure out what's going on first. Like you said, Keel, they're probably slave hunters."

His sharp, cool voice reminded me of Father from the first go-around, I say.

Keel oinked several times in response, nodding, before looking toward Lazy Pig. She was still in the carriage. She squealed loudly in response.

Lumo Slave Hunters

After the damage the wave of destruction caused, Melromarc soldiers went slave hunting in Raphtalia's village but also continued to search for slaves elsewhere. Lumo are a race of mole therianthropes, skilled with their hands. They usually take on miscellaneous jobs in villages.

Personally, I didn't see how these so-called slave hunters were any different from plain old thieves.

"Elena, you're saying that even Melromarc soldiers and knights are mixed in with the slave hunters? This really is a rotten country," Father said.

Then he cast a gaze in the filolials' and my direction and gave us a signal to go.

Lazy Pig sighed and grumbled a few meager oinks.

"You're saying even if we rescue the slaves then they'll be after us instead? Well, yes, but we need to help them anyway, right? We're deep in the mountain, so we just need to make sure that no one else sees us here."

Then Father looked at me again.

Aha—I understood what he wanted me to do.

"Liberation Fireflash!"

I chanted a spell to reveal any enemies that were hidden with concealment magic.

We couldn't see that well because of the dense woods, so we had no choice but to get closer to see any more details about what was going on.

"There don't appear to be any hidden enemies," I informed Father.

"That's perfect for us," he said.

"Stop your futile resistance!" bellowed a slave hunter. "If you want to die, then so be it!"

The moment the slave hunter was about to strike his sword through a mole, Father called, "Air Strike Shield!"

The swords helplessly bounced off of his shield, right before the moles' eyes.

"Huh! What the hell?"

"First let's prioritize stopping the attack," Father said. "Capture the slave hunters without killing them!"

"Anything for Motoyasu!" chirped Sakura.

"So many moles!" cried Kou in delight.

"Let's do it!" said Yuki.

At Father's orders, the filolials charged.

"Don't leave me out of the fray!" I declared.

"M-Motoyasu, make sure you go easy on them!" Father called.

Well, if Father commanded me to do so, I suppose I had no choice.

"Who the hell are these guys?" shouted a slave hunter, caught off guard by our attack from behind.

"Take that!"

With her sheath still on the sword, Sakura sent one flying with a powerful blow.

Kou went around kicking the hunters while keeping one

longing eye on the moles. And Yuki chanted wind magic spells to send attackers flying away from the moles.

"Paralyze Lance! Sleep Lance! Illusion Lance!" I groaned. "Man, this is so tedious. Aiming Lancer IV!"

The bloodcurdling, agonized screams of slave hunters rose into the air.

After paralyzing and putting to sleep countless slave hunters, I targeted those attempting to escape and stopped them in their tracks with Aiming Lancer. In an instant, all of the slave hunters were knocked out or frozen.

The moles stared at us blankly.

"Wow, it really only takes you and the filolials a second to finish everyone off," Father commented.

With that, we took care of the whole group of slave hunters so fast even we could hardly believe it.

"I've captured the ones that were trying to run away," Yuki announced.

"I'll tie them up and keep a close eye on them!" Sakura said.

It was almost like the filolials were playing a game of cops and robbers with each other. Of course, in that scenario, Yuki would always play the role of the cop.

The moles were staring at us with frightened eyes. Father finally took his hand off of the first mole that we encountered and gave him a signal to go ahead.

The mole glanced back at Father several times and, with axe in hand, hurried back to his companions.

"Is everyone okay?" he cried.

The moles chattered amongst themselves. There didn't appear to be any fatal wounds.

There weren't any captured slaves yet either, so it appeared that the slave hunters had just started their outing.

"Anyone injured, please come over here right away!" Father called. "Motoyasu, you come help too!"

"At once, Father!"

Right at that moment, Lazy Pig came out with medicine, oinking away.

Father turned to her with an exhausted expression.

"Elena, what are you saying? We didn't do this to sell medicine!"

The moles were still eyeing us suspiciously as we healed them, but since we had rescued them from the slave hunters, after all, they seemed to let their guard down somewhat. We finished treating all of the injured.

"So then," Father said in a tone as sharp as a dagger, turning to the captured slave hunters. "Are you really going to keep hunting demi-humans for slaves?"

"Just who the hell do you think you are?!" the hunter screamed. "You think we'll just let you get away with this?! No chance! You've underestimated us!"

"Answer the question," Father demanded.

Then Lazy Pig finally climbed out of the carriage and walked over to the hunters. She oinked a few times.

"Yeah, that's right!" a hunter snarled in response. "House Seaetto is done with! We're in a new era, a better one! What's wrong with hunting demi-humans? What's wrong with that?"

Father explained to me later that Lazy Pig recognized that the slave hunters were knights of Melromarc. After some of the Melromarc nobles who had fervently supported demi-human rights died, slave hunting in the country seemed to have increased.

"So that's it," Father said. "You really think that slave hunting is okay, then."

"Of course it is! We won't forget this! Hey, aren't you the filthy Shield Hero? So the Shield Hero attacked us—our friends in Melromarc won't let you get away with it!"

As if they had somehow won the battle, the captured slave hunters started grinning at us.

What unbelievable idiocy. They thought that they had found the Shield Hero, who had a bounty on his head, but had forgotten that *they* were the ones who had been captured.

Keel oinked angrily at them.

"Your day will come," the slave hunter snarled. "Aren't you one of the demi-humans who used to be in Seaetto territory?" he spat at Keel. "Typical demi-human. The Shield Hero and his demi-human companions . . . the whole country is after you!"

So this was the same lot that had attacked Keel's village, apparently.

They were a bunch of seriously bad guys, no doubt about it. That was proof enough that we couldn't just leave all of the justice and righteousness to Itsuki, because he'd never solve any of the real problems. Typical of any villain who would stoop so low as to support Trash, I say!

"Father, why don't we get rid of them?" I suggested. "There would be no witnesses or survivors."

If we got rid of them now, no one would have to know what happened, I say.

"What!?" All of a sudden, the slave hunters turned pale. Those fools had assumed that they would live to see tomorrow. How pathetic.

"How about no, Motoyasu?" Father said, and the slave hunters breathed a sigh of relief and started smirking again. They really didn't understand the position they were in.

"Motoyasu, can you go get that slave merchant and bring him here? I have an idea."

"What do you intend to do?" I inquired.

Keel oinked a few times.

"I'm going to sell them as slaves," Father announced.

"You imbecile!" sneered the slave hunter. "You can't sell human slaves in this country. It's against the law! You didn't even know that?"

He was acting so arrogant toward Father. Know your place, I say!

Father turned to the slave hunters with an ice-cold gaze.

"Whoever said I was going to sell you in Melromarc?"

Lazy Pig appeared to have guessed what Father was thinking and started to oink and snort a bunch of times.

Immediately, the slave hunters went sheet white and started to beg Father for their lives.

"Exactly," Father said. "You're going to experience what it's like to be one of the slaves that you've sold."

It was that same sharp, frigid tone that Father always used in the first go-around, I say!

"You think that will make us apologize or something?" the slave hunter screamed in desperation. "Are you insane! Don't do it! Please, don't do it!"

"What do you mean?" Father asked. "So when you sell others, it's fine, so long as you don't get sold? Let me give you some advice here. People who attack others need to be prepared to be attacked themselves."

"No, no, that's not how it works! There's no problem with lowly demi-humans suffering and dying! But we're noble humans! We would never be beaten by a pathetic—"

Should I stop his annoying babbling? Just as I thought about it, Father glanced at me and gave me the signal to go ahead and shut them up.

So I struck him with a Sleep Lance and he slumped over, having fainted.

"I think Yuki is doing her best dealing with the rest of the deserters, but I'm sure a separate group of slave hunters will come searching for their friends after they've been out of action for long enough," Father said.

Taking a deep sigh, Father turned to Lazy Pig to discuss something.

"So if the knights and soldiers in this country are caught up in the slave trade, we may have no choice but to hunt the slave hunters," he said.

"Oink oink," said Lazy Pig.

"I know it'll be almost impossible to take them all out. We also have to worry about our own standing." Father thought about it. "Well, let's worry about that later."

The moles seemed to have pretty much relaxed at this point. One of them, who appeared to be a leader of some sort, called out to us with an axe in hand and gave a deep bow.

"Thank you so much for saving us," he said.

"Of course," Father said. "I'm just glad that nobody was badly hurt."

Having sensed that it was safe, more moles appeared to be peering out at us from inside the cave. There were also little baby moles.

I noticed one little mole in particular glancing our way from the shadow of a mother mole, pregnant belly swollen. I couldn't help but feel like I had seen that little mole somewhere before.

I did remember from the first go-around that filolials thought they looked tasty and that they were skilled at making pretty accessories. I just got the vague sense that little mole was somehow important.

Father noticed that it was glancing at us repeatedly and waved at it with a smile.

The mole leader spoke back up. "When you were talking with the slave hunter, I heard that you are the Shield Hero."

I figured that the moles trusted us if they were going to bring that up.

"Uh, well . . ." Father nodded, as if trying to be intentionally vague. "That's me. My name is Naofumi Iwatani, the Shield Hero."

The moles all expressed their immense thanks to Father with prayers of gratitude. Then they showed us into their den.

"Really, we cannot thank you enough for protecting us," the leader mole said. "I wasn't sure what would happen if we hadn't encountered the party of one of the heroes."

"Don't worry," Father said. "I heard from Keel that some really tragic things have happened. I'm sure things have been difficult for you."

The mole leader frowned darkly. Maybe he was thinking about all the cruel things the slave hunters had said.

"Well, they might try to do something once they catch wind of what happened with those guys. But if Melromarc can change from behind the scenes, I think you'll be safe in the end," Father said.

We didn't really have much choice but to wait until the queen came around here and fixed things up for good, I supposed. Which meant another two months of being patient.

"Excuse me, Shield Hero," the leader said.

"Yeah?"

"I've heard a rumor in Melromarc about the Shield Hero being involved in some disgraceful activities. It may be better for the Shield Hero to go to some other demi-human land, in my opinion."

"Sure, you're not wrong."

"However, I don't think Melromarc will let you out without a fight," he continued.

I didn't disagree with the mole. That's what happened in the last two go-arounds after all.

"If you don't mind, I have a proposal."

The mole leader explained his idea. When the time came, the moles could take us from their village and out of the country without passing through the border fortress—by means of underground tunnels they had built.

I had no idea that those tunnels even existed. So it turns out that if we had befriended these moles previously, we could've had another way to secretly leave Melromarc. Well, from our experiences in the last go-around, it seemed like we had people working against us in Siltvelt anyway. So we probably would've been attacked either way, I guess.

"We built the tunnels so that demi-humans could escape from this country in a time of absolute need," explained the mole. "Please use our tunnels so you can flee this land!"

Father scratched his head. "I really appreciate the offer, but we still have some things to take care of here in Melromarc," he said.

"Is that so? I do apologize for going so far as to make a suggestion."

"Don't worry about it. More importantly, it seems like slave hunters know about this place, so make sure they never find out about the tunnels. Of course, we'll do our best to stop other slave hunters from finding it, but it's not like we're going to stay here forever."

"Certainly," said the mole.

"Even worse, it sounds like people are going to be after you here in Melromarc," Father said. Father glanced at me before turning back to the mole. "It sounds like you could easily get us into Siltvelt—why don't you do that?"

The mole cleared his throat. "Unfortunately, that's not possible. You see, we lumo had a low status in Siltvelt and Shield-freeden, which is why we came to Melromarc in the first place, when Lord Seaetto invited us here."

That's true. While Siltvelt was sympathetic to demi-humans in general, they had a strict hierarchy system among the different races. Even if the moles went to Siltvelt, they might attract unwanted attention.

And Shieldfreeden was out of the question. Even though they claimed that discrimination was abolished there, it was really a hotbed for racism. The obvious result of being led by that contemptible Takt.

"Oh, okay. Still, I wonder if maybe you could have a place there, if I advocated on your behalf . . ." Father trailed off. "I guess, in a worst-case scenario, there would be others getting upset at you out of jealousy, if anything." Father thought about it for a moment. "Regardless, until we clean up things here in Melromarc, I'd like for all of you to flee the country using the tunnels you built. Once things get better, of course, you can always come back."

The mole leader nodded. "Understood. Now that Lord Seaetto is no longer with us, in order to escape the slave hunters, we shall follow your wisdom and escape this country as quickly as we can."

"So sorry for mixing you guys up with our own problems," Father added.

"Not at all! You have given us a path forward when we had lost our way! Do not worry about us."

It sounded like they had built the tunnels without any of

the Melromarc nobles finding out, so pretty much no one knew about them other than demi-humans. Which was obvious, because if they had told anyone in Melromarc, others were bound to find out.

So the moles were there waiting for other demi-humans that needed to flee. Who, tragically made into slaves, never managed to come themselves.

With that, we secretly brought the monster trainer to the moles' den, and Father ordered him to sell the slave hunters as slaves. Then I forcibly added them to my party and I sent us all flying to Siltvelt with Portal Spear.

When the monster trainer heard what we were trying to do, I saw his face light up like I had never seen before. He gave us a letter of introduction to other monster trainers he knew in Siltvelt and told us where to find them. Since word had arrived in Siltvelt about people in Melromarc making demi-humans slaves, he told us that we could get a great deal in Siltvelt. But once we sold them, Father got into an unpleasant mood for a long while.

Well, it was only natural, as those slave hunters were scum filthy enough to make you vomit.

After we took care of all that, we went with the moles to the entrance of the hidden tunnel and waved goodbye.

"Shield Hero! Everybody! Thank you, thank you! We'll never forget your kindness!"

"Stay safe out there, and be happy!" Father called. "Please wait just a little longer and you'll be able to come back!"

Keel oinked excitedly and waved so hard I thought her arms were going to fly off her body.

"Moles," whined Kou. Certainly, he was sad to see them go.

"Lord Shield Hero," came a voice. It was the first mole whom we had met. He handed us a letter.

"Thank you so much for everything you've done," he said. "This was all I could do to thank you, but I heard you were friends with a weapon shop owner in Melromarc castle town. If you give him this, you'll be sure to get some favorable treatment."

Father accepted it. "Thank you. We'll use it carefully."
The mole nodded. "I can never say it enough, but thank you again!"

With that, the mole went scurrying away into the entrance of the secret tunnel.

Chapter Four: Experts Know Best

It was the day after we encountered the moles.

"All right, should we head for the dragon hourglass now?" Father asked me.

"At once, Father!"

I activated Portal Spear and sent us to Siltvelt. We set out for the dragon hourglass. It was located in a big building that looked like a church, similar to where the dragon hourglass in Melromarc was. I recalled fondly how Father had helped Yuki and the filolials class up in the previous go-around. With heroes as their companions, filolials also shed marvelous large feathers. But unfortunately, we didn't have any feathers this time around.

We entered the church with the dragon hourglass and went up to the reception area. It didn't appear like the people inside were particularly religious or anything.

"Excuse me," Father said. "We'd like to perform the class-up ceremony here."

"Letter of permission?" the receptionist demanded.

How rude. I supposed Siltvelt was known for its discrimination against humans. For showing Father such blatant disrespect, swiftly murdering this impudent receptionist was not out of the question. Disrespect toward Father is a crime punishable by death, I say.

"Uh . . ." Father paused. He pulled what the Siltvelt emissary had given us out of his pocket and handed it over to the receptionist.

At first the receptionist mechanically glanced down at the forms but then stared back up at Father with disbelieving eyes.

"L-Lord . . . Lord Shield Hero?"

"Yeah, that's me. Need proof?"

Father held up his shield and chanted Air Strike Shield.

"Will that do?"

"Of . . . of course! Then before the class-up, please, allow me to take you to the castle—"

"Sorry, but we're traveling here in secret. The people over there are already aware of our plans."

"Very . . . very well then, if you so command. It's written here as well, but it seems that you are in the midst of attempting to change Melromarc from the inside."

"Yup. That's why no one can find out about what we're doing. We can only head to the Siltvelt castle after we finish things on our end. Got it?"

We were here to level up in secret, I say. Of course, the top brass in Siltvelt would want to meet us if they found out we were here, but then we might get pulled into all sorts of avoidable trouble, so Father was smart to try to evade.

"U-understood." The receptionist bowed. "I am here to serve, oh Mighty Spear Hero."

"Sorry about that."

"In that case, which of you needs to class up?"

"Okay, Keel."

"Oink!"

At Father's direction, Keel stepped forward and raised a hand without any hint of shyness.

"Please, this way," the receptionist said, to which Keel responded with a few nervous oinks.

"Oh, you don't understand the Siltvelt language?" Father asked Keel. "I forgot that my shield was automatically translating everything for me. He's saying to come with him."

Father translated the receptionist's explanation to Keel. They went to the hourglass and Keel touched it. The hourglass faintly glimmered, and they commenced the class-up process.

"Once you close your eyes you should start to see it," Father said. "I can't decide your future for you, so think carefully and decide for yourself."

Keel oinked once in contemplation and then triumphantly.

Father did always have the policy of leaving class-up decisions up to the individual. I remember Father giving me the freedom to class up as I wished.

So Keel's class-up ended without incident, and we completed the ceremony for the filolials as well.

"So now you can all get even stronger, right?" Father said. "We have one week left until the wave of destruction . . . We'll need to work hard, so keep at it!"

A chime of robust agreement rang out around the room.

With his newly classed-up comrades, Father decided to level up until we had to get back to the carriage. I went to collect more materials to power up Father's shield and sell here in Siltvelt. Since Sakura had leveled up enough to help Father, I took Yuki with me.

It was important for us to save a lot of money, I say. There are power-ups that require an investment, for one, but more importantly, once we had finished cleaning up things here in Melromarc, I had to buy filolial eggs. A *lot* of filolial eggs.

There was a limit to how much money Siltvelt would just give me, after all. I needed as much money as humanly possible to have the best shot at finding my precious Filo-tan.

And then there was one big problem that I had forgotten about.

The next day, Keel and Yuki watched over the carriage while Kou went out with Lazy Pig to level up. We had just four days left until the wave of destruction.

But Keel was on all four knees in the carriage, groaning and focusing intensely.

"Yeah, like that!" Sakura chirped. "When I transform, I just focus really hard and get way stronger!"

"Sakura, I'm not sure if that's a helpful explanation," Father said.

"But Kou feels the same way!" Sakura said.

"What about Yuki?"

"That's simply how it works," called Yuki, who was pulling the carriage.

"What are you talking about, I say?" I inquired. I had been busy drawing a picture of Filo-tan.

Keel squealed and groaned about something or other.

"What is she saying?"

"She's saying she wants to be able to transform so that you can understand her," Father said.

That would certainly be the best possible solution, I say. She should've been able to transform by about now, but it seems like she couldn't yet.

"Oink oink oink!"

Father shook his head. "Motoyasu said that you could transform into a dog. But maybe you actually can't though."

Lazy Pig and Kou had just gotten back. Lazy Pig grumbled a few exhausted oinks, to which Keel squealed back furiously.

"Hey, don't start a fight, Elena," Father said.

Apparently, Elena had said that even if Keel transformed, it didn't mean that I would necessarily see her as a boy.

"I mean, I see your point," Father said. "I'm trying to tell him that you're a boy, Keel, so just keep at it."

ABOUT DEMI-HUMANS AND THERIANTHROPES

"Demi-human" refers to **species that look like humans on the outside but have qualities and features from certain animals**. Species that have much more animal-like features are referred to as therianthropes. However, some demi-humans **can transform into therianthropes at will**. Demi-humans that can transform are generally rare, but sometimes the ability can suddenly spring up.

Therianthropes also have **various special abilities depending on their species**. For example, Sadeena, an orca demi-human, when transformed can swim at great depths. And lumo, mole therianthropes, are skilled at digging tunnels.

Fohl became able to transform into a therianthrope after the battle in Siltvelt, a realization of the old legend that the Shield Hero brings out the true powers of Siltvelt citizens. Keel became able to transform in the first go-around after practicing with Sadeena. Every case is different.

When a demi-human classes up, either their strength in their human form or in their therianthrope form increases—but not both. Classing up can also grant special abilities.

"How do you think we can get Keel to be able to transform?" Father asked.

"It seems like being around the filolials as they transform isn't enough," I said. I recalled that Keel could already transform by the time I had arrived at Father's village, so I had absolutely no idea how she had developed the skill.

"Experts know best," I remarked. "Perhaps we should go ask some demi-humans in Siltvelt how they do it?"

"Yeah, that's a good idea. Let's try that."

Keel oinked in agreement. So we took Portal Spear back to Siltvelt. This time, Yuki and Lazy Pig kept an eye on the carriage.

"On second thought . . ." Father trailed off. He then raised a good point. If the Shield Hero just went up to a random demi-human on the street and asked them, they might raise a ruckus and alert the Siltvelt leaders. Of course, Father always had a way to escape. But we didn't want anyone to know we were here if we could help it. The word might always leak back out to Melromarc. So it would be better to figure this out after we fixed things in Melromarc.

In which case it would make the most sense to pretend to be ordinary travelers and ask around that way. But how many random demi-humans could transform in the first place?

"I guess we have no choice but to ask around and find out," Father said. "Motoyasu, just keep quiet."

"Anything for you, Father!"

Keel oinked and followed after Father.

A few minutes later, we called out to a passerby.

"Excuse me. We think he has the potential to transform into a therianthrope, but would you happen to know how to do that?"

But the demi-human just cast us a suspicious glance and walked away. These bigoted passersby didn't realize who Father was and ignored us as a result, even gripping their weapons and assuming a fighting stance. But since Father had excellent defensive powers, I wasn't particularly concerned.

We went on calling out to different people that we passed. One appeared to be a wolfman.

"Huh? How to transform?" He glanced at Keel. "So you can't transform? That's too bad."

At the least he had done us the favor of responding, I say.

"Do you think you'd be able to teach him?" Father asked.

"All right, sure."

"Oink!"

So that solved things pretty easily. But a bigger problem quickly emerged.

"Hey, so what language is that guy even speaking?" the wolfman asked Father.

"What?" Father looked confused for a moment. "Oh . . ."

"Oink?"

We had forgotten. Keel spoke Melromarc's language.

"I can translate," Father offered.

"Can you translate magical terms too?"

"Well . . ."

"Sorry, in that case, it's a no go," the friendly therianthrope said and disappeared like all the rest.

We were in quite a pickle, I say. It appeared that transformation required some complicated magic that could be difficult to translate. At the moment, Father couldn't use magic at all. We had to somehow find a demi-human that could transform and also spoke Melromarc's tongue.

"Motoyasu, do you have any other ideas about how we can get Keel to transform?"

"I'm sure Big Sis's Big Sis would be able to solve things, but . . ." I paused. In Father's village, how many demi-humans had there been that could transform? Keel, of course. I could remember her transforming a number of times, I say. After that, it was Big Sis's Big Sis, the orca demi-human. And then the tiger guy.

Between the two, I'd have to lean toward Big Sis's Big Sis. Filo-tan trusted her, for one, and she took care to look after everyone in the village. I remembered that she was kind to the filolials and a very reliable person.

Huh? All of a sudden, I remembered someone else, a person who was pretty similar to Big Sis's Big Sis. It was a tanuki therianthrope, someone who had been pretty close to Father, if I was remembering correctly.

Who the heck was that?

"Oink?"

"Come up with anything?" Father prodded.

"Someone from the same village as Keel," I said. "An orca-like therianthrope, a fisherwoman named Sadeena, I say."

"Oink oink oink oink!"

"Her name is Sadeena? Do you know where she is?"

"I couldn't even begin to guess," I declared. I hadn't the slightest clue where Big Sis's Big Sis could possibly be. She had already been there when I had arrived at Father's village, so I had no idea when she had met and joined up with Father.

"I suppose we have no choice but to put off Keel's transformation a little longer." Father sighed. Just as he said it, we could hear Keel's stomach grumble.

And then I heard a loud rumble coming from Kou's and Sakura's bellies as well.

"Well, let's go eat somewhere," Father said.

"I'll go slay some monsters, I say!"

"No, we can go to a tavern or something, and we'll go ask around if anyone's seen Sadeena while we're at it," Father said.

"Of course, Father!"

So we went straight to the nearest tavern. Siltvelt had plenty of nocturnal demi-humans, so places tended to get crowded at night, but even though the sun was still up, there was a decent number of people in the tavern. While everyone else started eating, Father surveyed the interior.

Keel oinked a few times.

"Don't worry about it, Keel," Father said. "My job is to figure out stuff like this for us."

"Oink . . ."

Just as they were chatting, Father's face lit up as he saw something. He tapped me on the shoulder and pointed.

"Motoyasu! Look—look!"

"Whatever could it be, I say?"

When I looked in the direction he was pointing, I saw a panda therianthrope heartily guzzling liquor.

"It's a panda!" Father said excitedly. "So there are even panda therianthropes in this world!"

The panda grunted and turned to us with an unpleasant expression. "Huh? Whaddaya want?" It stood up and thudded toward us.

What in the world was happening?

If that panda intended to do harm to Father, I, Motoyasu Kitamura, would lay waste to its vile existence.

But that panda . . . I had the strange feeling that I had seen it somewhere before, I say.

Panda Therianthrope	
One of the three champion mercenaries of Zeltoble. We first met her when we went to the Colosseum with Sadeena.	

I seemed to remember the panda speaking to Big Sis's Big Sis at some point.

"Calm down, Motoyasu," Father said. "He doesn't look like he wants to hurt us."

Father calmed me down before standing up and bowing politely to the panda.

"I apologize," Father said. "Since I'm from the faraway countryside, I'd never seen a panda therianthrope before and got overly excited."

"Hmmm," the panda grumbled. "So that's why you pointed at me?"

It had a high voice. Perhaps it was actually female.

"I'm truly sorry."

Then Keel oinked at the panda.

"Huh? You're the one who pointed at me!"

"Oink! Oink oink!"

"I was just enjoying myself, drinking, and then you went ahead and interrupted, with your weird fancy clothes."

"Oink oink oink oink oink!"

"So you're wearing those clothes even though you hate 'em? Just take 'em off. It looks pretty wimpy to me."

Keel was about to stand up but Father held her down. Sakura stood up at the same time and Father had to calm her down as well.

"Stop it! Everyone, calm down!"

Father turned back to the panda. "I just noticed it now. But since you were able to talk with Keel, does that mean you're able to speak the languages of both Siltvelt and Melromarc?"

"Huh? I am a mercenary, so I can pretty much get by."

"A mercenary, of course. So you've gone around to fight for different countries, right?"

"That's what a mercenary does, ain't it? And I'm a mercenary, so that's the life I've lived."

"Got it," Father said, nodding. "I just have one question for you then. It seemed like you noticed me pointing at you, so you came over here . . . But can you explain why even before that, you were looking at Keel the whole time?"

Oho? Now that Father mentioned it, she had been staring at Keel for a long while. Did something about Keel annoy her? Or was she staring at Keel longingly, like Kou, who wanted to eat her tail?

"Father," I said.

"What is it?"

I leaned over and whispered in his ear—my personal opinion of course.

"Oh, definitely," Father said, nodding. "That's definitely possible."

By the way, I had this strange memory of the panda in front of us doing sketch comedy of some sort with Big Sis's Big Sis, I say.

"Thanks. Let's see what happens," Father said to me and turned back to the panda, brimming with confidence.

Flustered, the panda was trying to answer Father's question. "W-well, you see . . . I hate wimpy-looking things, that's why!"

"Is that really your answer?" Father asked.

"What are you trying to say!" roared the panda.

Father produced the ribbon that Keel typically wore on the job and tied it into a bow. Then he handed it to the panda.

"It isn't because it caught your eye, is it? I mean, what he's wearing, of course."

"It *caught my eye* because I hate it!"

"So why did you accept the ribbon I just gave you?"

The panda grunted and shoved the ribbon back to Father.

"You've got it wrong! I wasn't looking at the damn clothes!"

"Motoyasu, can you make some cute clothes to suit our friend here?"

"I certainly can," I responded.

Sometimes there are filolials who want to wear cute clothes even in their filolial forms, I say. If I know what size to make it, I can make any clothes at all, I say!

"He's the one who made that outfit," Father said to the panda. "He'll make you some if you want. We'll make you something, so please forgive us."

"S-stop joking around! I'd never wear those wimpy clothes! They'd look terrible on me!"

Father was smiling brightly. Thinking back on my experiences chasing pigs, I felt like I somehow understood what was happening here. There were some pigs that cultivated a rough-and-tumble image and pretended to hate anything pretty, but deep down they loved girly stuff and actually owned lots of cutesy accessories. I could hear the panda's real intention with the last sentence that slipped off her tongue—that they wouldn't look good on her. Which meant the jig was up.

My suspicions had been correct, and Father had managed to rein the panda in perfectly.

"Really? I think they would look just fine on you," Father said.

"Shut up!" shouted the panda. "Everyone would just laugh at me if I put something like that on!"

Father approached the panda and put a hand on her shoulder. It was like Father was examining her closely.

"Your fur is stiffer than it looks," Father remarked. "You should wash it with soap or soy to soften it up. Then that outfit will practically suit you."

"What do you think you're saying?!"

"I just think a cuter outfit would suit you much better than rock-hard armor," Father said.

Dumbfounded, the panda took several steps back. I couldn't read her expression. She just looked flustered.

"I—I—I'm telling you to stop what you're saying!"

Then a group that appeared to be the panda's underlings started to chatter. "Are they trying to make the lady do something?"

"They're trying to make her become a mascot or something. It's like they're trying to get her to sell wares in the countryside!"

"Are you trying to make me some sorta toy to show off?" the panda demanded.

"I think you'd become a lot more than just that," Father said.

The panda turned around as if she had nothing more to say and walked back over to her underlings. Maybe she got sick of the conversation.

Then, with her back turned to Father, the panda tied the ribbon to her head.

"Whoa! What are you doing?" called out one of the panda's gang.

"I thought it looked nice."

"No! It looks awful!"

"Really? It seems fine to me."

I had absolutely no idea what was going on. The ribbon looked okay, I guess.

I supposed they were just playing around. But I noticed that the panda's underlings, rather than looking angry or surprised, had strange expressions on their faces.

"Isn't it a little too weird?" one of the underlings whispered.

"It's just . . . unexpected."

"Milady's got a nice face, so it does kinda suit her."

The panda silenced them with a vicious glare. Her subordinates glanced away uncomfortably.

Breathing a heavy sigh, the panda turned back to Father.

"Look, I'm sorry about that. What are you all doing here anyway?"

"No worries," Father said. "We were looking for a therianthrope that could teach Keel how to transform. Since you're a mercenary, would you happen to know someone like that?"

"Transform? You don't know? Where did you guys even come from?"

"Uh, we came from Melromarc."

"That's pretty much the center of anti-demi-human racism, ain't it? I get it now. That's why he uses the language of human supremacists." The panda walked over to Keel. "Watch carefully. I'll show you how to transform."

In an instant, the panda turned into a pig. Father widened his eyes in surprise. Had he been expecting something different?

"You *are* cute after all! Those clothes would definitely look great on you!" he exclaimed.

The ex-panda-now-pig oinked and slapped Father in the face but only hurt her own hand. Of course, it was pointless to try and hit the Shield Hero.

Unfortunately, the moment the panda transformed, I lost all ability to understand what she was saying.

"No one would laugh at you! I'm being serious!"

"Oink oink!"

The pig slapped Father again, to little effect, and transformed back into a panda.

"You need to think carefully about what you say!" the panda said. "I'm never going to wear clothes like that!"

The panda grabbed Father's shoulder and attempted to lift him up, but now that Father had powered up, he didn't move an inch. Keel oinked and squealed in protest.

"Shut up! This guy won't stop screwing around!"

"Milady's right! Get 'em!" cried one of her underlings.

"You all better scram! Or else I'll have no choice but to punish all of you!"

"No chance," said Sakura, quickly coming closer to protect Father.

"It's okay, Sakura," said Father. "You too, Motoyasu, just watch and listen."

"Oh, you're asking for it now, ain't you?"

The panda now tried to tackle Father with what appeared to be a bear hug, but even that didn't move him an inch.

"What the hell?! This guy's hard as a rock!"

"Satisfied yet? Is it my turn now?" Father asked. He pulled

out a cloth and wrapped it around the panda's neck like a little scarf. And then he wrapped another one around the panda's head.

"What do you think you're doing?!"

The panda took a step back and yanked off the scarf.

"How many times do I need to tell you to stop messing with me?"

"I'm *not* messing with you," Father insisted. "Men's clothes just don't look great on you."

"That's not the point, damn it!"

"Am I wrong? I just think you're cute . . . In a sort of imposing way, of course, but cute. You could really do well switching back and forth between your demi-human and therianthrope form."

Father had an honest smile on his face. The panda looked taken aback and sighed.

"I've had enough. Just stop trying to make me wear those wimpy clothes." Meanwhile, the panda slipped the cloth that Father had wrapped around her neck into her pocket.

Father had won a battle with words alone, I say! Impressive as ever.

The panda then transformed into her pig form and started teaching Keel. She put her hand on Keel's head and chanted some sort of spell. After finishing, as if Keel had known deep down all along how to do it, she transformed into a puppy.

"I did it! I finally did it!" she cried.

"That's amazing, Keel!" Father exclaimed.

"How do I look? Do I look cool?"

"More cute than cool, to be honest."

"Still? No way. I want to be cool like her!" Keel glanced at the panda, who was watching Keel with a peculiar expression on her face.

In my personal opinion, I agree with Father that Keel was on the cute side of the cute-cool spectrum.

Of course, the cutest of them all was none other than my beloved Filo-tan, I say!

"Hey, hey," Keel asked the panda. "How do I become cool like you? Teach me how!"

"Well, to become like me, first you gotta ditch that frilly skirt . . ." The panda glanced at Keel's maid outfit she had torn off after becoming a dog. "Wear tough armor, and fight a lot! That's what it takes."

"Got it! I'm gonna do my best!"

"Motoyasu, do you understand Keel now?" Father asked me.

"I completely understand now, I say. She finally stopped being a pig."

"From pig to dog, huh? You really are a weird one, Motoyasu."

"Yes! *Finally*, I'm a guy!" Keel said. Father frowned.

"Keel, I'm not sure if that makes you a guy to him," he said.

"Whaaat? Why not?"

The panda interrupted the conversation. "There must be some reason that we met each other here," she said. "Things have been pretty boring around here lately anyway. How about going monster hunting together?" The panda seemed to have cheered up considerably, I say. Maybe Keel's compliments had cheered her up.

"Yeah, I suppose it wouldn't hurt to do that until evening," he said, nodding.

"Great," the panda said. "Let's do it!"

So a monster hunt limited to Siltvelt. I remember doing stuff like this back in the games I used to play. I would go monster hunting with a group of friends. This wasn't much different, I say.

"I have something I need to take care of, so Kou and I will go separately," I informed Father.

"'Something'? All right, fine with me. Sakura!"

"Yeah!"

Sakura turned into her filolial form. The panda and her underlings all gasped.

"All right, let's get going," Father said. "Until the sun sets, let's take care of some monsters wherever you think is best."

"What in the . . ." The panda still looked shocked at Sakura's transformation.

"Oh yeah, I haven't asked for your name yet," Father said. "My name's Naofumi."

"Me? I'm Larsazusa, but I'm going by Lars nowadays."

"Nice to meet you, Lars."

"Good to meet you too, Naofumi."

Lars? That meant that Big Sis's Big Sis *did* know her after all.

I approached the panda. "Don't you go by Sasa?" I'm pretty sure that's what they called her.

The panda gave me an ugly gaze that felt oddly familiar.

"I mean, maybe you could say it that way as well," Father said.

"Oh? You don't like Sasa?" I asked.

"Don't you ever call me that again!" the panda demanded.

Hmm. I supposed that she hated being called that by anyone but people that she was really close with. It was a pretty cutesy nickname.

"Let's get going," Father called. With that, Father and the panda, now partners in crime, set out on their monster-hunting mission. Until they left, Keel kept excitedly asking me if I understood her, to which I repeatedly nodded yes.

After they left, I went monster hunting with Kou to level him up. I was glad that Father seemed to be enjoying the temporary company of the panda. The panda did seem like a reliable companion, I say.

When I got back, I found them all enjoying themselves at the tavern.

"Well, we better get going soon," Father was saying.

"Next time we meet, let's go monster hunting again sometime!" the panda said.

"Yep, it was a great time."

"I had plenty of fun myself."

"Thanks, Lars!" Keel called. "Next time keep teaching me how to be cool!"

"See ya!"

Father and the rest of them came over to me. Only Father would be able to build a great relationship with someone in such a short span of time!

"Well, back to Melromarc?" Father asked.

"At once, Father!"

Once we were out of sight, we went back to the carriage with Portal Spear.

"So what did you do, Motoyasu?"

"I was investigating how to grow a special type of bioplant in Siltvelt. You used them in the first go-around," I explained.

"We were talking about that before, weren't we?"

Lazy Pig glanced over in our direction and grumbled lazily.

How dare she interrupt our precious conversation! I strongly considered vaporizing her on the spot.

"Huh?" Father asked. "We can experiment with them on your family's land, you say? I appreciate the suggestion, but we can't afford anyone knowing what we're up to. It might make us look bad."

Father was right, I say. If we caused trouble, it would support the bad image that Melromarc was trying to project of Father. We had to avoid that at all costs.

"Oink oink!"

PEDDLING AND BIOPLANTS

Naofumi successfully began peddling in the Riyute domain. Since people would stop buying from him if they found out that he was the Shield Hero, who had a bad reputation in Melromarc, he let Raphtalia handle the negotiations and the selling.

They started off by selling medicine. They didn't have a wide variety of products, but they could sell them cheaper than the market rate and then sell special healing medicines and nutrients at higher prices. They bought herbs in villages along the way and mixed them into medicines as they traveled. Sometimes Naofumi delivered medicine directly to ill patients and powered up the effects of the medicine, demonstrating his own abilities. They went from village to village, from city to city, selling their wares.

About two weeks into their travels, rumors about their carriage started to spread. On the carriage, the so-called "saint of the bird god" prepared special medicines that magically cured the sick.

Somewhere along the way, they heard a rumor about someone who needed a massive quantity of weed killer. It turned out a group of villagers wanted to get rid of a plant that was proliferating at a dangerously fast rate.

This mysterious plant had been sealed away since ancient times. Motoyasu had awoken the seed from which this plant grew and caused a deadly famine in the village. The plant grew various fruits on its vines and vegetables on its roots. Motoyasu hadn't realized what he was doing when he gave the seed over—he simply thought it was the same as a mission in a game to get rid of famine in a village, and he didn't bother to look after the village once he delivered the plant.

While the plant certainly solved the problem of hunger, it magically replicated at a ridiculous rate and couldn't be stopped. On top of that, the plant was poisonous, produced a dangerous acid, and could create sub-species of monsters. Plants that possess these sorts of magical traits are referred to as bioplants.

Naofumi managed to stop the explosive growth of the bioplant and helped the village become free from the bioplant and from hunger too.

Now having received land from the Seaetto family as well as having learned how to deal with bioplants as well, besides making money by selling medicine, Naofumi and his friends added a new tool to their arsenal to help them revitalize their village.

Lazy Pig appeared to be in agreement with whatever Father said as she oinked.

"So long as we succeed, it'll be fine in the end. Well, I guess so . . . If you can guarantee us a place to grow it, then I suppose so long as we make good money, it's fine."

"Hey, Spear Bro! You understand what I'm saying now?" Keel asked me.

"How many times must I say it? I understand you, I say."

"Keel, you must look even more tasty than before," Father said. "Look at that drool coming out of Kou's beak."

"I'm not a piece of meat!" barked Keel at Kou.

"Kou, leave Keel alone," said Sakura, squeezing Keel in a hug from behind. "I'll protect him!"

Sakura had started to act like a big sister for everyone. You'd have expected that to be Yuki's role, but maybe Sakura was better cut out for it?

"We've gotten off topic," Father said. "So you grew a bioplant?"

"Yes, bioplants, I say! I took the letter of introduction we used at the dragon hourglass to a Siltvelt bioplant farm, and they gave me seeds."

Those letters of introduction were really helping out, I say. Ordinarily, Father could just go himself to get them, but we were trying to keep him in disguise. Thinking back on what happened in the last go-around, I realized that people in Siltvelt gave Father far too much of a warm welcome. Caution never hurts.

Regardless, the next time we had some free time on our hands, we ought to go see if we could get some seeds. From my gaming experience, I had known that bioplants have been sealed in Melromarc since ancient times, so I had been able to get my hands on some. Ideally, we could harvest enough that we could use them as materials for our weapons, but I'm not sure how feasible that would be. With only one bioplant seed, you can't unlock any new weapons or anything. We should experiment to find out how the weapons would respond.

"Did you remember something, Motoyasu?"

"Once you plant them, they grow extremely fast," I said. "Besides that, I know pretty much nothing."

"That sounds like we could make a ton of money selling them," Father said.

"Indeed. That's why we should experiment."

I remember from previous go-arounds that because of the waves of destruction, food shortages had become a problem. I believe that's the main reason Father was able to use the bioplants, since they allowed him to grow a tremendous quantity of food.

The problem of hunger is truly universal among all worlds, I say.

I had noticed that the price of goods was sharply on the

rise at the moment. I recalled that in the first go-around, when Father first started cultivating the land for his village, the food shortage crisis was fairly severe. In the end, Father managed to solve the issue with his flourishing agricultural lands, of course. If we could get a bioplant into Father's hands, it'd be nothing short of a money tree, I say!

It was no problem to go around selling medicine for cheap. That was as good as scattering Father's graces around the land and boosting his reputation. Our top priority had to be gaining the trust of the people. I'm guessing that Father in the first go-around became such a popular figure in the same way.

"Why don't you get some people from Siltvelt to help out and investigate bioplants, then?" Father said. "Do you want me to help too?"

"No need, Father. I merely sought your approval to move forward with this plan."

"Well, sure . . . I have to say that the bioplants sound pretty interesting anyways."

"All we have to do is regularly monitor their growth. We could always drop by to check things out when we leave Siltvelt."

"So let's just do that, then."

"The biggest problem is that if it becomes clear that you're the Shield Hero, you'll get summoned to the Siltvelt castle."

"I mean, it sounds like they might listen to me if I just say that I don't want to be summoned," Father said. "Based on what you told me about the last go-around, they arrange marriage proposals and try to poison Sakura, right?"

I did not want Father to have to worry. I recall how he exploded with rage when they attempted to poison Sakura. He looked pretty upset when I told him about it, so I doubted he trusted Siltvelt in the slightest. For that reason, I wanted to avoid the Siltvelt castle altogether.

"We only have a few days left until the wave of destruction," Father said. "At the very least, I'd like to discredit Melromarc's false rumors and try to stop any war."

"Agreed on all accounts, Father."

"And I know this is more about what happened after we have to deal with that Takt guy, but how on earth can we stop full-out war from happening?"

Our largest challenge lay there. Since I have no ability to identify pigs, if we were to defeat Takt, the best I could do would be to count how many allies he had. The soundest course would be simply to kill every last one of them.

If we moved forward in such a manner, when Takt tried to catch us in a trap, I'd turn the tables on him by killing them all in one fell swoop, fleeing the country, and hence avoiding war. The other option would be to try following what Father did in the first go-around and publicly execute Takt.

I'm sure there were other ways to proceed, but we hardly had the time to test them out.

Regardless, if we spent too much time in Siltvelt, war was practically guaranteed.

I also wasn't sure whether or not we should expose the Claw Hero as an imposter. The best-case scenario would be to do nothing and not have to worry about it. As much as possible, I wanted to take advantage of being able to go to Siltvelt without actually visiting the castle. By this point, the Siltvelt brass probably knew that Father had been there a few times. We just didn't want any strange encounters. And if they tried to force us to come, then we could just flee.

Since our objective was taking out Melromarc, Siltvelt's long-time enemy, I felt fairly confident that Siltvelt's leaders would ultimately let us do what we wanted.

"We just need to make sure that we're well trained for when we do have to head to Siltvelt castle," Father said.

"Right as always!"

And we spent the day planning and discussing in such a manner.

With three days left until the wave of destruction, we headed to the Melromarc castle town in need of supplies.

With the money we had earned from our peddling, we went to the familiar weapon shop. Lazy Pig and Kou watched the carriage for us in the meantime.

"Hey, you kids are back! How're ya doing?" It was the old guy.

"Same as ever," Father said. "We need some new equipment."

"Hey, Mister!" said Keel, running up to the old guy, eyes full of pride. "Spear Bro finally started understanding what I'm saying!"

The old guy looked Keel up and down. "By that voice, you must be the slave . . . You're Keel, right? Congratulations! You've become a fine therianthrope!"

"How about it? I look pretty cool, right?"

"More like an adorable pet!"

"Whaaaat? Get out of here. I'm a cool kid!" Keel grunted in frustration and Father patted her on the head. She really was a puppy, I say.

"Come on bro, don't treat me like a baby." Keel broke away from Father.

"All right, all right. We all know you're cool, Keel," Father cooed.

"Whatever."

"Just have fun with who you are!" the old guy said to Keel. He turned to Father. "So what can I do for you this time?"

"Well, we came to a weapons shop, so I'd say we're after weapons," Father said.

"Naturally. So what do you want and for what price? We could also trade in your old ones for something."

"Well, to start off, we could sell you these weapons that we stole from a thief way back when we started peddling."

"I could also create some order-made weapons for you if you have good materials."

"Wow, you do that too?" Father asked with a surprised smile.

"Now that's a happy smile, kiddo," the old guy said.

"Yeah, that's great. I mean, to have something made out of the raw materials that you collected, wouldn't you be bound to grow attached to it?"

"I certainly know the feeling."

"Although, now that I think about it, we might not have much left out of what we collected in between peddling . . ." Father trailed off. He showed the old guy the ingredients we had collected and still had left in his bag.

"Hmm, I think I can do something with this," the old guy said. "In fact, good stuff, better than your average equipment."

"That would be wonderful."

"No problem. So weapons or armor, which are you doing?"

"We should probably strengthen Keel and Sakura's equipment," Father said.

"What do you mean?"

"I want something sharp! Like the ones in Siltvelt—" Keel started to exclaim.

"Keel, zip it," Father advised. He was right, as always. We couldn't tell anyone we were fighting over in Siltvelt while we were here. Father and I were purposefully making sure to use different weapons in each country, using weapons we found as drop items over in Siltvelt. They had great attacking power, so I understood why Keel wanted to bring it up here. But if we disclosed that in Melromarc, they might send assassins after us or try to pull something weird.

"So for now, strengthen the weapons for Keel and the young lady?"

Father turned to me. "Motoyasu, are Yuki and Kou really fine as is?"

"Yuki and Kou have a monster fighting style," I told Father. "I'll get some equipment for them from the monster trainer."

"So we'll go there later?"

Excellent question, Father. I wouldn't say the situation for Yuki or Kou was particularly urgent. It would be good to get some monster claws, but we had to strengthen the equipment for Father and the others. Worst-case scenario, I could probably use a claw or two from the drop items I collected.

"No need to worry about it now, I say."

"Really?"

"Absolutely not, Father."

I'd rate the necessity of claws for Yuki and Kou as precisely zero, in fact. If we were going to head someplace where they might need weapons to fight stronger enemies, I'd be able to take care of things regardless. After all, we were trying to stay out of dangerous situations in Melromarc, and it'd be good to have a bit more money to spare. So we didn't need any weapons for Yuki or Kou after all! They had their claws and their beaks, as good as any weapon a human could ever wield!

"What would you like, young lady?" the old guy asked Sakura.

"Two swords, please."

"Oh right, you also fight with two swords, don't you?" Father said.

Now that he pointed it out, Sakura's fighting style was totally different from the previous go-around. It meant that Sakura had to stay close to Father at all times for defense. But according to what Father told me, she could fight like a dancing breeze with two swords. In both angel form and filolial form alike, a powerful force, I say. I could hardly wait to see her and Father in action!

"With all that, I'll also need some cash to finish the job," the old guy said. "The trade-in won't be enough."

"We could also sell this sword we took from the thief," Father said.

"What about you, Keel?" the old guy asked. "By doing something with a monster claw or fang, I could make something special for you. How about it?"

"I'm not some kinda monster! Sure, I bite, but not as my main weapon or anything!"

"So a human weapon, it is? What kind? I think anything light would work well for you."

"Nowadays Keel has been using a dagger," Father told the old guy.

"Yeah! Like one of Sakura's swords, but shorter!"

"Kiddo, you've sure got a lively group here." The old guy sighed.

So in the end the old guy was going to make four swords, two for Sakura and two for Keel. This was going to cut into our savings significantly. If Keel wanted two weapons, wouldn't using a monster claw and a fang be the better option? I noticed that she tended to stay in her dog form nowadays, after all.

Father laughed. "I sure do. Oh, I just remembered." He reached into his pockets. "We got this letter from someone for you. Do you happen to know him? It sounds like he also sells weapons here in Melromarc." He handed over the letter we got from the axe-wielding mole.

The old guy examined the letter carefully.

"Beats me! Isn't this from Tollynemiya?" And then the old guy let out a booming laugh and clapped Father on the shoulder. "I expected nothing less from you kids! I really appreciate you doing that for Tolly."

"Which means that . . ."

"That's right! They make the weapons that I sell! I owe you kids a little something extra."

"But you've already done so much for us," Father said.

"Don't even think about it! I'll get serious now. Don't think about the price or worry about me. Just choose whatever you want to do with them. What do ya think?"

"Hmmmm."

There was no need for indecision, I say! We also had the ingredients that I had collected for Father and that we had given to the old guy. A skilled craftsman could probably fool Father about the quality of a weapon. But the old guy was on our side here. He pulled out a blueprint of a sword design.

"I'll use the materials you gave me to make swords for the young lady. For Keel . . . I'll make one dagger and then give you another from my stock as a thanks."

The old guy winked at me. It was my cue.

I responded by giving a thumbs-up.

"Last of all, we need to get you kids some armor," he said.

"Motoyasu, don't you think you should get some proper equipment?" Father asked me. I had some armor that we picked up as a drop item in Siltvelt, and we also had some that we got from the thief. The next step for my armor was to put together some gauntlets for my forearms, I say.

"Father, we must prioritize your armor," I proclaimed.

"That's it!" the old guy exclaimed. "Since you guys are around so many filolials, if you gather some filolial feathers for me, I can make great armor for you. I know it."

"In fact, we're already making careful use of them," I told the old guy, showing him my creation: a beautiful cloak sewn out of filolial feathers! So long as I had my cloak, there was absolutely no further need for defensive armaments.

Naturally, I would much rather have made it out of Filotan's feathers. But alas.

I made sure to ornament my armor with feathers from all of the filolials. Every time I put it on, I felt a spark of happiness.

It would be amazingly fun to have a feathered headdress, like something Native American, to put on and dash gallantly as the filolials pull the carriage across the plain, I say! Maybe the old guy could make me something as marvelous as that.

I proposed my idea.

"Well, I'm not sure if I could do something like that . . ."

"And why not? So long as you use filolial feathers, you can't go wrong. And this is all that I have at the moment."

In the first go-around, I gathered countless filolial feathers and made many different goods and spare pieces of equipment.

"Hey, Spear Bro, your eyes are really shining now!"

"Just like you, Keel, when it's dinner time," Father said.

"You're telling me I look like that?"

"That's exactly right. You look like the happiest person in the world."

"My eyes don't sparkle like that!"

Armor made from the feathers of filolials . . . there is nothing more beautiful in this world, I say.

If the old guy could make equipment out of filolial feathers, he was nothing short of a master craftsman.

That reminds me of how in the first go-around, Father had a pair of fluffy pajamas that closely resembled Filo-tan herself! I would love to get myself a pair of those. It would be the purest happiness to wear my very own Filo-tan draped around my body, I say! If only . . . if only . . . The problem was that I hadn't the slightest clue where to get my hands on them.

"Uh, Motoyasu? I'm talking to you! Man, it's hopeless. Once he gets into his own world there's no coming back."

"That's just the way he is, huh? Well, with these ingredients, I could put together some rough barbarian armor."

"'Barbarian'? I suppose we can surprise everyone with how fierce I look."

"That sounds rad!" Keel chimed in.

"I guess . . . I would really like to get some armor for you and Sakura."

"I wanna breastplate!" Keel said.

Sakura shook her head. "That would be too tight on me," she said.

"Too tight? Okay. Elena has her own weapons and armor so she's fine for the time being." Father turned to the old guy. "Okay, I'll take that armor."

"Got it. You've got the letter from Tolly, and you're becoming reliable customers. Anytime."

Father shook his depleted wallet. "After all of our hard work peddling, the money is gone so fast. Well, it's all for the best!"

If Father was concerned about our finances, perhaps I ought to suggest raising the prices of our merchandise? Our current prices were far below market rate, I say.

We did have a potential solution on our hands with the bio-plant idea. And we didn't have all the time in the world after all. Our bigger goal was to stop Trash. The queen would be back in about six weeks, so we just had to stop him from taking over the whole world until then. After the second wave of destruction, he'll come after us forcefully. But even if we get taken in for questioning, I could use Portal Spear to get to Siltvelt and bring back help.

"All right, I think this will make for a decent bargain," Father said, concluding the order.

"Kids, I'm glad you could find reliable friends," the old guy said.

"I couldn't agree more," Father said, nodding with a smile. It was a smile that shone like the sun, I say.

After we left the weapons shop, Father turned to me.

"So what should we do now?"

"How about going back to the dragon hourglass? We can get information about the coming wave of destruction there."

"That makes sense."

"The only thing is that I heard that in the first go-around, you went there the day before the wave," I said.

"So I suppose we just went to confirm when the wave would arrive?"

Then I remembered something. "Aha, that's when you met up with Ren and Itsuki. And myself, of course."

The Crimson Swine and her lot had come to class up, I recalled. Ren and Itsuki probably came to class up their companions as well. As is a typical rule in MMO games, when players at low levels work only with other low-leveled players, it can take a while to get stronger. But when players work with people at much higher levels, they can power-level to speed up the process. Because I had leveled up Yuki and Kou so much, they and Father were already past level 40. I think I was also around level 40 by the first wave of destruction, but we had way more money and equipment this time around.

"I doubt we'd be able to really exchange information or anything, but wouldn't it be good to meet up with them all just to see what Ren and Itsuki have been up to? Aren't you curious?"

He raised a good point. Since I assassinated that vile Smoked Human, one of Itsuki's companions, it would be wise to observe what kind of change might have occurred as a result. We could see if anything had changed due to Smoked Human's absence or if maybe Itsuki himself was different this time around. I could only assume that he was working with the Crimson Swine. Surely, he wasn't doing as much damage as I did with the Crimson Swine in the first go-around. Since the variable of Smoked Human was also a factor, I wanted to learn more.

I was also concerned about Ren. He would be far more inclined to distrust Melromarc in this go-around, and I had no idea what kind of differences that might create. Of course, in Ren's case, the best scenario would be for things to stay exactly the same. If there were changes, we just had to respond accordingly. But I had definitely come to think that for the sake of gathering information alone, we had to meet up with Itsuki and Ren before the wave of destruction hit.

"Agreed," I proclaimed. "So let's slowly make our way over to the dragon hourglass, peddling along the way so that we arrive on the day before the wave of destruction."

"I can also study reading the language," Father said.

With that, we boarded the carriage and set off.

The day before the wave of destruction, we went back to the weapons shop. Father waved at the old guy, who was there waiting for us in the store.

"Hey! You're back!"

"How'd it go?" Father asked. "Is everything ready?"

"Pretty much," he said. "Check out the armor here."

The old guy had done quite a number on the armor with the materials we had given him. He used them here and there to supplement and strengthen Father's armor. With a base suit of armor already in place, the old guy could finish a custom set of armor in just a few days. He had also used the materials to strengthen Keel's breastplate.

The new weapons glittered in the light. Keel and Sakura tried out their new swords, which, while appearing to be cheap, had peerless cutting ability.

"Thank you so much," Father said.

"It really wasn't a big deal," the old guy replied. "Next time I'd love to make you a genuine set of custom armor."

"Of course. We'll need it at some point or another. When the time comes, I'm sure we'll come back to place an order."

"And I'll be sure to fulfill that order!" The old guy laughed. "I heard the wave of destruction is coming tomorrow. Stay safe."

"Don't worry about us!" Keel barked. "I'll crush 'em all with the swords you gave me! Thanks, bro!"

Keel was even more enthusiastic than Father, I say. Good for her, I supposed.

"Keel, don't swing that in here. It's dangerous!"

Sakura, meanwhile, was staring at her new swords blankly.

"This is sharp. I think?"

"Both of you need to be careful," Father said, turning to them with a concerned expression. "If you lose focus, you'll cut yourself wielding two swords."

Sakura and Keel nodded.

"Don't worry about it, bro!" Keel said.

I realized that Keel hadn't changed back to her pig form even once lately. I supposed it was all better this way.

"All right, let's get going, Motoyasu!"

"Yes, Father!"

"Come back again sometime, kids," the old guy said.

"We'll be back," Father promised.

Next up, just as planned, we set out for the dragon hourglass.

Chapter Five: An Underestimation

As our carriage halted in front of the building where the dragon hourglass was located, Lazy Pig grumbled about something or other to Father.

"Huh? You want to stay to watch the carriage? Again?"

Just how lazy could this pig truly be?

Lazy Pig oinked in response.

"You think they'll know who you are and it might give us unnecessary trouble?"

It appeared that this time she was using the excuse that because she was from a noble family, the Church of the Three Heroes or other nobles might find out if she showed up at an important site like the dragon hourglass. Another excuse to be lazy, of course. Most pigs are only concerned for themselves, I say.

"Okay, well, I don't think it will take us very long, so we'll be back soon. Thanks, Elena."

"Oiiiink."

"I wanna come!" Sakura chirped.

"Me too!" said Kou.

"It's not going to be any different from the one in Siltvelt," I told the filolials.

"Aw, man!" said Kou. "Then I'll wait out here."

"In that case, I shall accompany you," Yuki announced.

So Yuki and Sakura were coming with us. Sakura came, of course, because it was her duty to protect Father. She seemed to be getting along well with Keel too. Sakura was giving puppy Keel a big hug.

"Let's go!" barked Keel, wagging her tail in excitement. Father watched the scene with a bright smile.

Finally, we were off to the dragon hourglass!

When we entered the building, a pig came to greet us. She had a strict, unfriendly expression. I had to stop myself from impulsively grabbing my spear. I wanted to turn this pig into half-burnt charcoal as soon as I had the opportunity.

"We come because the wave of destruction is supposed to arrive tomorrow," Father explained to the pig.

The pig led us to the dragon hourglass. Since Father had seen the dragon hourglass in Siltvelt as well, he didn't seem particularly surprised.

Suddenly, I remembered something—in the first go-around, I had originally gained my Portal Spear skill from the dragon hourglass on my first visit there. Getting sand from the hourglass let me acquire the skill. This same pig had brought it to me after Father and Big Sis left in a terrible mood. I had requested to use the sand as an ingredient, after all. But that was the reason why Father never got to use the sand as an ingredient himself, because the pig made him angry and he ended up leaving! Father hadn't even realized that was how we got the portal skill until I explained it to him after defeating the High Priest much later.

The memory sparked an idea.

"Father, I must inform you of something," I declared.

"Huh? What is it?"

I whispered into his ear a potential plan.

"Really? Okay, got it."

Father nodded and stood in front of the dragon hourglass. A light shone out of the dragon hourglass and hit Father's shield. It informed Father of exactly when the wave of destruction would arrive.

Father nodded and turned to us. "Just as expected, it's coming tomorrow."

Since this would be the very first wave, I wasn't expecting it to be much of an issue. Once we handled the wave of destruction tomorrow, we could return our undivided attention to peddling and quickly wrap things up.

"I know it's your first wave, but don't be too afraid. I want you to fling yourself at it, headfirst, no fear," I told Father.

"No problem," Father said. "I think we're as ready as we can be."

"I'll protect you, Naofumi," Sakura said.

"And I'll kick some monster butt!" Keel barked.

And at that moment, just as we had been expecting, Itsuki called out to us from behind.

"Oh? If it isn't Motoyasu and Naofumi."

We turned around and saw Itsuki and Ren walking toward us.

Of course, if we hadn't thought that Itsuki and Ren were coming here today, then we wouldn't have needed to come in the first place. Father and everyone else turned around to face them.

Oho? I noticed that the Crimson Swine wasn't with them. Wherever could she be? I had wanted intel on her movements, too. I glanced around the room, but all I could see were Ren and his companions.

"What are you all doing here?" Ren asked. "Some sort of meetup?"

"No, not exactly," Father said.

"We haven't seen you at all since then." Ren glanced at Sakura and Keel. "It looks like you got some companions. That's good." As always, Ren's tone was completely cold and indifferent. Still, I suspected that Ren had been a little concerned about Father. He knew to mistrust Trash and the Crimson Swine this time around, so the concern was to be expected.

"Yeah, more or less," Father said.

"I don't like your tone," Itsuki said, casting an angry glare at Father. "Have you got something to hide?"

His accusation suggested we had no right to even speak in his presence. But really, it was Itsuki who had no right to talk down to us, I say! Itsuki and his damned messiah complex! He was a fool who could be swayed by nothing more than a few pig tears. Yes—just like my past self!

Pigs, those demonic beings capable of shedding fake tears for their own scheming purposes . . . They should all be eradicated from this world, I say! When the right time came, I would utterly destroy that Crimson Swine.

A long silence ensued. An ugly atmosphere, as Father would say.

But there was no need for silence! In the first go-around, once Father ended up leaving, all that happened was Ren and Itsuki classing up. So I decided to take the first step forward and begin to execute my ingenious plan.

"Did you two come to class up your companions?" I inquired.

"Well, yes," Itsuki said.

"What about you?" Ren asked.

"Uh . . ." Father hesitated. We had already classed up, but if we revealed to them that we had been acting outside of Melromarc, then it would ruin all of our carefully cultivated plans. So we couldn't tell them that we had classed up before coming here. I could sense that the pig that had greeted and led us here was sneering in the background. Perhaps she assumed that our levels were too low to even class up.

In response to that pig's vile arrogance, it was all that I, Motoyasu Kitamura, could do to suppress booming laughter! The sheer idiocy!

But this was all just a part of Father's scheme. If our enemy underestimated us, then they would become just that much easier to fight. And his scheme was working marvelously.

"We just wanted to find out how much time there was until the wave of destruction," Father said.

"Does it really matter?" Ren asked. "If you're that weak, you shouldn't bother dealing with the wave."

"Yeah, good point."

I could tell that Father didn't like getting looked down on by Ren. But he shut down the feeling and put on a smile.

"So do you think we can class up here as well?" I inquired.

"I'm not sure if you guys would be able to anytime soon," Ren responded.

"Perhaps not," I agreed.

For a moment, I saw Father's shoulder twitch and the shadow of a scornful expression cross his face. I mean, we were much more powerful than Ren and Itsuki from all of our training in Siltvelt. But please, Ren and Itsuki, go ahead—feel superior to us for the time being.

"What are you talking about?!" Keel growled, snapping

forward from behind Father to bite at Ren and Itsuki. "Big Bro is—" But Father held her back and calmed her down.

"There's no need. Right?" Father smiled. "Sakura, you need to calm down too."

Father had noticed that Sakura's hands were drifting toward the hilts of her two swords. If he hadn't, then both Ren and Itsuki would've ended up dead. They probably wouldn't stand a chance against either Sakura or Keel.

But they were heroes after all. There was no way they were *that* weak. Just based on my impression, they were about equal in strength, maybe.

Ren glanced at Sakura and Keel. "You've sure got some strange companions," he commented.

"Keel is certainly a bit of an oddball," I agreed.

"Me!?"

You don't often see a dog therianthrope like Keel, so I had nothing but the utmost affection for her, I say.

"Well, yeah, that guy, but also . . ."

Ren glanced at Yuki and Sakura.

Ren, just what did you mean by suggesting that Yuki and Sakura were strange companions? Filolials—this world's supreme, ultimate beings! Don't you dare put yourself in the same sentence, I say!

"Are they demi-humans with wings growing out of their backs? Their legs look kinda bird-like too."

Ren was examining Yuki and Sakura closely. He wasn't even close to correct. He may as well have been blind. He ought to have known from all of his gaming experience that filolials were not mere demi-humans. Well, I did also make unfortunate errors based on my gaming knowledge in the past, I supposed.

"The white-haired one looks way too young to be your companion. Are you forcing her to come along with you?" Itsuki demanded.

Father narrowed his eyes at Itsuki. "Why are you so intent on painting me as a criminal? We have no intention of making her fight against the waves of destruction, and we're protecting her at all costs."

"Yeah!" chimed in Keel. "I won't let anything happen to her!"

I understood how Keel was feeling. Father's words were so moving they made one want to lay their life on the line out of sheer loyalty!

"This is Keel," Father said to Ren and Itsuki. "Right now he's in therianthrope form, but he's a great demi-human."

"I've been able to transform for a while now!"

"So it wasn't just a monster capable of speaking our language then . . ." Ren muttered.

"That's closer to what Sakura and Yuki are," Father said, gesturing to the filolials, who transformed with a poof.

Ren's and Itsuki's jaws dropped. The filolials quickly reverted back to their angel forms.

"Keel lost his village in the first wave of destruction, before we were all summoned here."

"Yeah! Which is why I'm gonna stop the wave no matter what!"

"And I'm Sakura." Sakura introduced herself, stepping forward and bowing her head.

"You all didn't know?" Itsuki sneered. "Naofumi is a convicted rapist."

"Itsuki!" Father shouted, unable to contain himself. Ren let out a long sigh.

"Big Bro's a rapist?" Keel burst out laughing. "What a joke! He can barely bring himself to glance at Sakura when she's naked!"

"Keel!" Father glared over at her. "Look, I'm glad you believe me . . ."

Father turned back to face Itsuki.

"Look, I didn't do it, whatever you think I did. And don't even think about going after the people who actually trust me and are my friends."

Itsuki scoffed. "I wonder what they would think after seeing the tears rushing down Myne's face."

The tears of a pig. I didn't know what one was supposed to think after witnessing such a revolting sight.

Perhaps the time had come where I should think about putting an end to that disgusting creature.

"She's a pig," I spat. "That pig is the one who committed crimes against Father, not the other way around. Those were poisoned tears!"

"I couldn't agree more!" Yuki declared. "Naofumi is simply not that kind of person! I know because Motoyasu trusts him. And from what I've heard and seen myself, Naofumi would never do such a horrible thing. He's so peaceful and gentle that he'd sooner be the victim of such a crime than to actually commit it himself!"

Thank you, Yuki! Together we shall be Father's defense against the prosecution!

"Motoyasu, Yuki, please—if we make a big fuss, this isn't going to end easily," Father protested. "And Yuki—what do you mean I'd sooner be the victim?"

"There have been rumors about the horrible deeds you've committed," Itsuki said, ignoring Father's protests. "I hope you aren't thinking of coming to arms against your fellow heroes."

Yes, I had forgotten that Melromarc was spreading rumors about us. I supposed Itsuki believed every last word.

"When you accuse me of things I have no memory of, all I can do is tell you that I honestly don't know anything," Father said, exasperated.

"So you're practically admitting to your crimes," Itsuki proclaimed.

Father sighed. Why in the world was Itsuki so absolutely

convinced that Father was a rapist? I *was* the same way in the first go-around, but seeing it with my own two eyes made it hard to believe. He probably had come to think ill of Father from what the Crimson Swine had told him.

I also remembered Father calling Itsuki a slave to justice. His lone objective was to claim that others have done wrong, even if it was a lie.

Ultimately, Itsuki was working alongside the Crimson Swine at this point. He'd believe anything she told him, no questions asked. Otherwise, he wouldn't believe all the fake rumors about Father.

Ren butted in with an annoyed expression. "Just how long are you going to keep having this pointless debate? I want to class up already."

The pig who had up until now been watching on the sidelines with a smirk quickly assumed a serious expression. *But I saw you, pig! You cannot hide your repulsive behavior!*

Ren turned to the pig. "Can we class up now?"

"Oink oink," replied the pig and took Ren and his party members to class up.

"Make sure to do it fast," Ren told his companions. I remembered how Ren had always been like that. He didn't care about giving his companions the ability to choose like Father did. Even I had let my pig companions freely class up, I say.

So from a distance, we watched Ren and his team

finish classing up. Then, after they were finished, Itsuki and his companions went next. I observed his team. I had secretly assassinated Smoked Human, but what exactly was the outcome of that? And just as I thought, the Crimson Swine wasn't a member of his party either.

"What happened to the Crimson Swine?" I inquired.

"Crimson Swine?" Itsuki gave me a strange expression. "Who in the world are you talking about?"

His attitude was so irritating that if he hadn't been a hero, I might have just about snapped. Paralyze Lance would have been a good compromise to make him suffer without any real consequences.

"He's probably talking about the princess," Father chimed in.

"Princess Malty?" Itsuki asked. "She's helping us out from behind the scenes, but she's not a part of my team. When we visit the castle, she supports us."

I could hardly believe it. She wasn't a member of Itsuki's party?

"You should know, she wanted to help out the heroes, but after being nearly raped by one of them, she was traumatized and couldn't actually set out from the castle," Itsuki said, casting a glare at Father.

He was irritatingly stubborn. He continued to fixate a disgusted glare at Father, but Father had managed to ignore it so far, so I ignored Itsuki as well.

Still, when you think about it, it was a strange outcome. Originally, the Crimson Swine was working with me. So why wouldn't she just go with Itsuki instead?

Could it be that cooperating with Itsuki would actually interfere with her evil deeds? Or was it that Itsuki was in fact too annoying to cooperate with at all? When I thought back, she mostly supported us from behind the scenes, even when she accompanied me. She really was pathetic to her core.

When you consider Itsuki's aggressive fighting style as well, if things didn't go well, she could end up getting crushed with the rest of them. So she was taking care to separate herself from the battles and support only from the sidelines.

While I pondered such matters, Itsuki and his companions finished classing up. I wasn't 100% sure, but it did seem like he had different companions this time around. For example, I knew that one of his companions was that stalker pig, but I didn't see her anywhere.

Then again, I recalled that around this point in the first go-around, she hadn't been with him either.

Finally, Ren and Itsuki's companions finished classing up. After this, Ren and Itsuki would get the portal skill for their weapons, which meant that they would be heading to Zeltoble sooner or later. So first they had to get the sand from the dragon hourglass after finishing classing up. I remembered that in the first go-around, Ren had asked on behalf of Father when the

Shield Hero would get the sand. The pig responded by lying and saying that she would give it to him later. I also vaguely remembered Father complaining about how they wouldn't let him class up in Melromarc at the time. And so that was my plan: to get Father to try to class up. Then, when they rejected him, it would only give Ren more evidence to distrust Melromarc, I say.

"Let's class up your companions now, Father!" I proclaimed.

"What?" Father glanced at me in confusion. I gave him my signature leave-it-to-me glance, and Father nodded and understood. Yes, Father had already classed up, but this was an ingenious bluff.

The pig that had led us here oinked, squealed, and snorted in surprise.

"You can class up?" Ren asked.

"This glorious filolial Yuki here grows at a remarkable rate, so I think she should be able to make it, I say!"

If you get a filolial up to level 30, they should just be about able to class up. You might have problems depending on how you want to class up, but even in the game there was no strict minimum on what level you needed to be. I had used that knowledge in the first go-around, so I expected Ren would have the same knowledge.

He let us go through, unexpectedly, without a fight. This was the potential scenario that I had whispered about to

Father before, but Keel and Sakura were tilting their heads in confusion.

"Hey, Big Bro—"

"Naofumi—"

Father raised a finger to his lips.

"I'd love to at least take a look," Father said. "I know that at level 30 there may not be a lot of options, but the wave of destruction is almost here, and I think we'd fare better with a class up."

The pig snorted and squealed some confusing explanation.

"Huh? Why would Naofumi's companions have to get up to level 40?" Ren asked. "Some of mine were just barely level 35, but they could class up. So they shouldn't have been able to do it."

"Oink! Oink oink!"

It was exactly what I was aiming for. In the first go-around, Father had told me that the heroes didn't need any special letter of introduction or money in order to use the dragon hourglass. But for Father, they acted like he needed both. So now we had exposed the inequality right in front of Ren and Itsuki, who had just classed up for free.

What will you do now, eh, Melromarc? An attack armed with the wisdom from the previous go-arounds—take that!

"Naofumi needs to apologize to the king to get permission, you say?" Ren snorted. "Just how much are you guys trying to hold onto that farce of an accusation against him?"

"It is an undeniable fact that he tried to rape the princess," Itsuki interjected. "He shouldn't be able to get permission in the first place!"

"They had no real proof that he did anything," Ren replied.

"You're the only one who thinks that!"

Ren opened his mouth to fire back and then sighed. "Even if we were absolutely sure that he did try to rape her, it makes no sense not to let Motoyasu and Naofumi class up. We all have to fight the waves of destruction."

"So if he apologizes, they'll let him fight!" Itsuki shot back.

Itsuki really was annoying. He got so easily confused in the name of justice.

However, it was problematic that this pig had the wit to come up with an excuse so easily. They couldn't use money or a letter of introduction as an excuse, so they made it such that he needed permission from the king himself.

But Ren wasn't moved. He looked at me and Father.

"There's something strange going on here. Doesn't it seem like the king and princess are working specifically against you, Naofumi?"

The pig chimed in to oink on and on about some sort of excuse, but Ren didn't seem to believe a word she was saying. It wouldn't be a bad time for me to reveal the whole truth here, but that might cause more troublesome differences between now and the first go-around to spring up.

Ren shook his head at the pig. "Really?"

"It's all because he won't properly apologize!" shouted Itsuki, pointing at Father. "Do it! Apologize!"

"Why would I have to apologize to you?" Father shouted suddenly. "Even if I were to apologize, it wouldn't be to *you* of all people!"

This had gone far enough. Father had clearly understood my intentions and was pretending to lose his temper. His back was facing the dragon hourglass.

"Just forget about it," Ren said. "It's not like saying anything now is going to change things."

The real performance began now. After a moment of silence, the pig brought sand from the dragon hourglass, put it into bags, and handed it over to Ren and Itsuki.

Ren checked the contents and carefully applied it to his sword. "The sand of the dragon hourglass, huh?" He looked over at us and back at the pig. "What about some for Motoyasu and Naofumi?"

"Oink oink oink oink!"

"Is this some sort of joke? There's *way* more than enough for all four of us! Just what are you trying to pull?"

"The point is that Naofumi won't be forgiven for his sins, Ren!" Itsuki interjected.

"You say that, but Melromarc is supposed to provide it to *all* of the heroes. How else are we supposed to face the wave of destruction? How are we supposed to protect this world with only half our strength?"

Ren's argument even appeared to resonate with Itsuki. The pure unfairness of only giving two of the heroes items that clearly could have been distributed to all four was too evident.

"Itsuki, if you're feeling all high-and-mighty because you're getting treated favorably, let me give you one piece of advice. Think about what you would do if you were put in Naofumi's situation."

"That's enough!" Father interrupted, turning around. "This whole argument is pointless! Let's go, Motoyasu!"

"At once, Father!"

Ren gave us a final glance. "Whatever. Itsuki, you ought to be a little more suspicious of this whole thing."

I followed Father out of the building, avoiding the gazes of Ren and Itsuki and their companions. We left Ren in his ugly mood.

And after leaving, I realized I forgot to figure out who Itsuki's companions were. *Oh well.*

"That lady was seriously unhelpful," remarked Keel.

"I was *this* close to giving her a taste of my sword," Sakura said.

"Keel, Sakura, don't do anything that causes a fuss," Father said. "Yuki, thanks for staying cool."

"I could tell from Motoyasu's expression that there was no point in listening to the mindless drivel of such a repugnant creature," Yuki said.

"Big Bro! We can't just let her get away with it!" Keel shouted.

Father looked at Keel and smiled gently. "I'll tell you a little secret," he said. "Just don't tell anyone."

"What is it!?"

"Even I tend to lose my temper from time to time," Father said. "Motoyasu, do you think we can really trust Ren here?"

"I suspect he already has plenty of reasons to mistrust Melromarc," I explained. "He was bound to believe you sooner or later."

"Well, I'll take it. If we don't try using his mistrust against Melromarc, then we'll be leaving our knowledge of previous events on the table, so we may as well go for it."

I was happy that Ren didn't trust Melromarc, but if he ended up being unreliable as always, then it could backfire on us. Still, just as Father said, we had made the safest choice.

"So we finished our preparations, and now all we need to do is relax and wait for the wave of destruction," Father said.

"Time off! Yay!" Keel shouted. "Big Bro, please, cook us something?"

"All right, all right," Father said. "Let's go cook by the riverbed over near the plain."

"Woohoo!"

"I can't wait to eat," Sakura chirped.

"And I as well!" I declared.

"You always make the most wonderful food, Naofumi!" Yuki said.

Father looked over at me. "Motoyasu and Yuki, I have something I want to talk to you about really quick."

Father took us aside to give us a serious lecture. In short, he gave us a passionate speech about how he was *not* in fact the type to get dominated in bed but took the lead in romantic situations. Of course, only toward someone who he had feelings for and with appropriate consent.

And in the end, we enjoyed a pleasant rest of the day.

The next day, we were waiting for the wave of destruction.

"We've stockpiled a good amount of medicine and made sound preparations," Father muttered, fiddling with a bag of tools. "I know we have. But still, I can't help but feel nervous."

"Big Bro, you're such a worrywart!" Keel said, patting Father with her paws. "In the last wave all I could do was run, but with how strong we are now, it'll be no problem!"

"I won't fail you, Naofumi," Sakura said. She was practicing being able to draw her sword as fast as she could.

And as for me? I had been through the first Melromarc wave before, I say. I didn't feel nervous at all. Even the first time I had launched straight into the challenge, charging toward the fissure to start my first real fight. I had been excited to go straight to the boss, I say.

If I remembered correctly, Father helped evacuate civilians. He was focused on making sure that innocent people didn't get in the way of the fight.

It would be helpful to have a bigger force this time, but right now we simply didn't have many allies who would actually cooperate with us. And I couldn't predict how things would change in the future if we did.

"Father, what would you have me do?" I inquired. "If so desired, I could immediately destroy the entire horde."

"Hmm." Father scratched his head. "But wouldn't that reveal how powerful you are and potentially ruin our future plans?"

"You're not wrong. In that case, I'll restrain myself. Ren and Itsuki will also be at the wave this time, so it should be easy. Even if I do nothing, we'll handily win."

"Yes, that's true. But it would still be terrible to let people die just so we could avoid getting caught up in some scheme or another."

Upon witnessing Father's benevolence, I, Motoyasu Kitamura, burst into raging tears.

"Huh? Motoyasu—what's wrong? Did I say something weird? Why are you bowing to me?"

"Oink oink," muttered Lazy Pig.

"Because he loves me?" Father shook his head. "On the flip side, why don't you show just an *ounce* of energy, Elena?"

"Oink oink."

"Too much of a pain, I guess. Well, enthusiasm is the key to victory, so I need you to give me some!"

"Oink."

Lazy Pig shrugged and gave a small nod.

I wasn't sure if she was saying that she could or couldn't give any enthusiasm. Either way, I never expected much from her in the first place.

"Motoyasu, what would you have me and Kou do?" Yuki asked me.

"Simply whatever Father tells you to, I say."

"Understood!"

Following Father's orders would ensure everything went as smooth as possible. The first go-around was ample evidence of that. With his peerless skill and wisdom, a better future was practically guaranteed.

"In that case, by what Motoyasu says, it should appear near Riyute village. So let's prioritize evacuating the villagers. Motoyasu, you can help too. At the very least, we can minimize the casualties."

"The same strategy you used in the first go-around," I said.

"I guess," Father said. "But since we have your strength,

Motoyasu, once we finish evacuating everyone, head straight to the boss. Just make sure to hide your true power as much as you can."

"That I shall, Father!"

Before, I had rushed headlong into the fight, but this time I would prioritize saving lives, I say! I could feel strength bubbling up inside of me.

"I can't wait!" Kou said. "Are the wave monsters tasty?"

"Who knows?" Father said. "I do want to make sure we get the materials from the boss. They seem like they'll be high quality."

"In the process of defeating the boss, some of the materials got scattered and left behind," I said. "However, I think you should be able to find them all with your shield."

"I think we'll have that area to ourselves away from Ren and Itsuki, so let's get everything we can," Father said. "But if the materials are too big, we might not have a place to store them . . ." He trailed off.

"We should just bring them to the old guy," I suggested.

"Oh, good idea," Father said. "Although we're almost out of money, he should be able to use the bones and stuff for new weapons."

"The day after the wave, Trash gave us what he called 'support funds,'" I said. "Not to you, of course."

Father shrugged with a frown. It had been a move to drive Father away from us, after all.

But what an idiotic king he was, to drive away Father of all people, who was far more powerful and useful than Ren or Itsuki.

I couldn't wait to put an end to that king of fools, I say!

"Still, after the next wave of destruction, the Queen of Melromarc should come back and give you your money as well. So just be patient, Father!"

"I know. I get it. So long as I can get the money in the end, it'll be fine. Plus, we can always get money from Siltvelt."

"You're already wanted for questioning. Do whatever you want. We only have to hold on for a little more," I said.

I thought back and remembered fighting a really odd enemy at this wave.

"I know, I know," Father said. "When I think about the king and that princess as just being pathetic, it makes it easy to take it."

"That will have to do. I do believe it's almost time for the wave, I say."

Then I remembered something else from the first go-around. When I had been so foolish as to blame Father . . .

I wondered what exactly Father had felt the first time he faced a wave. It only made sense that he would come to resent the world. I had felt the same way when the Crimson Swine eventually betrayed me as well.

And Filo-tan . . . wherever could you be?

If I could just find you once again, I could come to love this world again!

Back early in the first go-around, Father didn't have a single person he could trust. So perhaps it was Big Sis who became the first person to actually reach out and help him.

Big Sis, am I doing a good job helping Father now?

Now that I had started thinking about it, I couldn't help but wonder where Father had met Big Sis in the first place. It seemed like we were at risk of not finding her at all. I felt like I remembered something about her ending up as a slave, but I just couldn't remember the details. I didn't remember seeing her anywhere when we went to buy Keel.

Well, whatever. I was sure she was safe and happy somewhere or other. A healthy, strong, and chivalrous individual such as herself would have no problem getting by.

I also recalled that once things had calmed down in Melromarc in the first go-around, Father had attempted to restore the village. I figured we ought to shoot for a similar outcome. I felt confident I could support Father enough for the both of us—Big Sis and myself!

"All right, it's time," Father said.

00:01

"Remember, try to make sure there are no casualties," Father said. "Our actions here will help us succeed down the line."

"You can count on me, Big Bro!" Keel said. "I'm going to make up for all the times you protected me before!"

Sakura, Yuki, and Kou all chimed in enthusiastically. Even Lazy Pig seemed to oink miserably about trying her best.

"All right, Motoyasu, cheer us on," Father said.

"Absolutely," I declared. "You've all become so much stronger in preparation for this day. Let's all fight our hardest to create a better future!"

Everyone shouted in agreement just as the clock hit zero, and the first wave of destruction in this round officially began.

Chapter Six: Emergency Evacuations

As I expected, we were sent to nearby Riyute, not too far from the Melromarc castle town. Ren, Itsuki, and their companions were racing toward the fissure. The whole scene felt very nostalgic.

In my first wave, without even stopping to hear what Father had to say, I had simply dashed straight for the wave. My heart had been racing to jump into battle! I had wanted to see just how far my training had gotten me.

"Oh, come on!" Father shouted. I had cast an illumination spell to show Father what Ren and Itsuki were doing. "It's just like you said! Ren and Itsuki jumped straight into battle without even thinking about bystanders!"

We could've intervened to try to hold them back, but we didn't want to get into an argument again. Just as Father had proposed, we remained calm and let them do as they wished.

"All right then," Father said. "Let's stick to the plan and focus on evacuating the villagers. Keel, Sakura, Yuki, Kou, Elena, fight off the monsters coming for the village and do your best to make sure no one gets hurt—Motoyasu and I will evacuate the villagers."

"No problem, Big Bro!" Keel said, tail wagging in

excitement. "And once we get everyone out, should we go fight the boss? I'll protect everyone! Arf!"

"Keel, calm down," said Father. "Sakura, keep your eyes on Keel and make sure he doesn't get hurt."

"You got it!"

"Keep everyone safe, Yuki and Kou," I told them.

"At all costs."

"Are the monsters tasty? I want Naofumi to cook 'em up once we're done!"

"I *told* you I would," Father said. "Can we even turn those monsters into food in the first place? Aren't they . . . what, ghouls, zombies, locusts, bees? I'm not sure if any of those would be any good. Maybe boil them in soy . . ." Father trailed off, muttering to himself.

The corpses of the monsters would probably rot fast, so once Kou saw them, I figured he would lose interest. He might be able to get a taste of the boss if he made it in time though.

"Oink oink," said Lazy Pig.

"Yep. I need you to help us out here, Elena. Keep an eye on the time so you can stop the others if they get too into fighting the monsters."

Lazy Pig oinked regretfully.

"Then let's get going!"

At Father's direction, we started evacuating Riyute. The filolials were so fast that we arrived at the village before any monsters had infiltrated it.

From the villagers' expressions, you could tell that they knew there would be a wave of destruction somewhere but had never imagined in their wildest dreams that it would hit so close. I also saw a number of adventurers assuming their fighting stances to face the monsters, but I could tell that their movements were slow. From the last go-around, I knew that if Father didn't come to protect these villagers, then the village would've been totally destroyed. However, I remembered that even with his help in the first go-around, the village still needed a lot of repairs.

This time, we'll protect them for sure!

"Are those filolials!?"

Of course! There was that filolial farmer in Riyute. If the filolials got caught up in the wave, monsters might kill them, since humans always prioritized their own lives over those of precious filolials.

"FILOOOOLIAAAAALLLS!"

"Motoyasu! Wait! Where are you going!?"

I sprinted as fast as I could to the filolial ranch, destroyed the fence, and herded the filolials out. Once I had evacuated all the filolials to safety, I returned back to Father and the others.

"Hurry, this way!"

Father was shouting at the villagers, pointing them in the right direction.

"You're back," Father said, turning to me. "What the heck were you doing?"

"I was rescuing the filolials, I say!"

"Oh, of course. I mean, I understand why you would do that, but we need you here. You're the strongest. Remember that, okay?"

And then, under Father's orders, I proceeded with evacuating the villagers. At first, they sneered at the detested Shield Hero, but when they saw the monsters pouring out of the fissure and storming toward the village, they quickly started to follow his instructions.

Meanwhile, Keel and Sakura fought the monsters that were racing toward Riyute and protected all of the villagers that they could.

"Get out of here, everyone!" Keel screamed. "If you don't, you're toast! Sakura! Look—a big one right there!"

A huge ghoul had broken through the crowd and reached the entrance to the village. If I showed my true strength, I could instantly crush all of the monsters in this area. Unfortunately, that was not the plan. I had to hide my true strength as best as I could, like Father told me to.

"Leave it to me!" Sakura cried, shifting into her filolial queen form, drawing her two swords in a flurry, and cutting down the ghoul in three swift blows.

"Incredible."

The other adventurers watched Sakura in amazement.

Was the dispatch from Melromarc castle not here yet?

There were so many monsters that if I kept holding back, sooner or later there would be some casualties. While I was trying to decide whether or not to eradicate the whole field of monsters with one spell, more and more giant insects and ghouls stormed in toward the village.

What in the world were Ren and Itsuki doing? Well, they weren't particularly strong in the first place, so whatever.

"Motoyasu! Don't let them get any closer!"

"Yes, Father! Air Strike Javelin, I say!"

I launched my spear with all my strength, scattering the approaching monsters.

"Heeeelp!"

I saw Father turn and rush toward the sound of a pig's scream. A monster rushed toward a pig, threatening to devour it whole. Father extended his hand.

"Shield Prison!" Father cried.

A prison materialized, trapping the monster and saving the pig.

"We need to get the rest of the villagers out!" Father shouted. "Anyone who can fight, protect the others!"

The nearby adventurers nodded, surrounded the villagers, and ran off with them, leaving Father scratching his head.

"So those guys are done too?"

"They're scared for their lives," I told Father.

Father sighed. "Well, no point in complaining over it."

"It would be much easier if they just swarmed us rather than going after all the little guys," I said.

If the people whose lives we were saving were just going to desert us, I didn't need any kindness from them, I say.

Father sent all of the nearby monsters flying with a Shooting Star Shield. Father's barrier shields came in handy for times like these.

Then, all of a sudden, a blaze of fiery rain came pouring down over Father and me. With my strength, it didn't hurt or even tickle, and Father didn't look like he sustained any injuries either.

"Hey!" Father and I turned to see a group of Melromarc knights standing across the village. "We're over here!" Father yelled angrily. The knights appeared to have cast the spell.

I could tell from their expressions that they had been hoping that their spell would take out Father. But his Shooting Star Shield had stopped the fiery rain from dealing any damage. *Should I teach those knights a lesson or two?*

Keel, Sakura, Yuki, Kou, and I all fixated our nastiest glares at those detestable knights.

"Hmph," one of the knights scoffed. "So the Shield and Spear Hero aren't paper-frail after all."

I was tempted to burn them all down in a raging tempest of flames. Just like I did last time. But when I raised my hand to start chanting the spell, Father pulled my hand down. Whatever

Father might say, I still wanted to take those knights out. I would've never guessed that they would actually attack us in the middle of the wave. I wondered if they attacked Father this same way in the first go-around, baptizing him into the world of magic. I felt a storm of anger start to rise inside of me.

"What in the world do you think you're doing?" shouted Keel, waving her dagger at the captain of the group of knights. "We're doing our best to save as many villagers as we can! And you attack us!"

"So the Shield Hero has stooped to working with lowly demi-humans," the captain responded. "You've fallen even lower than we could have expected, Shield Hero!"

"Who are you calling lowly?!" Keel shouted. "We're just fighting to protect everyone! If you attack us again, I won't hold back!"

Father was beating out the nearby blazing flames with his cloak. He ran over toward Keel and put his arm on her shoulder. "Keel, Sakura, I need both of you to calm down!"

In a flash, Sakura was in her angel form, her sword pointing straight at the back of the captain's neck.

The captain yelped in surprise. "How dare you!"

"Choose your words carefully, or this sword will cut straight through you." Sakura spoke calmly, even gently, but you could hear the bloodlust in her voice. "I'll slice your head clean off."

Classic Sakura. Hopefully, the captain would understand who really had the upper hand here.

"So you want to die, is that it?" The captain glared at Father.

I take that back—he did not appear to understand in the slightest. Personally, I would have no problem if Sakura sent his head flying.

"We only have one enemy," Father said. "And that's the monsters coming out of the wave."

The captain turned away from Father. Undoubtedly, his mission was not to fight the wave but to take out Father instead!

"What are you prattling on about, you criminal?"

"If you insist, I'll get out of here, so long as you take care of the rest," Father said, pointing to the countless monsters rushing toward the town. Sakura still held her sword to the captain's neck. Father walked up to him and grabbed him.

"What are you doing! Let me free, you fiend!"

"Yes, of course, I'm the enemy, aren't I?" Father said. "You all really don't even know how to extend basic courtesy, do you? We're here evacuating civilians, fighting monsters, and then all of a sudden you show up and attack us. Wouldn't that make *you* the enemy here? I'll let you go if you fight alongside us. And you don't even have to apologize to us. How about it?"

As he was talking, Father walked toward the horde of monsters, pulling the captain with him.

"Yes, and I know you *did* attack me behind my back, but it didn't hurt at all, so I'm not mad or anything," Father ranted.

"But when you look down at me for only being able to protect . . . Well, it just makes me want to give you the firsthand experience of just how powerful my abilities are."

What a glorious sight! His tone of cold, reserved fury stood toe to toe with that of Father in the first go-around, I say!

I was nearly moved to tears. While Father was usually kind and gentle-hearted, he would ever so occasionally show us a glimpse of his tough side. Yes, I should've expected this from the future leader of the Four Holy Heroes! Father, magnificent Father!

"L-let me go! Enough!"

Father finally let the captain go with a nasty look.

"You'll never get away with this!" the captain growled.

"Still worried about me? I would be more worried about the monsters coming after you!" Father shouted.

I wasn't sure it was because his threat worked or not, but the captain went running away as quickly as he could. What a repugnant sight.

I decided to assassinate that captain on the next pitch-black night. It would be a just punishment for his sins against Father.

The rest of the knights went fleeing after their captain. Now we had to face an even larger horde of monsters racing toward us. But working together, we managed to stop every last monster from reaching the village. Eventually, Melromarc reinforcements arrived, evacuating the rest of the villagers, and finally we finished our work.

"Motoyasu!" Father called. "We're all finished up over here, so would you mind going to face the boss now?"

"Absolutely. Yuki, Kou, let's hurry!"

"At once!"

"More food!"

"Don't let Kou eat too much!" Father added. Kou had his mouth full of insects.

I leapt onto Yuki's back and rushed off toward Ren and Itsuki, who had been slowly and unskillfully making their way through the enemies and toward the boss.

Yuki, Kou, and I arrived on the scene. Ren and Itsuki were using fairly weak skills, nothing more than Air Strike Bash and Dual Arrows. I supposed they had nothing better to work with at this point. They screamed at the top of their lungs as they put up a decent fight against the chimera boss.

Still, they were doing even less damage than I remembered. Maybe it had been much faster with three heroes rather than two? It wasn't a particularly powerful boss in the first place.

"Now you're here! Motoyasu, what the hell were you doing?" Ren demanded, dodging an attack from the chimera and coming up to me.

"Slacking off as always, I'd expect," Itsuki said.

"We were evacuating the villagers, I say! There was a village right in the path of the wave, so if we didn't do anything, the whole village would have been destroyed."

Ren scoffed. "You should've just left that to the castle soldiers."

"Our sole objective is to defeat the wave of destruction," Itsuki said. "Naofumi should've been able to handle it himself. The guy can't even attack, anyway."

How could Itsuki not comprehend just how disadvantaged Father had been this entire time? A group of Melromarc knights literally attacked him! I bet Ren and Itsuki didn't know about that!

"Please don't say such things about Father," I told him. "He may not be able to attack, but he can stop opponents in their tracks, which makes it much easier for the rest of us to take them out."

I wondered how Father might handle fighting this chimera boss. A scene easily came to mind: first, he'd stop the chimera's movement by grabbing it by the forelegs. Then, with his shield's counterattack, he'd send the monster's attacks bouncing right back at it. And finally, he'd ask Big Sis or me to land the finishing blow. Father would enable us to focus all of our energy on one powerful attack that was sure to take out the chimera for good. But Itsuki and Ren would have no understanding of something like teamwork.

"If it had been just you and Itsuki, the village would have gotten completely destroyed," I declared.

"Not if we defeat the boss fast enough!" Ren responded.

"The boss is the highest priority," Itsuki said. "Many more will die if we do not defeat it!"

I sighed. "Now I can understand why . . ." They really were the pinnacle of stubbornness.

And I had made a promise to Father and to my beloved Filo-tan. To treat everyone kindly, and to lead the world to a true peace.

That is the reason why I fight! Not for my own selfish reasons!

"What are you talking about?"

"If you've got something to say, go ahead and say it already!" Itsuki demanded.

"It's nothing whatsoever," I protested. "There's no point in saying it."

It was time to take out the chimera, already. The big problem was that if I revealed how much more powerful I was than Ren or Itsuki, it would prevent my knowledge of the future from remaining useful. So I had to fight without using any of my skills.

I gave Yuki and Kou a sign to hold themselves back as well. Yuki nodded and raced ahead in front of the chimera to attract its attention.

The chimera had three heads: a lion's, a dragon's, and a goat's, plus the tail of a snake. It let out a furious roar and its tail lashed out toward Yuki to attack her. The dragon's head puffed out a breath of flame as the goat's head wagged back and forth.

There was no need for any of my skills here, I say! I simply stabbed the chimera with my spear a few times. I slashed its fur ragged, broke its bones, and slowly went about defeating the beast.

"Motoyasu! Use your skills!"

"This is no time to be playing around!"

I heard their voices behind me and stopped. Even my normal attacks were far stronger than Ren and Itsuki using their best skills. I supposed they were utterly lost for words at the display of my power.

"Oh, I get it," said Ren. "Instead of learning how to use skills, you used a different skill to power up your normal attacks."

"Aha! You got your hands on that sort of skill!"

They must've been referring to what I knew from my gaming experience as the skill called Berserk. Unfortunately for them, they were incorrect. Any of my skills would've been far too much for them or this chimera to handle, of course. My attack power was simply on a different level. In fact, I had been holding back with all of my might and still dealt tremendous damage.

To mistake my strength with a skill . . . just how stupid could those two be? But they wouldn't believe me even if I explained the power-up methods I had used. These are my regular attacks, I say!

Finally, no longer able to bear the might of my attacks, the chimera collapsed, defeated.

Then I ran over to the fissure and thrust my spear into it, sealing it up and ending the fight for good.

"All right, that's just about it!" I proclaimed.

"That boss was no problem," Ren said.

"At this rate, the next wave of destruction should be super easy," Itsuki said.

"I wouldn't recommend thinking that way," I said. "You two are mistaken about that."

Ren turned to me. "All right, Motoyasu, time's up—what did you want to tell us before?"

"If you have something to say, hurry up and say it already!"

And now they were mad at me. I was simply trying to warn them that the next wave was in fact a close fight. And that Ren and Itsuki, as a matter of fact, were the ones who got knocked out by the enemies.

"Now to get the ingredients!" I had to collect my gifts for Father, I say. Back in the first go-around, I took the head of the chimera that seemed like it would make for the strongest power-up and added it to my spear. After the fact, Itsuki pretended like he had known to do the same thing and chose the goat head. We had also collected the hide of the chimera, if I remembered correctly.

"Let's split up the remains," I said. "I'll take the lion head and the tail."

"Hey! Who said you get to decide?" Ren demanded.

"Should I take a different part then? If you want to give me the dragon head, then I'll take that."

"No, that's not . . ." Ren trailed off. I knew he wanted the dragon head. Another instance where my knowledge of the future came in handy.

"Why do you get to choose first, anyway?" Itsuki asked.

"I was the one who landed the first attack!" Ren said.

"But I was clearly the MVP here," I said. My attacks had obviously defeated the chimera. They couldn't deny that. "And since Father was the one who saved me, I'm taking a piece of the prize for him too."

"Hang on a second," Ren said. "Naofumi was just protecting the villagers. He didn't help us here."

"Yes, because all you two could do was charge at the boss like a wild boar," I remarked.

"How dare you!" exclaimed Itsuki.

"In fact, we had almost finished evacuating the villagers when that group of knights came. If Father hadn't been there, the village would have been done for."

"What are you talking about?"

"Those Melromarc knights came to attack me and Father. They shot a sky's worth of fiery rain straight at us."

Ren glanced at me. "Is that true?"

I nodded, and Ren fell into thought with a deep frown on his face. Then he spoke in a calm voice.

"Well, the snake tail isn't worth much anyway. Since Motoyasu did protect the villagers . . . may as well give it to him."

But Itsuki came straight up to me, his face bright red with anger.

"Melromarc would never do that in a million years! Why would you tell such vicious lies?"

"Either way, we ought to give Naofumi something too," Ren said. "Naofumi and Motoyasu were the ones who protected the villagers. So they probably saved a lot of lives. You want that, don't you, Itsuki?"

Itsuki clenched his teeth. "Fine. Take whatever you want."

"Then I absolutely shall!"

I immediately slashed off the lion head and snake tail with my spear and took them.

"Now, Yuki, Kou," I said, turning to them. "Take this head to Father at once, I say!"

"Understood."

"All right! Let's do it!"

I added the snake tail to my spear and gained the skill Chimera Viper Spear. It appeared to give my spear a poisoned tip. It wasn't weak by any means, but I didn't exactly need it at the moment. I'll just get rid of it later.

"That was . . . fast," Ren said.

"How did you cut off the head in one blow?" Itsuki exclaimed.

As I started to take my leave, I heard Itsuki and Ren talking about something or other. My priority was to get the ingredients to Father.

"All right! Time to go!"

And with that, we concluded our battle against our first wave of destruction without much difficulty. When I got back to Riyute, Father, Sakura, Keel, and Lazy Pig were taking out some stray monsters. The Melromarc knights also appeared to be helping. Things were pretty much wrapping up.

"Father, my present to you!"

"Oh, you beat the boss? Then we'll have no problem from here." Father saw Yuki and Kou pulling the enormous lion head. "What the . . . That's enormous! A giant lion's head?"

"It's the head of a chimera," I said. "Now, hurry, Father, add it to your shield!"

"Okay, okay. Thank you, Motoyasu."

THE STORY OF THE FIRST WAVE OF DESTRUCTION

In the first go-around, the first wave of destruction that Motoyasu and the other heroes encountered hit near the village of Riyute. The other three heroes besides Naofumi could only think of increasing their renown and experience by launching a direct attack, so they rushed straight from Riyute toward the wave without a second thought for the villagers' safety.

Naofumi and Raphtalia had to handle the evacuation themselves, and Naofumi acted as a decoy in order to draw the monsters' attention away from the village. They defeated as many monsters as they could while protecting the villagers. They led the villagers to safety and worked to ensure a successful evacuation. They had trouble defeating some of the monsters, but nevertheless, by drawing the enemy's attention away from the village, Naofumi and Raphtalia were able to help all of the villagers escape to safety.

Still, the number of monsters had barely diminished, so Naofumi confronted them in order to draw them off. More than ever, Naofumi was faced with the challenges of having a shield as his primary weapon. Still, he managed to use his shield creatively to repel the monsters.

Then a particularly large zombie appeared. Raphtalia paused from evacuating the villagers momentarily to help Naofumi in the fight—and at that very moment, a rain of fire came crashing down on them.

The Melromarc knights, finally having arrived on the scene, attacked Naofumi and Raphtalia with a spell instead of attacking the monsters.

The captain of the group also looked down on Naofumi. Melromarc had chosen now, of all times, to take out the Shield Hero for good. But Naofumi managed to stop that plan in its tracks.

Afterward, Raphtalia finished evacuating the villagers, and Naofumi, thanks to the cooperation of some of the knights, had been able to keep damage to a bare minimum as their first wave of destruction came to a close. The other three heroes, who had defeated the chimera boss, were chatting about how easy the battle was. Naofumi could tell that the next wave wasn't going to be nearly as easy as the others were expecting.

Meanwhile, the Riyute villagers thanked Naofumi from the bottom of their hearts for protecting their village. Raphtalia, who had lost her own village in one of the waves of destruction, also expressed her gratitude for focusing on protecting the innocent. Watching Raphtalia's smiling face, Naofumi felt something strange pull at his heart as they set out for Melromarc castle.

THAT WAS A TOUGH FIGHT BACK THEN.

I WILL NEVER FORGET MY OWN IDIOCY, I SAY!

Yuki and Kou dropped off the lion's head and Father added it to his shield. That should really help bring out the true power of Father's shield, I say.

"Oh wow, this . . ." Father held up his shield. "Apparently, I have to use some more ingredients to be able to unlock whatever skill is attached to it."

"Yes, I have some more right here!"

"I really appreciate it, Motoyasu. Did you get a new skill?"

"I've already unlocked everything I need, Father. No need to worry about me!"

Now Father would be one step closer to my level of strength. Did I get Chimera Lion Spear, maybe? I remember that I had gotten a powerful skill.

Still, it paled in comparison to the spear I had at my side today.

Chapter Seven: Rebirth of the Paradox

"Looks like we got past the first wave," Father said.

"That was easy-peasy!" Keel said. "And if that obnoxious group of knights hadn't butted in, it would've been even easier."

"I think so too," Sakura said, and Yuki and Kou nodded in agreement. I couldn't disagree. The first wave had been nothing short of a marvelous success.

"Let's not get too ahead of ourselves," Father said. "Based on what you said, Motoyasu, the waves are just going to get more dangerous from here on out, right? We can't get careless."

A chorus of agreement rang out.

Meanwhile, the captain of the group of Melromarc knights went over to Ren and Itsuki.

"You did well, heroes," he told them. "The king has officially invited you to the castle in honor of your deeds today. You will also receive a generous reward."

That's quite the attitude to take toward Ren and Itsuki, considering how he greeted me and Father. Of course, Ren and Itsuki should still take all the money they could get. It would become their funds to use after they left Melromarc, and 500 silver coins was nothing to scoff at. Although 500 silver coins was chump change compared to what Siltvelt would give the

Shield Hero, it was still enough to get some weapon power-ups, so there was certainly no harm in taking it.

"The wave went well, but still . . ." Father was murmuring to himself. "The real show starts tonight, I think . . . Motoyasu is still here, and the best-case scenario is nothing happens."

Father appeared to be worried about going to the castle. Naturally, it would be the best-case scenario if Trash and the Crimson Swine left us alone, but there was a possibility that they would try to pull off some dastardly scheme.

And if I immediately disrupted whatever they tried to do, it could have a serious effect on future events.

The good news was that Father was much stronger than he had been in the first go-around. That's a significant change. And of course, I was far, far stronger as well. If we decided to, we could put an end to their schemes instantly.

"E-excuse me," came a voice. One of the Riyute villagers who we had evacuated came up to us.

"Hi—can I help you?" Father asked.

"I wanted to thank you for helping us," the villager said. "If you hadn't been there, our lives would've been in danger."

"You're very welcome. Was anyone injured? If so, we have some medicine . . ."

"No, no, we're fine," the villager said. "Nothing serious—and all thanks to you."

Father nodded. "That's great to hear."

"Again—thank you so much!" The villager bowed deeply and hurried off. The villagers were truly relieved to be safe. There was no serious damage to Riyute either, beyond a few ruined buildings. It wasn't as bad as the first go-around.

Still, back then, Father had done an impressive job minimizing damage without any of the other heroes helping him. It was a remarkable achievement.

"So I guess we're off to the castle now," Father said. "It seems like they'll be putting on a feast for us, so enjoy yourselves."

"Heck yeah! Food!" Keel shouted.

"I can't wait!" Sakura exclaimed.

"No one here has *any* modesty," Yuki declared.

"You're not looking forward to the food?" Sakura asked. "Kou's basically drooling with excitement. I wonder if there will be food as tasty-looking as Keel!"

"I'm telling you I'm *not* some kinda snack! Leave me alone!"

"Oink."

Oh yeah. I had totally forgotten about Lazy Pig. What had she been doing this whole time? Was it possible that she hadn't helped out during the attack at all? If so, I'd have no choice but to send her flying as far as I could.

"Yep, thanks so much for all your help with the evacuation," Father said.

"Oink."

"Your instructions were just right," Yuki chimed in.

"You didn't fight much though," barked Keel.

That point was obvious. Well, it's not like I was expecting anything more from her. But if Father said that she had been helpful, then I had no choice but to raise my estimation of her. Slightly.

And as we chatted and as I got lost in thought, we continued to follow the knights toward the castle, staying on guard as much as we could.

"You've done splendid, fine heroes!" bellowed the king in excitement when we arrived. "This wave of destruction did nothing compared to how hard the last one hit us before you arrived!"

We were taken straight to the banquet hall, where a feast was laid out for us.

Did nothing in comparison, you say? Indeed—the greater damage was done by your own soldiers, Trash! We knew just what happened to Keel and Big Sis; innocent demi-humans were taken captive as slaves!

Incidentally, the soldiers let us know that there was not even a single casualty in the fight.

Before we got to the castle, Father asked that I stay quiet about whatever the king might be scheming against us and let events proceed as naturally as possible. Of course, that was my intention from the beginning, so I would put all of my trust in Father's wits, I say. In typical Father fashion, he was anticipating that they might try to do something or other.

"Food! Yes!"

Keel shoveled dishes onto her plate and gobbled them up, one after the next. She had quite the appetite, nearly on the same level as a growing filolial, I say.

"You all sure can eat fast," Father observed.

"This isn't as good as your stuff, Big Bro!" Keel said. "Make us something tomorrow!"

"All right, all right."

"I want it too!" Sakura added.

"And me!" Kou shouted. "I wanna dip you in sauce, Keel!"

"Why won't you stop talking about wanting to eat me!?" Keel barked. "Come on and fight me if you wanna eat me so bad!"

Kou was drizzling some sauce on Keel and licking her all over.

"All right, Kou, stop it already," Father said.

"Aw, man," Kou said. "Can't we get another Keel so I can eat him?"

Father shook his head. "Even if we get another Keel, you can't."

"What do you mean 'get another Keel'!?" Keel shouted.

What a delightful scene. I was having fun just watching from the sidelines. Seeing Father take care of the others cleansed my heart and soul, I say!

Keel, Yuki, and Kou all gobbled up the food with glee. However, I did notice the other groups watching us coldly. Did they not understand how many lives we had saved?

But as the meal unfolded pleasantly for the most part, I had more important things to be thinking about. In the first go-around, now was around the time that Father and the Crimson Swine betrayed me.

Oho? Itsuki was walking over toward me with a grim expression. Apparently, even without me on the Crimson Swine's side, Itsuki was fulfilling my role to a tee.

But what exactly would he try to pull? I couldn't just let him do whatever he wanted, so I decided to make the first move and walked over to him.

"Itsuki, is there something wrong?" I inquired.

"I have to talk to Naofumi," he said. "Please step aside."

"What about? I can tell him for you, I say!"

"Motoyasu, this is none of your business!"

He tried to push me aside, but even a hard shove from someone as weak as Itsuki wouldn't make me so much as flinch.

Then Father came hurrying over. I saw Father glance at Itsuki, and I could tell that when Father saw Itsuki's unpleasant expression, he understood just what was going on.

"What's up?" Father asked.

"Nothing is *up*!" Itsuki pointed at Father. "I heard everything, Naofumi!" Itsuki raised his voice. "That you—you bastard—enslaved your own companions!"

Father and I met eyes for a moment. "I did, and so?"

Keel, Sakura, Yuki, and Kou all looked over toward us. Lazy Pig, seemingly too lazy to get involved with anyone else's business, looked away as if she hadn't heard anything at all. Father was looking surprised, as if to say, *Itsuki, what in the world are you even talking about?* But since Father and I had discussed the possibility that this might happen beforehand, I knew that Father wasn't the least bit surprised.

"So you admit it!" Itsuki's face flushed with the glee of victory.

"Keel is a slave, and Sakura and Kou are monsters," Father said, with his confused expression a contrast to Itsuki's joyous determination. "Is there a problem with that?"

Itsuki suddenly looked lost as well. "How . . . how could you just say that? Like it's a matter-of-fact thing?"

"Well, it is matter of fact," Father said. "Of course, it's immoral, but it's not against the law. Given the circumstances, I didn't have much choice—"

But Itsuki was quick to interrupt. "You enslaved a human being and forced them to fight to the death on a dangerous battlefield! How could someone who takes slaves call themselves a hero? Let them go—and if you don't, I'll make you!"

"What are you talking about?" barked Keel. "We fought because we wanted to! Alongside Big Bro!"

But Itsuki shook his head. "Of course you have to say that—you're being controlled by the slave seal to do whatever Naofumi commands! But don't worry, I'll save you!"

Father sighed. "I'm not sure what to tell you. Is it wrong for us to use slaves? Maybe, but in this country, demi-humans are by and large enslaved to begin with. There are some exceptions, some adventurers, but it's hard to find them in Melromarc. And one of the only regions with free demi-humans was completely ruined in the first wave of destruction. And then the people from that village were enslaved by none other than the knights of Melromarc!"

Itsuki didn't appear to be listening to a single word that Father said. Trash and the Crimson Swine appeared to have noticed the commotion and moved over toward us as well. Surely, they had whispered all sorts of dangerous lies to Itsuki beforehand.

"Keel told me himself," Father said. "It was Melromarc knights that enslaved him."

"And that's the truth!" Keel interjected. "It was Melromarc soldiers. We were trying to rebuild our village and they killed every last one of the men and took the rest of the women and children into slavery!"

Of course, Keel was telling the truth. But Itsuki had heard

Trash and the Crimson Swine's side of the story first, so he would never believe her. Itsuki was neck-deep in their lies. Just like me in the first go-around.

"Itsuki, we're in another world," Father said. "When in Rome, do as the Romans do. Slaves exist in this world and we have to make do with it."

"'We have to make do with it'? Surely we can do something! Naofumi, this . . . this is just wrong!"

"Honestly, I agree with you. It is wrong. If we were back in Japan, I couldn't be more wrong. But we're not in Japan. We're in a country where demi-human slaves are the norm."

Itsuki's expression was resolute. He would not back down. I could tell.

Back then, I looked at Father the same way Itsuki and Ren were looking at him today. And yet Father somehow found it in his heart to forgive all three of us. To take the point to its logical extreme, there is no such thing as an absolute right or wrong. Something done for the right reasons could kill countless people. And while the way we treated Father was wrong, Father recognized that he needed our strength as heroes. So he let us live.

It was all in spite of Itsuki's cruel treatment of Father.

Yes, for better or worse, the world has never revolved around right and wrong alone.

This makes my promise to Filo-tan a bit of a paradox. In order to do the right thing, I might have to do things that would otherwise be wrong. I learned that from watching Father.

"Itsuki, I couldn't help but overhear your noble words!" Trash exclaimed, breaking through the crowd to join us. But he was the one who made Itsuki think this way in the first place. His pestering alone was nearly enough to drive me to action. *Should I kill him on the spot?*

But I couldn't. It would cause too many changes to the timeline.

"I had heard a rumor that one of the heroes was using slaves, but I couldn't believe my ears!" Trash said. "And since Itsuki disapproves, I command it: you two will duel!"

Father let out a heavy, exasperated sigh. A duel against someone who can only use a shield? What a ridiculous concept. Of course, Trash pit me against Father in the first go-around, but I realized now just how stupid I was. And since we had suspected just what was coming, there really was nothing we could do but sigh in the face of the absurdity.

"If Itsuki wins, then you must release your slaves at once," Trash continued. "And if the Shield Hero wins, then we'll let the incident pass without punishment."

"I really don't think there's any point," Father said.

"Of course there's a point!" Itsuki exclaimed. "Justice will be done!"

"Justice?" Father shook his head. "There's no benefit to fighting me and you know that I have pretty much no way to beat you in a duel, right?"

"I see benefits for both of us," Itsuki responded. "If you win, you get to keep your slaves, and we'll leave it at that."

"I already have that right," Father said. "Why are you trying to make it into some sort of lucky prize?"

Father was right to get angry here. But there was no point in arguing with Itsuki. Even though Father already had slaves, Trash was stepping in after the fact to try and act like he had the right to give Father permission. I nearly lost my cool myself.

"How about I fight you instead of Father, eh?" I proposed. "I too am little more than a slave to Father's will, I say!"

Indeed, for I am the Love Hunter, a slave to my love! I will do anything that my beloved Filo-tan asks of me! And since Filo-tan was Father's slave, any order from Father is an order from Filo-tan!

"What are you talking about, Motoyasu? You're not my slave—"

I held out my hand. "I appreciate the good word, benevolent Father. But it's true. I, Motoyasu Kitamura, the Love Hunter, live to serve your will. I am a slave to love!"

"I have no idea what you're trying to say," Father said.

"Regardless," I said, turning back to Itsuki and Trash. "There will be no problem if I fight Itsuki in this duel as Father's representative. Am I wrong?"

Itsuki had no chance of defeating me. The biggest challenge would be to avoid killing him by accident. And he had seen me take out the chimera before. He was sure to admit defeat easily.

"Why would the Spear Hero be able to fight in the Shield Hero's place?" Trash asked. "I will not permit such an exchange."

"Yeah!" Itsuki said. "This matter is between me and Naofumi! Stop trying to interfere!"

Now I was starting to get angry. *I'm sorry, Father, but I may just need to kill Itsuki.*

But of course, that would reset the time loop all over again. So maybe I could chop off his hands or legs without killing him. We could always get him back up to shape with healing magic, and I was sure that he would never try to take action against Father again.

Meanwhile, the castle soldiers had to hold Keel, Sakura, Yuki, and Kou back from attacking Itsuki right away.

"Let me go!" Keel barked. "No way! Big Bro, don't listen to 'em!"

"Calm down, you brat," shouted the soldier, struggling to hold Keel down. "Hey! Ouch!" The soldier kicked Keel away after she bit him, and Keel hurried to Father's side.

"Stop bullying him!" Keel yelped. "If you don't, I'll teach you a lesson!"

"Keel, it's not quite . . . bullying." Father sighed, patting Keel on the head. Keel growled angrily at Trash and Itsuki, and you could sense her bloodlust.

The filolials had also broken away from the castle soldiers and Sakura had even drawn her swords.

"You aren't thinking about biting me, the king of Melromarc, are you?" Trash said to Keel. "So you're one of the Shield Hero's companions, I see. But you do have a slave seal. You must not be able to speak beyond whatever your master commands you. Call magicians who can undo the curse, immediately!"

Then Father clapped his hands loudly to capture everyone's attention.

"All right, I get it! You want me to fight Itsuki one on one, is that it?"

"Who said anything about a one-on-one fight?" Trash said. "It will be a fight between you and your parties! And my orders are absolute! I'll confiscate your slaves by force if I have to!"

Father's jaw dropped in surprise. A duel between their whole parties? Somehow, Trash was always even more idiotic than I could've expected.

I may end up breaking my promise to Father, but I couldn't just let this unfold without intervention. I supposed now was the time to just wrap things up and kill Trash.

And just as I started charging up my spear to launch an attack, Itsuki interjected.

"But that is an act of cowardice!" he cried. "Of course it's a one-on-one fight!"

"What the hell is going on?" demanded Ren, finally coming over to the discussion. Ren didn't really react to much of anything until much later in the first go-around, but I supposed that this time he had many more reasons to mistrust Melromarc. Maybe now was the right time to give him the full story.

"Itsuki is unhappy that Father has been using slaves, so he complained to the king, who's trying to force them into a duel," I explained to Ren.

"Slaves? Naofumi, you've been using slaves? Are all of your companions slaves?"

A bit late to the issue, aren't you, Ren?

Ren looked over at Keel and the filolials. "I mean, you and your companions all seemed so close, so I would never have guessed that they're slaves."

"I may be a slave, but I respect Father as a hero!" Keel barked. "Unlike the rest of you lot!"

Ren paused. I saw him giving Itsuki and Trash some unpleasant side-eye, I say. It seemed like things could start getting out of hand at this rate.

"And when Father was about to agree with Itsuki to have a one-on-one duel, the king interrupted to say that it was actually a battle between their entire parties and that it was his absolute command," I continued.

"What the hell? Isn't that totally unfair?"

"Absolutely it is," Itsuki exclaimed. "For the likes of him, alone I'm more than enough!"

I should've expected that Itsuki would be overconfident. I could tell that Trash had realized things were starting to spiral out of control. He wiped sweat off of his brow as he tried to remedy the situation.

"No, that's not what I meant," Trash said. "A one-on-one duel it is, between Itsuki, the Bow Hero, and the Shield Hero. I command it!"

Well, it's not like that would be enough to make Ren suddenly trust Melromarc again.

Realizing that they wouldn't be able to hold down Keel and the rest, the Melromarc soldiers finally backed away.

"Big Bro! Are you sure you wanna do it?"

"But of course," I said. "This is similar to events that happened in the first go-around, but Father is stronger and better equipped. It should be no problem."

And even though things were shaking up in a different way this go-around, it was quite similar to the first go-around in that Ren and Itsuki were still as clueless as ever. Itsuki was determined to protect his own version of justice at all costs, and Ren was just a little more skeptical of Melromarc this time around.

"I would rather have Sakura and Keel be there with me," Father said. "But still, it sounds like Melromarc just wants to see me fail no matter what. There's really no point in negotiating with them."

"Are you saying that you're considering losing on purpose?" I asked.

It was undeniable that no matter how strong Father was, he didn't exactly have a wealth of attack moves at his disposal. And even if Father lost and we released Keel, Keel would simply come with Father regardless.

I remembered my duel with Father from the first go-around. Good times, good times. After they released Big Sis from the slave seal, Big Sis gave me an honorable slap across the face, I say. And I figured things would be the same this time around. It's not like Keel or the others were going to appreciate Itsuki's savior complex.

But Father shook his head at my question and cast a glare over at Itsuki.

"Don't worry about it. I do have some idea of what I'm going to do. Just because I can't attack doesn't mean I can't win. I want to show Itsuki what I can do. He's been an accomplice to Melromarc this whole time, and his attitude is starting to seriously piss me off."

"But, Naofumi . . ." Sakura and Keel looked worried, but Father patted them on the heads and gave them a smile.

"Don't worry about me. I'll be fine. I'm going to win. I promise."

So Father and Itsuki went to stand in the center of the castle garden, with spectators gathered around them to watch the fight.

But what was up with Father's shield? It looked like it had thorns stuck onto it. Did he get it in Siltvelt? And if he did, wouldn't that make Melromarc start to suspect us?

What exactly would he do? Simply block Itsuki's attacks until he gave up out of exhaustion? Father hadn't learned any spells yet, for one. And they probably wouldn't let him use any of the medicine he had made during the duel.

Going against mighty Father was as good as a public execution for Itsuki. I started to have flashbacks of when I had my own duel against Father. It nearly broke my heart to think of it.

"This is a duel between the Bow Hero and the Shield Hero! The duel will end when one of them completely corners the other or one of them admits defeat!"

Father cracked his knuckles and adopted a fighting stance. I nearly leapt out into the ring to defend Father, but I reminded myself that he would surely be fine. All I could do was sit here and watch.

"It feels a bit like bullying to take on someone as weak as you, but it's all in the name of justice," Itsuki declared. "I'd recommend simply admitting defeat as soon as possible."

Father shook his head. "I'll show you, Itsuki. In gaming, tanks are always tough to take on. Soon you'll understand just how terrifying an unbreakable shield can be!"

Father might have significantly more gaming experience than even me or Ren. I remember hearing that Father was ranked third in a major guild on one server. And it wasn't just his experience—he also had instincts.

The rules may have been different in this world. But Father had a weapon capable of adapting to almost any situation. While everyone assumed that the shield was the weakest weapon, they forgot that Father himself was the strongest out of all of us. So while I did feel a tinge of anxiety, I nevertheless believed that Father would find a way to win.

And then the judge screamed, "Let the duel begin!"

Chapter Eight: Bad Status

Both Father and Itsuki let out their battle cries as Father, raising his shield, charged at Itsuki. Itsuki responded by leaping back, activating a skill, and firing his bow. The arrow bolted toward Father, but Father held out his hands and snatched the bow out of midair.

"Impossible!" Itsuki cried in astonishment.

But it only delayed him for a moment before he shot several more arrows at Father. There were so many of them that for a second, I doubted that even Father could handle them.

"Airstrike Shield!" Father cried. The volley of arrows bounced helplessly off of Airstrike Shield.

Itsuki's main role in battle was to attack from a distance, while Father's was to prevent harm to his comrades. Their roles couldn't have been more different. It seemed like Father couldn't hurt Itsuki any more than a mosquito.

But just like the time that I had dueled Father, he had tricks up his sleeve. Father had defeated me by using balloon monsters he had hidden under his cloak. In the gaming world Father might be what you call a monster-player killer—someone seemingly powerless who is still capable of taking down powerful foes. Father had really gotten me good. His strategy had been nothing short of first-rate.

Still, this time around, as far as I knew, Father didn't have anything hidden under his cloak. I simply could not wait to see what Father would do, I say!

"All you can do is shoot arrows at me while scurrying around?" Father called. "You camper! Maybe it would work in a mainstream console game, but you'll see just how far it takes you, Itsuki!"

The taunt spurred a vague memory I had. Something about enjoying an online shooting game. In games like that, I had heard players were called campers when they just hid and shot at other players.

"Now you've done it!" seethed Itsuki. "Suck on this! Bunker Shot!" Itsuki ran closer to Father, aimed at his chest, and launched the attack.

Perhaps it was an attack that grew stronger the closer you were to the target. Just based on Itsuki's play style, I knew Itsuki was unlikely to use an attack like that very often. It was probably an early-game type of skill—something to use in case of emergencies when the enemy gets too close. Based on what I knew, a skill like that might be pretty strong with a special status condition, but if you wanted to attack from close up, why bother with the bow class in the first place? If you were a solo player, the skill certainly wouldn't hurt. You may as well have it at the ready. But still, it was a skill so useless that I had never heard it used even once in the first go-around.

The attack thudded against Father where Itsuki had aimed.

Father bore the brunt of the attack without flinching. "Hm," he said. "It didn't even hurt."

Itsuki's smile quickly fell apart. "Not . . . not even a scratch?"

The difference between their levels of strength was like night and day. Father had applied all of the power-up techniques I had taught him to his advantage. But even if Itsuki had also acquired the four holy power-ups, he would still be no match for Father.

"I think it's my turn, isn't it?" Father said.

"And just what in the world could you possibly do to me?" Itsuki sneered.

In a flash, Father grabbed Itsuki by the collar and raised his shield. Armed with the sharpened spikes on the front of his shield, he plowed his shield into Itsuki.

Itsuki grunted in pain, but they didn't seem to pierce too deeply. I guessed it was light damage at most.

"What . . . what was . . . ." Itsuki raised his hand to his head as if he was dizzy.

Father then shoved Itsuki over and grabbed him by the arms and legs so he couldn't move. It wasn't a particular martial arts locking technique or anything. It looked more like Father just climbed onto him. But Itsuki was completely unable to move.

Now I remembered. Father had used the same move against me. His strategy was to aim for the face and the groin. It almost looked like Father was starting to get excited, but maybe it was just my imagination.

I, Motoyasu Kitamura, burst into tears upon witnessing Father's peerless courage.

"If you surrender now, I'll stop," Father warned.

"S-surrender? No chance!" Itsuki cried.

"All right then, that's your choice." Father looked down at Itsuki. "From here it's simple. I'm going to hold you down until you surrender."

"As if! I'm not going to surrender to the likes of you!"

"Let's see just how long you keep saying that."

Held down by Father, Itsuki kept trying to use his skills, but Father seemed to have him locked completely in place. I remembered being in Itsuki's exact position. As much as I tried to overcome him, Father's strength had held me locked in place, and there was nothing I could do. At this point it just seemed like Father was holding Itsuki in place and drawing out the match. But that couldn't be all.

Every time Itsuki tried to resist, his movements just got weaker and more sluggish. Itsuki opened his mouth and started to groan out a spell, but Father grasped him by the mouth and at the same time hit him again with his shield to stop any further counterattack.

"So you can use magic, huh?" Father asked. "Not like it would have much effect anyway."

Most likely Father had applied some sort of paralysis toxin to his shield. It looked like Itsuki was losing his ability to speak as well. The poison was sapping away Itsuki's strength, and he gradually stopped resisting.

I was blown away. If Father had used the same poisoned shield against me in the first go-around, he would've won even before the Crimson Swine was able to interfere. I did have a memory of getting bit by a shield with two dog heads, but this was far more formidable.

The strength of the Shield Hero was on full display. Upon witnessing Father's heroic deeds, I could no longer stop tears from uncontrollably pouring out of my eyes. I wept. The same ingenious nature he possessed in the first go-around was on full display!

"Spear Bro, quit crying, won't ya?" Keel barked.

"He's expressing the profound depth of his feeling," Yuki said. "Naofumi's heroic deeds have simply moved Motoyasu to tears."

"I get that! Big Bro's incredible!"

Then, the very moment that Itsuki could barely move and Father stood on the cusp of victory, I heard a strange sound and saw something move underneath Father's cloak.

No, it was before Father's cloak started moving—everyone could see that something had happened along with the strange sound. I had no doubt it was the Crimson Swine, hidden somewhere amid the spectators, who had used a spell against Father—Wing Blow.

But unlike in the first go-around, where Father's level was barely enough to get by, he was plenty strong. Even though the attack hit him square on, Father didn't even move. Father was invincible!

I looked around the crowd to find the Crimson Swine. Everyone could tell that the spell came from her direction, but the judge was acting like he didn't even notice. Or rather, he was so flustered that the attack did nothing that he didn't know how to react.

"Hey! Unfair!" Keel started barking, pointing at the Crimson Swine.

Suddenly, the king stood up. "Everyone! We must save the Bow Hero from the Shield Hero!" And not just Trash, but all of the nearby spectators that could use magic started to chant incantations.

"Stop it! That's not fair!"

They aimed their various spells at Father and attacked. A variety of attacks went hurtling toward Father: fire, wind, earth, water, thunderbolts, beams of light. But the moment they launched the attacks, Father raised his shield.

"Shooting Star Shield!"

The shield crushed Itsuki beneath it and rendered him completely unable to move, and the volley of spells dissolved into smoke as they collided with the barrier that Father had raised.

Then I heard Ren's voice.

"What the hell?!"

Ren had been watching from a distance. He then started to race toward Trash and the Crimson Swine. I was glad that I didn't have to speak up on behalf of Father and Ren did so voluntarily instead.

Soon enough I would give them their just desserts, I say. Soon enough.

"What the hell are you doing?! Why are the royalty and magicians interfering in what was supposed to be a fair, evenly matched duel?"

"The Shield Hero used a cowardly, poisoned shield," Trash responded. "Which means that Itsuki is in fact the victor!"

"Poison is a perfectly good battle strategy!" shouted Ren. "Naofumi doesn't have much choice, does he? Otherwise, it's just not a fair fight!" Ren drew his sword. "Stop your attacks against Naofumi at once. Because of your overt interference, anyone with eyes can see that Naofumi has won the duel!"

"The Shield Hero unfairly stopped the Bow Hero from being able to move or attack!" Trash said. "This cannot be called a fair fight!"

"So why didn't you set any rules for the fight in the goddamn first place? What the hell kind of joke of a duel is this, anyway?"

At this point Ren had completely lost his cool.

Then the Crimson Swine started crying and moved toward Ren, but he held up his sword as a warning.

"You really don't know where to stop, do you?" Ren hissed. "There's nothing more cowardly than getting the spectators to attack one of the participants! That was your last resort, wasn't it? I've seen enough!"

"Oink oink oink oink."

"Now she's saying that you couldn't bear to see Itsuki, who had rescued her before, about to lose," Yuki interpreted for me.

"Then why resort to sending a whole damn volley of spells at him! As a princess, you have the power to stop it and let it be a fair fight! But because of you, we all know that Itsuki lost!"

Now that Ren was blaming the Crimson Swine, Trash reluctantly raised his hand and stopped the barrage of magic attacks.

When the dust cleared, Itsuki was still completely held down under Father's Shooting Star Shield. And Father remained unharmed.

"That was a surprise," he said. "So? Did I win yet?"

"I . . . I won't . . . surrender . . ." Itsuki croaked.

"Impressive, given your position," Father said. "I guess that's what it takes to be a hero."

"Unfortunately, thanks to the princess and king here, you've lost this duel, Itsuki," Ren called. "And even if they didn't try to cheat your way to victory, the poison will eventually take you out."

"No . . ." Itsuki groaned and fell unconscious.

After checking to make sure Itsuki was knocked out, Father stood up and let go of him. Immediately, the Melromarc court magicians hurried over to Itsuki and started using magic to heal him.

"Satisfied yet?" Father called up to Trash and the Crimson Swine.

Trash clenched his fist and the Crimson Swine grumbled out an oink.

I saw that Ren was still staring at them suspiciously. It made sense—he saw the blunt favoritism right in front of us. He was a little slow on the uptake, but still . . .

Pretty much everyone looked angry and uncomfortable.

"When Itsuki wakes back up, I'm going to force him to admit that Naofumi won," Ren said. "And since Naofumi's slaves really seem perfectly content with where they are, he'll have no choice but to let it go."

This is the most overt Ren has been so far, taking Father's side this way. He must've seen how wholeheartedly Keel was supporting Father during the duel. I didn't need to say anything at all.

"You did it, Big Bro!" cried Keel.

"I'm so glad you're safe," Sakura said. "I wanted to help you so bad."

"Thanks so much, Keel and Sakura," Father said before waving to me and starting to walk over.

I didn't see any need for us to stay in Melromarc any longer.

Father turned back to Trash and the Crimson Swine and gave them an evil grin. That's right, you fiends—your plan backfired!

"My god, even after seeing all that, they still wanted to attack me," Father said. "Itsuki's sense of justice is a bit off. He really has some huge blind spots, doesn't he?"

"I could not agree more," I said.

"Hey, Motoyasu," called a voice. It was Ren. He seemed to have something he wanted to say to me.

"Naofumi," Ren said.

"What's up?"

"You had nothing but your shield, but you came up with a great strategy. I didn't realize you'd be able to pull off something like that. Nice job."

"Oh, uh . . . thanks?"

"Itsuki just didn't have it in him. I never thought he would lose to a shield, of all weapons." Ren shook his head.

I saw a flash of anger cross Father's eyes.

"Big Bro is strong!" Keel shouted, hurrying over.

"Yeah! Naofumi could beat you up," Sakura said.

Father held up a hand, as if to apologize for the interruption.

"Well, we're all finished up here, so we should get back to the carriage," Father said.

"Agreed," I said. "Let's come back to the castle tomorrow though."

Because of the change in events here, I wanted to find out what Melromarc's next move might be.

We hurried our way out. All the spectators were quiet and gloomy, as if Father had spoiled the mood.

I heard later that Trash and the Crimson Swine were so angry they completely lost it, but who even cares?

Chapter Nine: Unfair

We slept that night at an inn near the castle and went back to the castle gates the next morning. We were taken to the throne room, where Trash was waiting for us. Itsuki was there as well. He seemed to be grumbling something about how he hadn't really lost the duel.

"At this rate we'll never be able to abolish slavery here," he mumbled.

But from what Father had told me, it was his full intention to get rid of slavery as soon as he could. Itsuki's point was that so long as a hero had slaves, abolishing slavery would be difficult. And for that reason, Itsuki glared at Father as if Father were his mortal enemy. And Ren was staring at Itsuki in turn with an unpleasant expression.

But it was too late for them to steal anything else from Father, I say! Even with a large group of castle guards surrounding Keel, Sakura, Yuki, and Kou, if push came to shove, we'd have no trouble defeating Trash and Itsuki. I nearly burst into laughter.

Still, I noticed that Father seemed to be proceeding cautiously. I remembered him mentioning last night before going to bed that although he lost his temper and ended up winning, it might have made things easier in the long run to lose on purpose since, if the course of events deviated too far from the first go-around, we might end up in a tough spot.

We had a month and a half until the next wave of destruction. That was when Father's name was finally cleared in the first go-around. So to get there, we'd have to continue to pretend like we were staying in Melromarc for the next six weeks.

Trash looked over the four of us from his throne and cast Father and me a glance as if to say we were rubbish.

"Now I will be giving out some funds to help you prepare for the next wave of destruction," Trash said.

One of his attendants brought out pouches of coins. I could tell that they were all of different sizes, but even the smallest should have about 500 silver coins.

Father had warned me last night that because of the incident yesterday, Melromarc might try to start something new. But if they did, that would just further accelerate Ren's suspicion, as he had already observed plenty of unfairness toward Father. In fact, it seemed like Ren had already broken off from Melromarc entirely.

"Dispense the funds," Trash said, and the attendant passed the bags out. I glanced inside, and as expected, there were around 500 silver coins. Father's pouch was about the same size as mine.

So what to do with this new money?

Based on how far along we were in the timeline . . . it was the perfect time to find Filo-tan, I say!

Oh yes! I know for a fact that Father first purchased Filo-tan around this time. In the previous round as well, this was when I had bought up all the filolial eggs from the monster trainer. But Filo-tan hadn't been among them.

Just what had Father told me about the time he got Filo-tan?

All I could remember was him saying that he bought her from the monster trainer. The specifics were unclear.

Maybe it was actually the monster trainer who had told me that, not Father. I couldn't exactly remember. Either way, I knew that the timing was right.

Since we were still caught in a situation where we couldn't trust anyone, I had to consult with Father first.

"To begin, Sir Itsuki," Trash said. "Your noble deeds have been felt across the realm. You've taken on difficult missions and fought hard for the benefit of our nation. As a result, we've awarded you 7,600 silver coins."

Father's jaw dropped. 7,600? That's 76 gold coins! It was the amount I had received from Melromarc in the first go-around, plus more. I guess this time around Trash gave even less to the rest of us.

Itsuki raised the enormous pouch of jangling coins and showed it to us. "This is the reward for following the path of justice," he said.

Itsuki seriously irritated me. No, you were simply following the path that Trash and the Crimson Swine laid out for you, you fool!

"Next to Sir Ren, for fulfilling the mission and fighting the wave of destruction, we've awarded you 3,800 silver coins."

"Half of what Itsuki got?" I muttered.

That was the same as what Ren got in the first go-around. Since he had no reason to be mistrustful of Trash and the Crimson Swine, he had taken it without complaint. But now, he undoubtedly felt that it was unfair that he had gotten less than Itsuki. He didn't outwardly make a fuss about it, even though the rumors spreading around Melromarc were all focused on the deeds of the Sword Hero and the enigmatic bird saint.

Ren's companions could tell that Ren was angry and didn't even try to say anything to him.

"Next up is Sir Motoyasu. Since you didn't achieve anything of particular note, we've awarded you 500 silver coins."

Much, much less than Itsuki and Ren. I supposed that from Trash's perspective, I was as good as Father's accomplice, so he was doing everything he could to slow me down. Unfortunately, Father is way ahead of you, Trash!

I felt a slight urge to kill him and be done with it, but patience is a virtue, I say. Only another month and a half, and we'll be done with it.

I saw the Crimson Swine sitting next to the king with a pleasant smile on her face. What a revolting sight.

Last up was Father.

"Hmm, we would've appreciated a bit more effort from the Shield Hero," Trash said. "We've also subtracted the cost of healing Sir Itsuki. That was 200 silver coins."

So Father was only getting 300 coins? I supposed they added that portion to Itsuki's reward. They really had no shame.

"The cost of healing was 200 coins?" Ren asked, glaring at Trash. "You mean the result of forcing them into a duel? And Naofumi did just fine in the wave of destruction."

I could tell that Ren was pretty much fed up with Melromarc at this point.

Ren turned to Father. "It sounds like they're mad that you haven't done any jobs for the guild yet," Ren said. "You heard of it?"

Father glanced at me. It's not like Trash would've given Father the chance to do a job if he had wanted to. But what was the best response here? I didn't want to send Ren out of control. It wasn't hard to imagine a scenario like that, if we answered wrong here. If Ren did snap, he would still trust us just fine, but his relationship with Itsuki would be totally severed.

I sensed that we were losing our last chance to keep Ren calm and on track per the events of the first go-around.

"You see, we met with the guild, but they didn't offer us any work," I said.

"Gotcha," Ren said. "Well, it is Melromarc, so I honestly shouldn't be surprised."

It would be hard to lie to Ren in this position. We would risk all of our hard work going to waste if we told a lie and got caught. And we couldn't just say that we hadn't heard of the guild either. This whole scenario was a gamble from the beginning.

I wasn't sure what he would do next, but I had to keep in mind that Ren staying alive was also crucial to our success. We knew from the last go-around that Itsuki was prone to falling in line with Melromarc. Which meant we had to protect Ren as well.

If Ren were to flee, I figured he would go to Zeltoble. But would Melromarc go after him? He hadn't done anything beyond simply be suspicious yet, so I think they would let him move freely. He hadn't totally turned on Melromarc. But it was certainly a possibility that they could go after him like they had done with Father, making him an enemy of the state.

As I had done with Itsuki last time around, it was worth considering killing off Ren's companions.

When I thought back on the last three months, it was clear that the Church of the Three Heroes had been hiding a lot of their suspicious activities. I decided that I could simply sit back and watch their plans backfire and see how Ren reacted to the news that the princess was helping Itsuki from behind the scenes. And in the meantime, Trash would still want to drive us away.

Which means that, ultimately, not too much would be different from the first go-around.

Ren turned to Trash and pointed at him. "You should be giving a minimum . . . No, you should be treating the heroes equally."

Trash crossed his arms. "Hmph. It seems like the guild may have let their personal feelings toward the Shield Hero interfere with their treatment of him. On their behalf, I apologize."

He may have said the words, but I didn't sense an ounce of sincerity there. Trash simply wanted to see Father lose and suffer, and there was nothing else we could do about it.

"So the guild believes the nonsense rumors about Naofumi and wouldn't give him a job, and you punish him for it?" Ren asked.

"For the inconvenience, I shall increase the Shield Hero's reward by 300 silver coins," Trash said. "I would suggest simply taking it."

So Father got an extra pouch of money. I could tell by Trash's body language that he was reluctant to hand it over, and by the Crimson Swine's obviously manufactured smile.

Like Ren, I, Motoyasu Kitamura, was tired of this farcical charade! It was all I could do to hold in my vomit.

"That concludes our little gathering today," Trash said. "Until we meet again, I hope that you continue to make a great impact on our nation!"

Oho? This time, he didn't say that Father's reward was consolation money for him to leave the country. I supposed that Trash understood that if he went ahead with that, Ren would give him a hard time about it.

Which meant that we had to do something to make Itsuki start to mistrust Melromarc. It seemed impossible at this point.

Regardless, we had to do something.

And with that, we left Melromarc castle.

"Hey, get out of the way! Move it!"

"I'm sorry—but wait, just a moment—"

Ren appeared to be on his way over to us when one of his companions had gotten in the way. Father noticed it and quickly started to walk over to meet Ren.

"Hey, Ren," Father said.

"Naofumi," Ren said. "I was trying to talk to you, but this idiot keeps getting in my way."

The companion had followed Ren over and finally backed down.

Judging from the last go-around, I knew it would be pretty risky to start a conversation in the middle of the street here.

"If you want to talk, may I suggest going to someplace quieter?" I interrupted. "Away from your companions?"

"Yeah, that sounds good. Let's go somewhere else. You all, go wait for me at the pub," he said to his companions.

"B-but, Sir Ren! Wait . . ."

Trembling, the companion who got in the way still didn't leave. Ren let out a deep sigh.

"What is it already? Something that you have to tell me about? Well, I've got to tell something to the other heroes here. If I told them right in front of everyone, we wouldn't get very far, would we?"

It seemed like a single adventurer wouldn't be enough to slow Ren down.

"If you insist on following me everywhere I go, I'll dismiss you," Ren said.

"B-but, Sir Ren! Don't do that to us!"

Reluctantly, Ren's companions went away. Ren was prone to assertive action from time to time, after all.

"I can explain everything," I said.

"Please do, Motoyasu."

"At once, Father!" I declared. I gestured to Yuki, Kou, and Sakura to come over and I whispered to them.

"Make sure that no one is hiding nearby to overhear us," I said. "If someone is, give me a cue."

"At once," Yuki said.

"So like hide-and-seek!" Kou said.

"Let's go and take a look," Sakura said.

Filolials had an excellent ability to detect hidden people and objects. It didn't mean that it was completely impossible to hide in their presence, but if someone were detected hiding, all I needed to do was find them myself with a spell and eliminate them.

So we took Ren into a back-alley to continue our conversation. This alley seemed like it would work just fine.

I lowered my voice so no one could hear me and chanted a fire spell: "Liberation Fireflash!"

It was the same spell I had used back when we were in the mole village, which revealed the presence of anyone hiding nearby. The spell depended on how skillfully hidden the people were, so if anyone had sloppily hidden themselves, the spell would set them on fire instantly.

"This is better," I announced. "So, Ren, what can we do for you?"

Ren cleared his throat. "Just based on everything that happened up until now, it's all too obvious that there's something up with this country. The blatant discrimination I saw against the Shield Hero made me want to ask you guys about it."

"Sure," Father said and glanced at me.

Ren appeared to be confident that Melromarc was a bad actor. So it was about time to tell him a few things.

"Well, it seems that in Melromarc the Shield Hero is actually the antithesis of their religion," Father explained. "But if they officially do anything against me, the other countries in the region will get mad at them. So behind the scenes, they're making up crimes that I committed to give them an excuse to try to assassinate me. At least, that's what we've come to think."

Ren nodded several times. "That definitely seems to fit with everything we've seen so far."

If you thought about everything that happened objectively, it would be hard to doubt Father's conclusion.

"And the whole rape thing is just another one of their accusations?" Ren asked.

"Yep," Father said. "I didn't do anything to Myne. And while some of the people on my team are technically slaves, I'm definitely not forcing them to fight. Given the circumstances, I had no choice but to buy companions as slaves."

"That's right!" Keel interjected. "Big Bro hasn't forced me into anything I didn't want to do!"

"Got it," Ren said. "So why don't you just leave Melromarc?"

"Well . . ." Father trailed off.

I wasn't confident that Ren would believe us. The whole time loop thing. About how if we went to Siltvelt, Melromarc would eventually declare war on them. That the heroes would end up fighting all sorts of pointless wars. It was a lot to ask someone to believe.

"It's complicated," Father responded. "I want to try to change Melromarc from the inside. That's why I'm sticking to peddling for now."

It was the best response we had, and it wasn't a lie either. No one in the universe could come up with on-the-spot answers like Father, I say!

"It sounds like a pretty annoying way to go about things to me," Ren commented.

He wasn't wrong about that. Every step of the way had been annoying.

When I thought about what Trash and the Crimson Swine had done, it was all I could do to repress my rage. And Itsuki had become nearly as bad! Thinking about how Father had defeated him brought a smile to my lips.

"Wait! Look!" At that moment, fire from Liberation Fireflash blazed up behind us. Had Melromarc sent an assassin already?

"What's wrong?" Ren said. "There are all sorts of random fights in alleyways like this."

"I suppose you're right." Ren didn't appear to even remotely realize that someone had been secretly approaching us.

"Look, I'm going to have to pass on getting involved in these ridiculous power struggles," he continued. "I'm going to take a guild job and get out of here and go to Zeltoble."

"I understand," I said. "I think that we should be able to resolve things in Melromarc pretty soon, so why don't you meet back up with us here then later?"

"Maybe. Do you know when?"

Ugh. I didn't want to have to explain things in detail.

Since Ren tended to be a contrarian person, I wondered whether he would end up going to Faubrey instead of Zeltoble if I told him that he definitely should not go to Faubrey. But Zeltoble wasn't bad either in terms of a place for Ren to wait while we took care of things.

"I'm not exactly sure," I admitted. "From what I've heard, when Trash's power reaches a precarious state, there could be a regime change. If that ends up happening, do you think you would come back here so we could work together?"

"It's certainly not a bad idea," Ren said, nodding. "In Zeltoble, I'll probably hear rumors about what happens over here anyway, so I can just pay attention to those and respond on the fly."

I supposed that trying to cooperate too much with Ren was ultimately pointless.

Ren looked at Father. "And nice job beating Itsuki. How'd you pull it off?"

"About that," Father said, "I was meaning to tell you, Ren. There are a lot of different power-up methods for our weapons. What I did for the fight was use one of those methods." And Father went on to teach Ren about the power-up method he had used. But it was a waste of time. Ren was too confident in his own knowledge of the game, and Father's wisdom went in one ear and out the other.

"The system isn't really that complicated," Ren said. "You just fought harder."

Ren kind of tried the power-up methods. But since he didn't really believe they existed, they wouldn't work for him.

"It's not that I think you're lying to me," Ren went on. "I guess they just work for your weapon but not mine. Just like each of us came from different worlds, the games we played were different too, and that affects the way our weapons work."

Ren nodded as if that settled things. Well, in that case, I couldn't expect Ren to get much stronger than he was now.

"I can't implement them with my weapons, and you were just stronger according to your level," Ren continued. "I guess that's pretty much how the system works. All right, you two, stick together."

"Well, that's not quite . . ." Father tried to cut in, but Ren steamrolled over him.

"I have no idea why you would bother trying to change this country from the inside, but I'm sure you can do it." Ren nodded. "See ya later."

As noncommittal as ever, Ren waved and went running off.

I supposed it was pretty difficult to comprehend the strength of the Shield Hero. It sounded like as soon as Ren finished his guild jobs, he planned to leave Melromarc. Melromarc certainly wouldn't let Father leave, but maybe Ren would be able to get out without an issue. It felt a little bit dangerous to me, but even though he had expressed his doubts about Melromarc, I suspected that they would still let him do what he wanted. But if they went after Ren's life as well, maybe he would come back to us for protection.

At this point, Ren was strong enough that the average soldier or adventurer wouldn't pose him any danger. Enemies that could use ritual magic were another story, but those enemies would almost certainly go after Father before Ren.

Without a doubt, sooner or later Melromarc would pretend that Father had captured the second princess and attack the heroes and try to deal with Ren then. But we still had plenty of time until that happened.

Chapter Ten: The Egg Raffle

"Well, Ren's out of here," Father said. "What should we do now? I don't think it's a bad idea to just keep peddling until the right time comes. But how should we spend our money?"

It seemed like Father wanted to discuss our next steps now. But that would be better done back in the carriage.

"I'm going to find Filo-tan, I say," I proclaimed.

"This Filo again? Well, if that's what you want to do, I won't stop you. So we'll go looking for Filo, whoever she is."

"Indeed. In the first go-around, I believe you bought Filo-tan with the money you got from Melromarc after the first wave of destruction."

"So the problem is where and how I ended up with her?"

"Quite so," I said. "In the previous go-around, I tried buying every single filolial from the monster trainer, but Filo-tan wasn't there."

"Every single one?" Father shook his head. "You do some pretty crazy stuff, Motoyasu. But that's tricky, then. If there was some sort of sign or special characteristic that could help you recognize Filo . . ."

"She has the exact opposite coloring as Sakura," I explained. Filo-tan was white with pink mixed in, while Sakura was pink with white mixed in.

"Oh yeah, didn't you draw a picture of her before?"

"That was her angel form. She's the same height as Yuki and Kou, with blonde hair and blue eyes. She is a beautiful, heavenly creature!"

"Sakura has blue eyes . . . but her hair is pink. It is pretty unusual that Filo-tan would look so different in her angel form, isn't it? I remember that drawing you did."

What an amazing memory! But he was right. Even among filolials, having different coloring depending on the form was extremely rare.

Even if Filo-tan had ended up in someone else's possession, the best we could do was identify her based on what she looked like. We also know that she can't turn into her queen form unless she is with one of the heroes.

The only way we had to find her was her appearance. And after that, her smell, but that would be trickier to verify.

"So you were talking about how in the first go-around I didn't have anyone who would help me or that I could trust, right? So I needed to buy someone who seemed trustworthy and reliable. I have no doubt that I bought her from the slave trader. But I was frustrated, so it must've been an impulse purchase."

"You bought her from that same slave trader?" Keel interjected.

"I just get that feeling," Father said. "Thinking about this

Filo . . . I think I wanted something that was worth my money, worth the investment, to give me strength."

It was starting to make sense now. Since we now knew that the monster trainer had become Father's ally in the first go-around, he must've wanted to help Father out behind the scenes.

I think that Father also met Big Sis through the monster trainer, if I'm not mistaken, and that she used all her effort to gather the other slaves from her village and restore it. She also made a lot of stuff happen in Zeltoble, or so I heard.

And then, as a consequence of our duel, Father released Big Sis from slavery. But wasn't Big Sis still a slave when I met her the next time? Which meant that they might have gone back to the monster trainer to reapply the slave seal on Big Sis.

"I'm not really a big fan of the monster trainer's tent, but if you really want to go, shouldn't we head back there?"

"Thank you, Father. Thank you with all my heart!"

We would do everything we could to find Filo-tan, I say! So we set out to visit the monster trainer.

When we got there, the filolials hesitated to enter. The tent did have a gloomy atmosphere inside, so it only made sense that they would be reluctant. Lazy Pig seemed to say something about staying outside with the filolials because it was too annoying to go in.

As soon as we entered the tent, the monster trainer came to greet us and rubbed his hands together.

"Now what do we have here? It's the heroes, yes sir!"

So, I faced Father and rubbed my hands together too, I say!

"Uh, Motoyasu, what are you doing?"

"Rubbing my hands together!" I declared.

Now, now. Show me my precious Filo-tan, I say!

This felt just like a capsule toy machine scenario. Father was going to be the lucky one who finds the ultra-rare Filo-tan!

"Hey, Spear Bro, maybe you should . . ." Keel started to say.

"Keel, there's no need," Father replied. "Let him do what he wants."

"All right then."

Keel seemed to be concerned about my mental well-being, but I didn't care in the slightest. Sakura was looking absent-mindedly around the inside of the tent.

"What do we have here?" The monster trainer was looking at Keel and tilted his head. "So you had the ability to transform into a therianthrope all along? Yes sir. I'm happy to buy back this one at a higher price."

"What!? You're not gonna sell me to buy filolials, are ya, Big Bro?" Keel shrieked.

"Hang on," Father protested. "Why . . . why are you talking about buying Keel all of a sudden?"

Father seemed anxious to shut down the conversation as soon as possible.

"I should've expected nothing less of the Shield Hero,"

the monster trainer said. "You've chosen and raised your slaves well. Your wisdom is peerless, yes sir."

Somehow the monster trainer seemed to have figured out just how much stronger Keel had gotten.

"But still," the monster trainer continued. "With that glossy fur, despite his frail physique, I do believe he would fetch a high price on the market as a pet, yes sir."

The monster trainer was playing with some tool of his. An abacus, maybe?

"This is just my initial appraisal, but how about something to the tune of nine gold coins? And back in his demi-human form he would fetch even more. That lovely fur . . . with some grooming, I could go all the way to 17 gold coins. How about it?"

"Big bro!"

Keel was looking desperately at Father, like a filolial on the selling block.

Oho? I heard Yuki and Kou singing from outside the tent. They must've gotten bored. By some leap of association, they were singing that old song about the calf that got sold.

"What are they doing?" Father muttered, casting a glance toward where Yuki and Kou were outside of the tent. "Even if that was by accident, they should read the room." He patted Keel on the head and continued. "Sorry. Even though he's grown up a lot, I have no interest in selling him."

The monster trainer frowned. "That is . . . quite a shame. But still . . ." The monster trainer looked Keel up, down, and all over. "I thought we had struck a marvelous deal before, but it seems that I was mistaken."

Keel now was practically clinging to Father out of concern. Was this really that worrisome?

"You appear to misunderstand me," Father said. "The job of a real slave owner is to increase the value of his slaves."

Father appeared to have entered his negotiation mode. What was he trying to say? Was he talking about filolials? They should all be loved equally, I say!

Real job? Increase value?

Father must be trying to lay a trap! He knows that just like human children, whether they're fast or slow, strong or weak, sharp or dull, filolials must all be raised and equally loved! This was no place to be talking about value!

Every filolial is special, I say! There was no need to make it a competition. They are all number one.

"To you, slaves are just to be used and thrown away," Father continued. "But that's just a waste of resources. My friends here, whether or not they are my slaves, swear an oath of loyalty to me and fight to the death on the battlefield. Is that not an impressive use of slaves?"

"Hee hee. Is that so? You've given me goosebumps!"

The monster trainer appeared to be satisfied with Father's response.

Keel had gone sheet white.

"B-big Bro?"

There was the whole incident with Itsuki yesterday, after all.

Father glanced over his shoulder at Keel and raised his forefinger secretively as if to tell Keel that it was okay. Then he looked back at the monster trainer.

Keel nodded as if she understood.

"So what can I do for you today, yes sir?"

"Ah, yes. This time . . ." Father looked around the tent. "I was thinking about raising a new monster. I need strength on the battlefield."

"A new monster, you say! And what type of creature do you desire?" The monster trainer huddled in close to Father, talking quickly. "Perhaps a flying dragon? They're not cheap, but would you like to have a look? Yes sir."

Father shrugged and returned the perfect response.

"A dragon . . . Well, that's not bad, but I was thinking about a filolial as well. How about it?"

"So you're undecided, I see? Well, what do you think about taking your chances on an egg lottery? Yes sir."

"A monster egg lottery, huh?"

The monster trainer pointed at a wooden egg crate in the corner of the tent. It appeared that you could buy a random egg for 100 silver coins, but you couldn't be sure of what was inside.

"So it's a game of chance? That's nothing better than a nasty sales trick."

"What! You think that my operation is unfair, Shield Hero?"

"Am I wrong?"

"I take great pride in my merchandise!" the monster trainer declared. "Certainly, I don't mind tricking a customer that is trying to take advantage of me, but I would never misrepresent my products!"

"You say you don't mind tricking people but don't misrepresent things . . . Anyway, tell me more," Father said.

"To put things simply, they are knight's dragons."

"Hm, so you can ride them like a filolial or a horse, but they're dragons?"

"Yes, and some of them can even fly—the flying-type dragons. They are quite popular, especially among nobles, yes sir."

Knight's Dragons
A dragon that can be ridden by a person. Flying-type dragons are especially popular.

Father shrugged. It was a smart negotiation strategy to act disinterested. I kept quiet and watched the scene unfold.

"Maybe . . . maybe if I didn't have Motoyasu here or only had a single slave . . ." Father muttered to himself. I could tell that he was thinking very carefully about the right move here.

Then Father raised his head and spoke up. "How much for a filolial?"

"For an adult, 200 silver coins at minimum. Their plumage has all sorts of uses. Yes sir."

"So if that's the price for an adult, a chick must be cheaper. And even more so for an egg. So raising filolials must be extremely expensive. Am I right?"

"Not at all," the monster trainer said. "The eggs go for the same price."

"So it's a random lottery, like you said," Father said, nodding. "How much for a flying dragon?"

"On the current market, a flying dragon is 20 gold coins."

"What are the chances of drawing one in the raffle?"

"We currently have 250 eggs in the raffle," the monster trainer said. "Among them is a single flying dragon egg."

Father frowned and paused to think.

A 1-in-250 chance. Pretty tough.

Still, it's not like we needed a dragon or anything.

"You can't tell what kind of monsters are in each egg by the appearance or weight either. Be sure to buy with the expectation that it really is a 1-in-250 chance."

"You're a smart merchant," Father said.

"I'll be sure to publicize the name of the winner and use them in advertising as well," the monster trainer said with a grin.

Father scratched his chin. "Still, the chance is just so low . . ."

"If you buy ten, you'll almost definitely be giving yourself a fair shot and can choose from these lottery tickets," the monster trainer said, gesturing. "Yes sir."

"It's like a game where you focus on buying stuff," Father muttered to himself. "Is there really a knight's dragon in there?"

"There is. In fact, every egg in there has a value of at least 300 silver coins."

Father sighed, slumping his shoulders. He mumbled to himself about how it was like a capsule toy or something.

"Hmmmm . . ."

Father glanced over at me.

"Motoyasu," he said, beckoning to me.

"What is it, Father?"

"You might not have heard it from me before, but I'm pretty sure that in the first go-around, I bought an egg lottery ticket here. Which means that I likely ended up with Filo-tan in the lottery."

"How do you know?"

Would it really be possible to draw Filo-tan's egg out of a random lottery? I didn't understand in the slightest.

"Even if we don't end up with her, we can always make an exchange with the monster trainer. I must've been thinking that even if I got a useless monster, I could always train it and sell it back here. Just like how the monster trainer told me about how Keel's price had gone way up this time, he must've said something similar to me in the first go-around about another one of my slaves."

And after a moment's pause, Father pointed at one of the lottery tickets.

"And it would be hard on my other slaves if I buy a new one when they're standing right there. So I must've decided that a monster I could train would be the best move."

Hmm. So Father was saying that there was a high probability that he won Filo-tan in the lottery, it seemed.

| The Egg Lottery |
| A lottery of monster eggs that Naofumi tried his hand at for 100 silver coins. He drew the egg that had Filo in it. |

When I bought up all the non-lottery eggs from the monster trainer the last time around, Filo-tan's egg must have been among the lottery eggs, which would explain why I didn't end up with Filo-tan then. But why didn't the monster trainer tell me about the lottery in the last go-around? Had my timing been off?

For example, could someone else have played the lottery and gotten Filo-tan just before I had arrived?

"Then how about this?" Father said. "We'll pay 200 silver coins rather than 100, and you remove all of the other eggs besides filolial and dragon eggs from the lottery."

The monster trainer shook his head. "Even for the heroes, that I cannot do, yes sir."

"Then let's strike a deal."

"Which is?"

Father leaned over and whispered in the monster trainer's ear. Then he pointed at Sakura.

"Sakura, turn into your filolial form!"

Sakura looked around. "Right now? I don't really wanna here . . . But just because *you* asked me to, Naofumi, I'll do it."

With a poof, Sakura transformed into her filolial queen form.

The monster trainer widened his eyes in amazement.

"What in the world . . . I do remember thinking that you had a strange companion the last time that you visited here, but I didn't realize that she could do this!"

"So?" Father asked. "How about it? Take out everything besides the filolial and dragon eggs? No matter what we get, we'll come back here to show you how it develops. Is that sort of information valuable enough to you?"

The monster trainer thought about it for a while and then nodded.

"Understood. I'll take out all of the other eggs. Yes sir!"

"Okay, Sakura, you can switch back."

"Got it!"

Sakura turned back into her angel form.

As always, Father had come up with the perfect strategy. Since he didn't have the money, he offered information instead. I would have never come up with something like that on my own.

The monster trainer took out many of the eggs from the lottery crate.

"Now then, here is a lottery with only filolial and dragon eggs. Yes sir."

The once-full crate of eggs was full of holes. Father looked at the pile and beckoned me over. He was trying to figure out if Filo-tan was among the eggs, no doubt. But I couldn't remember exactly what she smelled like as an egg.

I could tell there were all sorts of strong smells mixed together in the crate. But as I learned in the previous go-around, this mix of smells alone wouldn't guarantee that Filo-tan was among the eggs. Unfortunately, there was nothing I could do about it.

I eliminated some of the eggs that were obviously not Filo-tan, leaving a few remaining. I pointed at the ones I was considering, and after Father thought about it for some time, he pointed at an egg.

We're not buying all of them?

I glanced over at Father in surprise, but he shook his head and whispered that it could cause problems for us if we got too many. I supposed he meant that we would stand out too much.

There was also the problem: filolials' enormous appetite. While they could acquire their own food, that would end up impacting the local ecology, which Father in the first go-around had also been highly concerned about. With the bioplants, we eventually managed to put that problem behind us, but we didn't have the same agricultural system in place yet.

Very well. I'd yield to Father's decision.

"I'll take this one," Father said to the monster trainer. "But this one and this one . . . and the ones over here, I want you to save them for me. I'll buy them later."

"Of course. Yes sir."

Once again, the perfect plan! I have never seen Father err, I say, not ever!

Certainly, things will turn out differently from the last time, where I simply bought every last filolial and still Filo-tan wasn't among them. Since the monster trainer was keeping some of the eggs on hold for us, we also reduced the chances that someone else could buy Filo-tan and snatch her away, in case the first egg wasn't Filo-tan.

"Since I see that you already have some filolials in your possession, I assume that you are already aware of the registration process, yes sir."

Father placed the egg in the monster trainer's incubator.

"If it doesn't hatch properly, I'll consider it a breach of contract and come for a remuneration," Father said.

"I tip my hat to you, heroes!" the monster trainer said. "You never miss a beat when it comes to negotiating."

Father definitely impressed the monster trainer. It was a completely different atmosphere compared to when I came last time.

But I could tell that Father was reaching his limit for playing along with the monster trainer. His tone had started to sound strange.

"I take verbal promises seriously," Father said. "If you play dumb, the Spear Hero is my slave, and he'll do whatever I tell him to do to you."

"The Spear Hero is your slave? Surely heroes can't become slaves!"

"Hmph. Well, there's no binding magic on him. But he does whatever I tell him to. Right, Motoyasu?"

"That is 100% true," I proclaimed. "If Father so commands it, I will see it through, no matter what!"

If Father so commanded, I, Motoyasu Kitamura, after stealing every last one of the monster trainer's filolial eggs, would happily burn this tent to the ground, I say!

"Amazing! You are even better than I thought you were, Shield Hero. You even took another hero as a slave! Yes sir!"

Father paid the monster trainer the 200 silver coins. And now we had another filolial egg in our possession.

Father let out a long sigh after we left the tent. "Man, that's always rough. I can talk on his level, but I don't like the guy in the least."

"You really made him like you, Big Bro," Keel commented.

"He's not difficult to play, but the longer I have to do it, the more I get scared about getting pulled into his world."

"It is remarkable," I said. "He was cold and reserved to me in the last go-around."

Father shrugged and nodded knowingly. "Well, you're you, Motoyasu."

What exactly did he mean by that?

"He was nice to you, but he totally gives me the creeps!" Keel said.

"I feel the same," Father said.

"I hate it in there," Sakura said.

Nevertheless, just as Father had told me in the first go-around, there was no doubt that it was an amazing store. There were other good places to acquire filolials, but still . . .

"Now that you mention it, he's pretty different from the other nasty merchants. He's got his own kinda weird atmosphere," Keel said.

"What do you mean?" said Father.

In Melromarc, there is a custom of enslaving demi-humans. In the first go-around, I visited other monster trainers as well, besides just the one that we just went to. If I had to put my finger on it, there was a clear difference in how this monster trainer and the rest of them treated their slaves.

"Before you bought me, there were even times when I got whipped by other demi-humans!" Keel snarled. "I don't know if they wanted to keep me or I just didn't sell, but they were laughing and smiling when they hit me!"

"That's awful . . ."

That monster trainer, while he didn't exactly treat his slaves well, at least saw them as valuable and would never whip them. He also had a few brawny guys as his workers, as opposed to the other monster trainers, who tended to use demi-humans to do the dirty work. Perhaps he was more moderate in some ways.

"But that was all before I ended up at that guy's shop," Keel continued.

"So it sounds like that monster trainer doesn't use a hierarchy of slaves to control one another," Father said. "I get the sense that he would leave any abusive treatment to the customers."

"He's not the worst, but he sure is creepy," Keel said.

"You're not wrong there," Father said.

"So what shall we do next?" I inquired.

"Shouldn't we go back to Riyute to help with more of the cleanup?" Father suggested. "We ended up leaving yesterday just after everything finished, and there's no way the soldiers would've done anything to help, right?"

"I haven't the slightest idea," I declared. "But since you say so, Father, I think it would be prudent to go and see."

"That settles it, although since we're not planning to come back to the Melromarc castle town anytime soon, why don't we go visit the old guy first before we head over? I want to thank him for the weapons."

"An excellent idea. Then let's get going!"

We left the back alley and went to say hello to the old weapon shop guy. Father gently open the door and called out to him. The rest of us waited outside.

"Wouldn't ya know! If it isn't you kiddos! I heard you kids did some great deeds!"

"More or less," Father said. "But it was only thanks to the weapons you made us."

"I'm happy to hear it," he said. "Anything I can do for you today?"

"Oh no, just stopping by to say hello . . ." Father trailed off. "Well, we did get some money from Melromarc, so it might not be a bad idea to get some more weapons made."

"What kind of weapons this time?"

"Honestly, I haven't thought about it." Father scratched his head. "I figured we wouldn't be back for a while, so it made sense to say hi before we left. We'll see you next time."

"Wait now, wait now!" the old guy exclaimed. "I remembered something!"

As soon as Father turned to leave, the old guy stopped him. *Whatever could it be?*

"What is it?" Father asked.

"I have a colleague who wanted to thank you for what you did in the wave of destruction," he said. "He wanted to at least see you."

"Oh, that's not necessary," Father said.

"He said that thanks to you kids, Riyute managed to avoid the worst of the damage. And he doesn't want to get back to his merchandise without thanking you first."

"He feels like he owes us something?" Father asked. "Well, that's really not necessary. That would mean that we owe you something for all the help you've given us."

"No, no, you've done plenty for me. There was the thing with Tolly, too, and all."

"And you've already sold us so much good stuff for cheap," Father said.

"All I want to do is do a good job. Favors don't come into it."

"All right. Fine with me."

Father and the old guy were like fast friends. He was a good man. Father trusted him in the first go-around, after all.

"So who is the person who wants to thank us?"

"It's the man who runs the apothecary and the woman who runs the magic shop," the old guy said. "You been there?"

"The apothecary? Yeah, we went there a few times before we started our peddling. And we went to the magic shop when we got Sakura's clothes. Okay, we'll go there."

We left the weapons shop and went over to the apothecary.

"Excuse me, the man from the weapons shop told us to come over here . . ." Father called out to the owner. I supposed

Father was holding back since we had only come a few times before. But the owner had a kind expression, very different from what we had seen before.

"So you already heard?" he asked. "Well then, this won't take long. You saved the life of one of my relatives in Riyute. He said he wanted to do something to help you."

"Oh, no kidding."

It seemed like the owner planned to give us some recipes for medicine. Father had mentioned that he had been practicing the Melromarc language and had just started to be able to read a little. I took a quick glance at what he gave us: a book chock-full of lists of medicinal ingredients and their uses, how to mix them properly together and in what ratios, the differences between different herbs, and much more.

"I'll also give you some more advanced recipes," the owner said.

"Wow, are you sure?" Father asked. "This seems . . . so valuable. Aren't these secret recipes?"

"Aren't you the ones who saved our village from being destroyed? For that, these recipes are fair payment."

"Okay, if you insist."

"Anyway, I've seen you taking a peek at us make our medicine. This is your chance to learn the recipes officially."

Father looked taken aback. So he had been watching them make the medicine to learn how to make it himself. The apothecary owner must have heard that Father was selling medicine from the old weapons shop guy and figured out what was going on.

"Y-yes, of course! I'll keep that in mind."

"From what I've heard about your operation, I have no problem with it."

The book would definitely be useful. When we made them by hand as opposed to with our weapons, there was a clear difference in quality. It would help pass the time in the carriage to learn to make the medicine from scratch. But since we were spending a lot of time leveling up in Siltvelt, we could always just let our weapons handle it in the end. Father was so fastidious, so he'd likely learn the recipes to perfection, I say.

"I hate medicine! It's too bitter!" Kou said.

"Then all I need to do is rub medicine all over me so you'll stop trying to eat me," Keel said.

Father turned around to spot Kou and Keel sniffing the various medicines.

"What are you two doing?"

Yuki was smelling the perfume, and Sakura looked like she was about to fall asleep.

"What a marvelous perfume," Yuki said.

"So you sell perfume as well?" Father asked the owner.

"The best of the best. The recipe's in there as well, so give it a try if you're interested."

"Of course. I'll give it a shot."

"Did you visit the magic shop yet?"

"Not yet," Father said. "We're headed there next."

"Be careful," the owner said. "I never know what that cheapskate is up to."

"I thought she seemed like a nice lady."

"That's just what she wants you to think," he responded.

"G-got it . . ."

Dealing with the merchants and shop owners is Father's specialty, I say. There's no one who would be able to take advantage of him.

When we got to the magic shop, the pig who was apparently the owner appeared to call out to Father in a friendly manner.

"Oink oink!"

Unfortunately, I hadn't the slightest idea what she was saying.

I hate dealing with pigs who have business smarts. I never understand what they're saying. But was she really up to something here? All I could register was a bunch of snorting and squealing, as per usual.

"Thank you so much for your help with Sakura's clothes," Father said. "So did you need something from us?"

The pig oinked a few times.

"What about magic types?"

A few more oinks.

The pig was looking at Keel, I noticed.

"So you want to see what kind of magic Keel is capable of?"

"Huh? I can't use magic," Keel said.

"Oink oink oink!"

Father picked up Keel and held her up so that the pig could divine her magical potential with a crystal ball. After she was finished, Father looked over at me.

"Motoyasu, do you want to learn any magic?"

"I can already use magic, Father," I declared.

Up to the powerful Liberation-class magic reserved for the heroes, I say! There was no need for me to pay any attention to what was going on at the moment.

The pig appeared to have oinked something else at Father.

"You want to see his magic?" Father asked. "Motoyasu, can you use some spell or something that is harmless?"

"No problem. Here it goes."

My magic types were fire and healing. I couldn't use the type of powerful healing magic that Father could, but I went ahead and chanted a high-level healing spell.

"Liberation Fireheal!"

The pig oinked and squealed and fell backward in shock.

"A-are you okay?" Father asked, rushing over to the fallen pig.

The pig stood up and crossed her arms, shaking her head.

"She says your magical power is incredible, Motoyasu," Father said.

"Not nearly as amazing as your own magic, Father," I said.

However, I must admit, I was the best when it came to offensive spells. But in terms of basic healing spells, I had a long way to go.

If some simple magic was this surprising, there wasn't really any point in showing her anything else.

Lazy pig oinked at the other pig, who oinked back.

"Yes. Motoyasu and Elena here can both use magic, so we don't really need to learn anything new at the moment."

I forgot to mention that Lazy Pig had joined up with us again. As usual, she kept yawning.

The pig oinked and pointed at the filolials.

"Motoyasu, should Sakura and the others learn some magic?"

"They know magic by instinct, so I'd say there's no need."

Filolials even know powerful magic like Drifa-class spells naturally. Depending on the situation, you might want to teach them some other magic too, but I had never felt the need.

"Oink oink."

"Yep, so just me and Keel. Why are you asking this?"

The magic shop owner gave a few books to Father.

"Is this what you recommended for us to buy before?"

"Oink oink."

"I see. Thank you so much!"

From what Father told me later, it was her way of thanking us for protecting Riyute village.

Finally, the pig handed Father a crystal fragment. It caught a flash of light, and Father blinked, examining it.

"And what is this? It feels strange . . . I can't quite put my finger on it."

"Oink oink."

"Oh, a fragment of a magic jewel? Thank you. So it's useful for learning magic. I can't thank you enough."

"Oink oink oink!"

The pig clapped Father on the back enthusiastically. She seemed very informal.

"Uh, y-yeah, my bad!" Father stammered.

So we left the magic shop behind. We loaded the book. Father got into the carriage and wiped the sweat off his brow.

"They're all so nice!" Keel said.

"Yep. It looks like we've really started to gain their trust. It feels good to help people, but also a bit weird that these people have gone so far out of their way to help us."

"You just need to repay kindness with kindness, I say!"

"You're right. So after we go clean up Riyute, back to our selling, then."

Keel grinned. "So we're gonna go back to selling medicine and helping people?"

"That's right. We're going to keep at it, help as many people as we can, and, just like I told Ren, see if we can change this country from the inside!"

"Let's go!"

A cheer of support rose up from everyone in the carriage, and we set off.

It seemed like everything was going well. There were some small differences from the first go-around, but I felt confident that we were headed in the right direction. As Father had said, we were off to help more people!

Just as we expected, the streets of Riyute were filled with the corpses of monsters. The villagers were in the middle of gathering the corpses and dragging them to one pile.

"Kou, you wanted to eat them, didn't you?" Father asked. "Do you still want—" Father stopped suddenly and looked over at the remains of the chimera.

The remains were crumbling and missing a lot of parts—people appeared to have taken plenty more parts from the monster after I had finished with it.

"It looks pretty much taken apart at this point, but is that the boss?"

"Indeed," I said.

"So you took the head, right? But it looks like the villagers are having trouble."

Father got off the carriage and went over to meet them. He talked with them for a minute and then gestured to me.

"They're having trouble getting rid of it, so let's help out. Motoyasu, can you help me take this thing apart?"

"Leave it to me, I say!"

So Father and I quickly took the chimera remains and cut them up. My spear was so sharp that it easily cut through the chimera's bone. And if necessary, we could've just added everything to our weapons. Like an interdimensional trash box.

"I want to give some remains to the villagers, so can you get the meat off the bones?" Father asked me.

"No problem," I said.

I disemboweled the beast, added the organs to Father's shield, and separated the meat. We put some of it into Father's shield. But what should we do with the rest? Father looked conflicted.

"Can we really eat this stuff? It might be good for the new filolials' feed."

"Hmm . . . The meat is a little tough for filolials, I must say."

"We can just process it, so there should be no problem."

I supposed so. There were various kinds of monster meat, but they tended to be pretty chewy. It was remarkable that Father was able to figure out what to do with the remains of a monster he had never even seen before. Since chimeras were a combination of multiple beasts, I wondered if we would be able to eat it. Well, they did sell mixtures of ground beef and pork back in the Japan I'm from, so surely it wasn't an impossibility.

"Oh Motoyasu, did you destroy the ranch fence? You should probably go apologize for that."

"I'll do that right now! Don't worry about me!"

I certainly had destroyed the fence in order to save the lives of the filolials there. But no matter the reason, I ought to apologize. I got onto Yuki's back and rode over toward the ranch.

"I came to apologize for breaking your fence yesterday," I called over.

"Oh, it's the Spear Hero!" The rancher came over with a warm expression.

"I did it to try to save the filolials, but nonetheless, I apologize from the bottom of my heart for destroying your fence with magic, I say!"

"I was so busy running to save my own life that I ended up forgetting about all my monsters here! But thanks to you, they're unharmed. No need to apologize."

"So all the filolials managed to escape unharmed?"

"Yes, as soon as the monsters were gone, they all came back here."

Filolials were truly unmatched in terms of intelligence. They understood who their owners were.

"That is most important to me," I said.

"Thank you," the rancher said.

I laughed. "Filolials are the jewels of this world. I only did the right thing, I say!"

"Gweh! Gweh! Gweh!"

The filolials rushed up to the fence to greet me. Yuki raised her hand and saluted.

When I got back from the ranch, Father was scratching his head about how to load the rest of the chimera remains on to the carriage. I think that Father had given some of it to the villagers, but there was still just so much left.

"I can load that onto the cart that we got from the villagers," I suggested.

"Oh really? That'd be great, I guess . . . Is one filolial going to be enough to pull both the carriage and this extra cart?"

"Oh, no problem. Even in angel form, a filolial could carry both the carriage and an extra cart easily."

"Naturally!" Yuki said, and the filolials chirped their agreement.

The single carriage was actually more troublesome since it was almost too light for them.

"Great, then let's go with that."

So we loaded the rest of the chimera meat in a pile onto the cart.

A large group of villagers came over to us. "We cannot

thank you enough," one of them said to Father, bowing.

"Is there anything else we can do to help?" Father asked.

"Nothing," he replied. "Our buildings escaped undamaged thanks to your efforts, and besides getting rid of the monster corpses, we've been able to return to normal life."

"No lasting harm is what matters most," Father said, smiling. "We appreciate you putting in a good word for us at those stores over in the castle town."

"Not at all. You're the ones who protected us. I'm also glad that the Shield Hero and Spear Hero were different from the rumors that were spreading around. We're the ones who should be doing whatever we can to thank you."

"We gladly accept your thanks," Father said. "All right then, stay safe!"

Another villager hurried up to Father just as we were about to leave.

"Excuse me, Shield Hero!"

"What is it?"

"Isn't there anything else we can do to help?" he asked. "If you're going to embark on a journey peddling, we could help you get a commercial bill of passage."

"Thank you, but we already have one."

"I see, that's good to hear. Please take care. Thank you, Shield and Spear Hero!"

All of the Riyute villagers gathered to see us off, and we finally departed.

"So it seems like I probably got a peddling pass in the first go-around from the Riyute villagers here," Father commented.

"You think so?"

"Most likely. It just kinda clicked for me. This is where we got it. I think there was more damage to the village then than this time around, so I probably stayed a while to help them repair their village, and eventually they gave me the peddling pass. Doesn't that make sense?"

Perhaps. I remembered that now was about the time in the first go-around when I first met Filo-tan. To be precise, two or three days from now, I believe.

I can still remember it so vividly. The first time I laid my eyes on Filo-tan. That was when it all really started.

At the time, I had just gotten some land from Trash and was still cooperating with the Crimson Swine.

"Father, I do believe we'll encounter Itsuki and the Crimson Swine tomorrow or the day after. He'll have just gotten land from the king."

"Huh? Does that mean Riyute?"

Indeed, it was a domain that included Riyute. And for the purpose of restoring the land, the Crimson Swine had decided to institute a heavy tax. That's when we encountered Father and his companions. When the Crimson Swine realized things weren't going to go her way, she made Filo-tan race against her knight's dragon.

That's when I first saw Filo-tan. Something came over me, and I just started laughing.

Even now I'm not quite sure why I laughed so much. It really was a mystery.

Most likely, I laughed so much because I had a totally incorrect image of filolials before meeting one. I had assumed that horses and knight's dragons were superior, but the moment I saw a filolial—the moment I saw Filo's beautiful color and shape—everything changed.

Before that, I had probably foolishly assumed that having a white dyed with pink as opposed to a monotone looked cheap.

Oh, my Filo-tan, how delightful your lovely colors are even in my mind!

Simply remembering her is the pinnacle of joy.

Filo-tan punished abusive, guffawing me with a hammer-strong kick straight into my nether region. I was sent flying like a mighty spaceship blasting off, and as the world drifted gently by, I felt as if my body had been seared by a mighty thunderbolt.

My beloved Filo-tan, wherever could you be?

"Is something wrong with Motoyasu? He doesn't seem like he's here," Sakura said.

"He's okay," Father said. "He seems happy to me."

"Spear Bro, what are you thinking about? Something tasty?"

"Why don't we add some Keel sauce?" Father said with a grin.

"Hey, stop making that joke!" Keel shouted. "Arf! Arf!"

"Oink . . ."

Watching the conversation from across the carriage, Lazy Pig let out a long sigh.

"So Itsuki and the princess might be on their way here, huh?" Father mumbled to himself, deep in thought. "Based on Itsuki's personality, I normally wouldn't expect him to go along with a hefty tax, but you never know. Maybe we'd be better off just getting out of their way and let him oppose it. We'll keep watch for two or three days, and if anything happens, we'll just have to do what we can. I'm sure it'll be fine."

"Got it!" I declared. "We'll see if Itsuki is really on the side of justice!"

"I'm just hoping that Itsuki isn't as dumb as he seems," Father said. "By the way, Motoyasu, that new egg we got, who's going to be the owner?"

"I despise dragons."

"Okay, but I think it's going to be a filolial. Do you want to raise it?"

A good question indeed . . .

"Understood! Then I shall register the egg, I say!"

"Maybe there's a way to co-register it or something, but it's probably safer for you to do it yourself."

I went ahead and completed the registration, and we spent the rest of the day clattering down the road in the carriage.

We didn't hear anything about Itsuki and the Crimson Swine taking over the domain. Maybe the Crimson Swine figured out Itsuki's personality. The idea that her manipulation skills were getting even better was a nauseating thought.

Chapter Eleven: Dressing Up the Panda

The next day, deciding we had some spare time, we took the portal over to Siltvelt. Kou and Lazy Pig stayed back to watch over the carriage. I wasn't 100% confident in that combination but figured Kou would probably handle things well.

When we got to Siltvelt, we went to the tavern where we had met that panda before.

The filolial egg hadn't hatched yet, but I could tell it wouldn't be long.

We went inside and saw the panda there, who waved over Father.

"Hey! Been a while. How ya doin'?"

"You know, the same. How about you, Lars?"

"We're just sittin' here waitin' for the scent of war to kick up, but there's been no word, so we're startin' to get bored out of our minds," the panda replied. "If ya wanna go out huntin' or something, we were thinkin' about headin' to Zeltoble."

"War . . ." As soon as Father heard the word, he appeared to space out.

He was right to be concerned. Considering how Melromarc had treated Father, if Siltvelt found out, there'd be war in no time.

"Ya see, there's been rumors around about how Melromarc has been mistreatin' the Shield Hero. It's startin' to get the people riled up for a fight. Stay safe out there."

"We'll be careful," Father said. "Now that Keel can transform, as long as we have her, we'll be safe."

"A little puppy might not be enough. Just saying."

Keel growled at the panda. "What are you saying?! That I can't be trusted?"

"Settle down now," Father said. "Anyway, that's why we came over to see you, Lars."

"You wanna hire me or something?" The panda chuckled. "Don't get on your high horse just because I did ya a favor one time. I'm pretty busy."

"But you're just sitting there playing cards," Father said.

"S-shut up! I'm too busy to help ya out again."

"Okay, well, since you mentioned it, do you want to go hunting with us? That's the real reason we came to visit you, anyhow."

"You say that now . . ." The panda trailed off.

"We'll be sure to make it worth your while. Look, we made you something. Motoyasu?"

"Of course!" I took out the clothes that Father had asked me to prepare for the panda. It was pretty similar to the maid outfit I had designed for Keel.

As soon as the panda saw the outfit, she spat out her drink.

"Idiot! What . . . what the hell kinda outfit is that?"

"Isn't this what you wanted? It's just what we made for Keel."

The panda's entourage started speaking up.

"That's what the lady's gonna go for? Not sure if it fits her personality . . ."

"Don't overthink it," Father told the panda. "It's just like Keel's, and it'll look great on you."

"I'm not wearing this outfit 'cause I want to!" barked Keel. "I'm only wearing it 'cause you asked me to!"

Even in her dog form, Keel was wearing the maid outfit. It was about time that we considered making a version with magic thread.

"Didn't I tell you before I wasn't interested in that girly outfit? Are you deaf?"

"You did, and I told you it'll look good, so Motoyasu went ahead and made it. I mean, you're already cute, so it's a natural fit."

Father took the outfit from me and handed it over to the panda.

"It's . . . that's . . . it's not my type!" the panda protested.

She looked like she was blushing, or was it just my imagination?

"I think once you have this on, all you'll need is a ribbon on your head, and voila. However, a hat wouldn't be bad either.

Keel looks great in his maid outfit even in therianthrope form, and I think the same would go for you."

"Why don't you ever listen to me?! If ya don't shut up about this nonsense, I'm gonna get pissed!"

"No need to get upset," Father said. "Okay then, well, how about just a plain old bandana on your head like this?" Father wrapped the bandana around her head. The panda didn't resist and appeared to have resigned herself to Father's fashion whims.

"Great, and now we add a ribbon," Father said. "We can put a big one right on your waist here for a nice accent." She was starting to look like a pirate with a friendly, big-sisterly disposition.

I had to say, it looked great. It was fashionable too.

"Why are you doing this to me?" the panda groaned, glancing down at herself with a bored expression. "What's so fun about dressin' me up like this, anyhow?"

"I wanted to see if it was as cute as I was picturing it," Father said. "I mean, it's fun to dress up like this. You're really pretty in your demi-human form, so try it out."

"P-pretty! I'm not pretty!"

But when Father held up a mirror, the panda stopped.

"Huh? That's me?"

"That's you all right. Cute as can be! I can tell you're caring for your hair now, like I mentioned before. It's looking really fluffy!"

"That . . . that doesn't look like me at all."

Just then, a bunch of the panda's mercenaries came over and one of them grabbed Father by the collar.

"Hey, you. Just whaddaya think you're doing?! If you keep messing with us, we'll kick your butts and send you flying!"

"Yeah, leave her alone!"

The panda shouted at her mercenaries to calm down.

"You tryin' to turn her into some sorta lewd pig? She's started to pay attention to the way she walks, taking care of her fur, stuff like that! She ain't nothing like she used to be!"

"A lewd pig? Jeez, no need to turn into Motoyasu."

Huh? Did I do something? Oh right. I ought to clarify the matter so no one gets confused.

"Please do not be mistaken of our intentions," I declared.

"What're you talking about?"

"That panda is *not* a pig, I say!"

"That's right!" Yuki chimed in. "She's a panda, black and white! And white is the most noble of colors!"

Father stared at us blankly and sighed.

"Motoyasu, please shut up and don't say anything. Yuki, you're fine."

"Yes, Father!"

Father turned back to the panda and her mercenaries.

"L-look, we just want you to leave us alone!" one of them shouted. "You keep trying to take the lady and make her dress up and look at herself in the mirror and stuff! We're mercenaries!"

"That's right," the panda agreed. "I don't need clothes like that anyway! I don't even know how you got me into this ridiculous outfit—"

"But, my lady, you're . . . you're a goddess now! You can never go back!" called another one of her subordinates, giving a big thumbs-up.

"What?" Father glanced over at them.

"You're perfect in that outfit!" another one shouted, giving the thumbs-up.

"Perfect!" A rousing chorus of mercenaries agreed.

What was going on? Everyone seemed to be changing their minds all of a sudden.

One of the mercenaries even had tears in his eyes. "My lady . . . to think that you were this charming, this beautiful!" He turned to Father. "Unbelievable! You're a guiding light for us. Thank you, sir. Thank you!"

"Hang on!" shouted the panda.

Father smiled. "My pleasure. Her beauty is all-natural. In her original demi-human form and her therianthrope form alike, she's as lovely as they come."

"Y-you really think so?" gasped the mercenary. "You're our guiding light—no, our hero! Don't stop now! Make our lady a more luscious, more alluring woman! We pledge to be her loyal pets! But please, don't stop now!"

"I've had enough of all of you!" bellowed the panda, storming after her mercenaries and Father alike with a series of powerful punches. Of course, her punches didn't hurt Father.

The panda finally relented and sighed. "What on earth is even happening?"

"You just have that natural charm," Father said, smiling. "I'll help you. It'll be the Lars Improvement Plan!"

"Whatever." Now the panda just looked bored. She scratched her head. "Let's just get going."

Father and the panda took a moment to organize their parties and calm everyone down.

"So where to?" the panda asked. "How about the same monsters that always make us money?"

Father thought about it. "Motoyasu, where do you think would be good?"

"I recommend going after the dragons that live deep in the mountains," I declared.

"Dragons!" exclaimed the panda. "Just what kind of insane hunting trip are you trying to take us on? Are you trying to get us killed?"

Personally, I wasn't aware of any dragons strong enough to kill us. At Father's current level of strength, even a dragon capable of beating an adventurer at level 100 would be a piece of cake for us.

"Before we go, I'd like to check on my bioplants," I said. I had gone ahead and planted some before the wave of destruction.

"Oh right. If we do it right, we can solve food supply issues, right?"

"Precisely. To be on the safe side, I planted them away from any human settlements, so I think we should go check on it while we have the time."

"Okay, so we'll go hunting after we check on the bioplants. Lars, do you want to come too?"

"I guess so," the panda said, crossing her arms. "You guys are plain nuts."

With that, our team and the panda and her mercenaries went over to the field where I had started growing bioplants. I had picked a stretch of wilderness that even demi-humans from Siltvelt wouldn't wander into and planted them there. Just a few weeks later, there was already a dense forest growing on the plot of land. The seeds had already ripened tremendously, and now an immense, fantastic forest had grown, bringing with it an abundant harvest and monstrous, terrifying creatures.

From afar, I could see vicious humanoid-like flowers present deep in the forest. I think it was what was known as PlantRiwe.

"Hey, this is just what everyone was freaking out about

lately!" the panda exclaimed. "What the hell did you guys do? Somethin' about a rapid expansion of plants way out this way—so it was you?"

Father frowned. "I didn't know it was going to turn into this." He turned to me. "Motoyasu, what do we do now?"

"This is no problem at all," I said. "We came at just the right time to do some logging, I say. I, Motoyasu Kitamura, can handle it myself!"

It had certainly been the right decision to not grow it in Melromarc, where the land was fertile to begin with. Even in the Siltvelt wasteland, it had grown this fast. Fortunately, I had been careful to choose an area that was known as restricted, uninhabited territory.

And if anyone dared to come near, they'd receive their just reward, I say! Plus, the plot was too narrow for there to be any real risk of malignant variant plants getting out.

Now I had to take out the monstrous plants to get the useful seeds at their core. There appeared to be flowers as big as trees wandering around.

I remembered that Filo-tan and Big Sis and Father had told me about their adventures with bioplants, but they didn't say anything about them looking like this. The kind of plants they grow into must depend on the environment.

"Let's get started, Yuki!" I called and leapt onto her back. As we rode out to the forest, I could see that the PlantRiwe was like a giant pea plant. There were other monsters as well.

But the PlantRiwe was our core concern. I would have to destroy it first.

It was like a giant tree that grew nasty, sharp-toothed flowers. They whipped long tendrils armed with gnashing teeth in our direction.

"Too easy!" Yuki cried, somersaulting out of the way and on to one of the long vines. She scrambled up the vine toward the PlantRiwe.

I pointed my spear at the sharp-toothed flowers. "Gungnir!"

A loud crack and tear sounded, and I saw that while I had blown all of the flowers away, the vines were still moving.

That was troublesome. Maybe I had to find some specific part in the plant that was controlling them. Since Father had used bioplants in the first go-around, he must have fought them at least once. How did he take care of them?

If it meant destroying the plants altogether, that would be easy. I could just burn the whole wasteland to the ground. But we needed to harvest the seeds from these plants, and I couldn't destroy them altogether. Even if I did, they might just regenerate.

"Motoyasu!" Father called. "Try a strong herbicide!"

Father and the others had also come closer to the forest of bioplants. Father took out a bottle from his shield and tossed it to me.

"I would've never expected studying herbs to come in handy now," Father said to himself.

It was a good idea. They were plants, after all.

"Impressive," the panda shouted, "but I'm gonna show you what I'm capable of!" For some reason, the panda was treating it like a competition.

She crossed her arms and concentrated.

"As the source of your power, I command you! You monstrous plants, listen and understand reason! Protect us fools! Spite Bamboo Spike!"

The panda pressed her hands to the earth and massive poles of bamboo blasted out of the ground, skewering nearby monsters.

"No way! You *are* cool!" Keel barked excitedly. "I'm gonna fight too!"

"Keel, wait!" Father cried. "It's dangerous here—don't go far from me!"

Sakura yawned, drawing her short sword. "I'm in." She danced with her sword like a whirlwind, slicing through any monsters that approached. But she was sure to never stay separated from Father for more than a few seconds.

As always, Sakura was doing a flawless job protecting Father, I say!

I was starting to get a good idea of just how far the bioplants had spread their roots. I just had to apply the herbicide and let it do its trick.

"Keel, Sakura, take this herbicide and spread it all over this area," Father called, pointing.

"Got it, Big Bro!"

Keel leapt on to Sakura's back, took the herbicide, and rode around scattering it. Meanwhile, I used my spear to shoot the herbicide all over.

The plant let out a ghastly shriek.

The damage seemed to be racking up. But even though parts of the PlantRiwe had started to wither, other vines and flowers were quickly regenerating.

"This plant appears to have developed herbicide resistance," I called. "I'm not sure if it will be enough!"

"What the hell kind of plant is this!"

The panda had returned back to the rest of her mercenaries to protect them, beating down any of the approaching monsters or vines. I must say, she had some strong arms.

"Motoyasu!" Father called. "You said this was originally wasteland, right? I'm guessing the bioplants need to dig their roots deep into the earth. The real heart of the plant is down—deep underground! Can you get there?"

"Leave it to me!" I declared.

That sort of wisdom went far beyond any simple knowledge of the game, I say. Father's guess was likely spot on.

I targeted several of the surrounding roots and attacked with Aiming Lancer. Clumps of dirt and chunks of bioplant exploded into the air. I supposed it may have been smarter to determine where exactly the heart of the bioplant was before attacking.

In the meantime, our attacks were finally starting to slow the bioplant down. I just had to aim underground and launch a final attack.

"Just one thing left to do, I say!"

I plunged my spear into the earth and attacked.

"Fissure Strike!"

The ground shook and rumbled, swelled up, and shot up earth and roots like a volcano. In the game, Fissure Strike was typically used to fire magma out of the ground, but you could also use it to force out anything that was deep underground. A massive budding sprout shot out of the earth, exposing what appeared to be the core of the bioplant.

"Brionac X!" I cried, aiming my lance at the large root and instantly disintegrating it.

Almost immediately, the rest of the bioplant started to wither away.

Then tiny sparkling seeds appeared to rain down from the area where I had shot the large sprout. So a single bioplant seed had multiplied into many.

"Quickly, get the seeds! Don't let them sprout!"

We ran around picking up the fist-sized seeds before breathing a sigh of relief.

The panda came over to us with a bunch of seeds in one massive palm. "Now *that* was something."

Father nodded. "For us, it's really not too out of the ordinary."

"So you're always up to weird stuff like this?"

"More or less. Don't worry about it too much."

"Is making me wear those weird clothes another one of your little adventures?" The panda looked at Father. "You said you come from Melromarc, right? They say that the Shield Hero was over there . . ." She trailed off.

"Uhh . . ." Father muttered. Had she guessed who we really were? Since we did go hunting together, I supposed she would be able to figure it out from his sturdiness.

"That's right!" Keel barked. "Big Bro is the—"

"Keel, that's enough," Father said.

"I'm a soldier too, ya know. I don't like getting into dangerous situations that I don't have to. I guess it was an experience though."

The panda's mercenaries nodded in agreement. They were a stoic bunch, like Ren's companions.

"Well, we did it," Father said, adding the bioplant seeds to his shield. We were really stocking up our inventory nowadays. "We need to modify these seeds somehow," Father muttered to himself. Father picked up his shield and used an ability. It must've been a power that would improve the plants that the seeds would produce.

In the meantime, I took the rest of the seeds and stored them in my spear. So these seeds would produce PlantRiwe, huh? Since we had gotten them from that plant-type monster, they seemed to have a power-up effect as well.

Regardless, I'd leave it to Father to figure out exactly what to do with the seeds. They were no different from drop items from monsters, so we could just add them to our weapons and take them out later. Father confirmed this by taking some of the seeds back out of his shield. I didn't really understand why that mattered, but whatever, I say.

"So what are you gonna do now?" the panda asked.

"Well, we took care of this, so we could go monster hunting with you guys now," Father said. "Or we could go to a store somewhere."

"Either is fine with me." The panda appeared to have gotten used to Father and wasn't on guard as much.

Father turned to me. "Lars and I are going to head out then, Motoyasu," he said.

"Understood! We'll meet up again when the time comes!"

Father nodded. "Let's go then."

Taking the panda by the arm, Father led the way, followed by Keel and Sakura.

Yuki and I went to explain to the bureaucrat who administered the wasteland what had happened. I thought about trying to learn some plant modification abilities myself, so I would be able to make something out of the bioplants without Father's help, but it sounded like a real pain, so I decided against it.

And at that moment, the egg in my breast pocket suddenly hatched. I heard a chirp and quickly withdrew it.

It was a navy-blue filolial, I say! A female, if I wasn't mistaken.

Which meant that, unfortunately, it wasn't Filo-tan.

What should I name her?

She sure was a cheerful little chick. Hmm, what to name her? I decided to let Father choose her name later.

I passed her over to Yuki. "Yuki, please go ahead and get her some food and level her up."

"At once, Motoyasu!"

"Let's race to the nearest mountain, I say!"

"It would be my pleasure! My heart is racing with excitement!"

Yuki seemed to really love racing. With that, we spent the rest of the day hard at work leveling up the new chick.

Chapter Twelve: The Fruit of Idleness

"Tweet! Tweet!"

When we got back from our day of leveling, Father and the others were already back at the carriage.

"You want me to name another?" Father asked.

I nodded. "Well, if you want to name her like you named the others, what about Navy-chan?"

Father shrugged. "Maybe. Were there any filolials that were a similar color in the first go-around? Maybe 'Ai' from the Japanese word for 'indigo'?"

"There was. Which is why I wanted to ask you to come up with a new name, Father."

"I'm not sure." Father examined the new filolial. He extended his hand to pet her. She closed her eyes and chirped happily.

Navy blue. You certainly couldn't call her black, although it was a shade of blue very close.

Father spoke up. "How about using the old Japanese word for 'navy,' then? 'Kokihanada,' and we can make it 'Hanada' for short."

"Father, your knowledge never fails to amaze me," I said. The depths of my admiration for Father had no bounds. His imagination soared far beyond mine!

"It was the name of a hidden dungeon in a game I used to play," Father said. "That's the only reason I knew it."

"Then shall we call her 'Hanada'?" I asked.

Father paused. "Saying it out loud, it doesn't really sound like a girl's name."

Lazy Pig oinked a few times.

"Since she hatched after we defeated the bioplants, we should name her something to do with that? That's not a bad idea."

"Oink oink oink."

"Right, name her after the place she hatched. That could be good."

Upon Lazy Pig's suggestion, we pulled out a map.

"Big Bro!" Keel suddenly exclaimed. "Big Bro! Since her color is like a deep, beautiful night sky, what about 'Yozora'? That means 'night sky'! Whaddaya think?"

"Not bad, not bad." Father scratched his chin, thinking about it.

"Tweet?"

Father struggled over what to name the new filolial chick. Choosing a name is no easy task, I say.

"Oink oink," continued Lazy Pig.

"What? This is all just a pain, so we should call her *Shutsuran-no-homare*, from the literal translation, 'honor from indigo'?"

"Naofumi! I suppose filolials are kind of like horses, but that name is the worst!" Sakura said.

Oho? Lazy Pig came up with a name that was not half bad. After all, a lot of filolials have names like racehorses. So I wasn't totally opposed to it or anything.

I supposed a name like Kuro, which meant black, wasn't too different from that.

"Let's keep thinking," Father said. "Keel, you suggested the night sky before. I like that. How about we name her after the moon. Maybe Luna?"

"That's a lovely name!" I declared.

"It's beautiful," Keel agreed.

"Oink oink."

I think that had to be it. Without thinking any harder about it, I decided to name her Luna.

If it had been totally up to me, I would've just gone with Navy-chan. But since Father said so, it would have to be Luna.

"From now on I shall call her Luna!" I declared.

Luna chirped in agreement.

Father smiled and looked around. "You all look hungry. How about I cook up some of the chimera meat for dinner tonight?"

"Yes please!"

We all gathered around the dining table to enjoy Father's delicious cooking and passed the rest of the day.

Lately, I had been teaching Father magic at night, but we took a break to investigate the bioplants. Well, Father did all the hard work, but I was there.

"Now that we've got some of the safe seeds, it'd be great if we had a place to experiment with them."

"Oink oink," Lazy Pig interrupted.

"We can use your family's land? Really?"

"Oink oink."

Lazy Pig offered her family's land to us. That's just what a pig would do—rush to the scent of an opportunity to rake in some cash. In the world I came from, they used pigs to sniff out truffles. It must be something like that. They must have a talent for it.

"Yes, I'm able to control everything pretty precisely," Father said. "Why do you ask?"

Lazy Pig oinked some more, and Father nodded in agreement. I supposed they were still talking about bioplants.

"Oh, I got it. That's a good plan. Just so you know, any final adjustments will be made on your family's land."

"So what did you decide to do?" I asked.

"Okay, so we were talking about changing the structure of the bioplant seeds, harvesting some food for ourselves, and selling the rest."

Father went on to explain the full plan to me. Basically, when you restructure and improve bioplants, you reduce their malignant tendencies and increase their productivity. But it would take a while to wait until that happened. Regardless, once we got them under control, we would easily solve the problem of food and food shortages.

When people were hungry, they got lazy and could start stupid wars by accident, I say. It was a brilliant plan to sell the seeds. Happiness self-earned is far more marvelous than happiness given to you by someone else, I say!

"So we'll take the seeds from our first harvest and go around selling them," Father continued. "Once food becomes more abundant accordingly, we just need to make sure people manage the seeds properly so they don't get out of control. And if all goes well, we'll have solved the problem of hunger altogether."

"Will we sell them at a high price?" I asked.

"Well, we do need the money. But if we sell for cheap, more importantly, we'll continue to gain the people's trust. No matter what the high priest says about us, the people will know the truth—that we're good people. And if there's an emergency anywhere, we can quickly go help."

Lazy Pig oinked again.

"Based on what Elena is saying, this year is a bad harvest, thanks to all the waves of destruction. It sounds like food shortages are really an issue."

So our plan was to go around selling the seeds and food to further win the trust of the people. Any famines were of great importance for us to solve. In the first go-around, as well as in the previous one, there had been a lot of hungry people out there.

"That's why we need to sell the seeds—it'll take too long for us to grow the food and sell it to people, at least right away. They should trust us enough to listen to us about how to manage the seeds properly. Still, you never know what people will do, and we have to be careful who we trust with them," Father explained.

Now that he mentioned it, I remembered something. After I had given the bioplant seeds to the village and Father cleaned up my mistake, the once dense forest around the village had been turned by and large into farms. Father told me later that he had been improving and taming the bioplants. At the time, I knew he had done a good job, but I hadn't realized just how dangerous the bioplants started off as.

But if we were going to give the seeds to the villagers right away, then they wouldn't have to go through nearly as much refinement as in the first go-around. If they slacked off and didn't care for them, the bioplants might grow out of control and ruin everything. Those extraordinary plants would pose a real test to anyone growing them. You had to take them seriously, I say. They could even end up threatening other villages.

But as long as they were managed properly, there shouldn't be any problem.

Father seemed to be thinking about just the right way to spread the seeds around. We couldn't just let everyone have them.

I did remember Father carefully managing the quality of the soil in the farms back in his village. He took charge of a bunch of monsters to keep the earth in good shape.

"We don't want anyone screaming, 'At first everything was fine, but then thanks to the Shield Hero, our village was destroyed!' We really need to decide carefully who we give the seeds to."

While he was talking, Father was making the modifications to the seeds.

"Each individual we sell to needs to take full responsibility," Father said. "Since we're preparing them so that they don't just destroy the land where they're planted, they'll be fine *unless* the people don't take care of them. We need to remind the people that they could literally be killed by the plants if they don't."

Listening to the conversation was starting to make me feel guilty. If I had known how dangerous they were, I would've never given the seeds to the villagers in the first go-around. But Father managed to clean up after me then, as well. The Church of the Three Heroes would be all too happy to blame it on us if something went wrong. But Father seemed to be keeping that in mind, so I decided to stop worrying about it.

"Done," Father said, standing up. "These are safe enough

to make food and sell. So we'll use your land to test them out, Elena. Thanks."

"Oink oink."

"Yep. If all goes well, we'll make plenty of money out of it."

With that, our next plan continued moving apace.

After a while, we arrived at a town in Lazy Pig's family's territory.

But wait—this town—I knew it!

This meant that Lazy Pig was one of my companions in the first round. That's right—Elena!

I had known that for some reason, Father always called Lazy Pig Elena, but only now did I realize that that was because Elena was the pig's real name! I would have never guessed!

And this was the very town in which I entrusted a store to that traitor, I say! So Lazy Pig was the very same person as that vile traitor!

If anything went wrong, she was bound to betray us again. Was there some way that I could kill her off without Father noticing?

Or perhaps the smarter move would be to ensure that we didn't get into the same circumstances that led her to betray us. She was reasonably powerful, after all.

In our peddling, the evacuation during the wave, bioplant cultivation, and more, she has continuously been helpful to

Father. She has some talents that I am unable to offer to him. It would be unfortunate to simply kill her.

But perhaps she didn't want to betray Father in particular. The events of the first go-around suggested that.

I remembered Father telling me that in the first go-around, he was accompanied by all sorts of unsavory characters, including monster trainers and thieves. So long as it benefitted everyone involved, he made the partnerships work.

I could take the same perspective with Elena. And if things took a turn for the worse, all I had to do was cut her down.

Perhaps there were some advantages to working alongside these kinds of people. Of course, so long as they were competent.

So I decided to continue to allow Elena to serve Father. If she betrayed us, I was prepared to execute her on the spot.

Her betrayal happened shortly after the battle against the Spirit Tortoise. I still trusted Lazy Pig at the time and had gone to meet up with her. I remembered Father had used Elena to catch me in a trap so he could talk to me, but I escaped with Portal Spear.

In the meantime, after arriving in Lazy Pig's domain, we went into a store and Lazy Pig went straight to the back, discussing something or other with the owner. Afterward, we went to her family mansion and got permission to use some of their farmland. At least that's what Father told me.

After Father planted the seeds, they quickly sprouted and grew. Soon enough, they sprouted big red fruit, completing stage one of our plan.

Laborers employed by Lazy Pig's family harvested the fruit and loaded it into our carriage.

"Elena said that she can go around selling to the local merchants here," Father told me. He turned back to Lazy Pig. "I think it'll be fine, but we can't be too careful."

"Oink oink." Lazy Pig issued a command to the workers, and we set out on our journey to sell food around Melromarc. And some medicine too.

The villages in southwest Melromarc in particular were stricken by poverty, so we sold tons of food there. In fact, rather than selling, Father ended up giving it away free of charge or for promises to be paid back later.

As a result, instead of money, we started to accumulate all sorts of random objects. That meant a heavier carriage, which Yuki and Kou very much enjoyed.

Along the way, Luna grew up quickly and turned into her filolial queen form before we knew it. Rather than her original pure-navy shading, she ended up having a white coat with navy mixed in. It was a combination reminiscent of only Filo-tan, I say, and she was about to reach her angel form too!

"Luna-chan, I can't wait for you to become an angel, I say!"

And upon my request, Luna instantly transformed into her angel form.

"Motoyasu, we're in the middle of a town!" Father protested.

Oho? What was the problem? For some reason Father was covering up Luna with a towel and directing her back into the carriage.

Once back in the carriage, Luna paused. "I'm . . . Luna."

"Uh, okay, well, no need to pull the carriage right now," Father said.

"Okay."

She had the same youthful appearance as Yuki and Kou, I say, and was completely different from how Sakura had turned out.

I took a closer look. First, I noticed that her eyes were a deep navy-blue, like the color of the sea at night. The same eye color she had in her filolial form. Next, I observed her hair, which was a glistening silver, sparkling as it caught rays of sunshine. It was a combination of colors unlike anything I had ever seen.

Haircut styles also depended on the filolial. Father listened to Luna's preference and gave her a haircut to her liking. Luna ran a hand through her hair and nodded.

"She's definitely a little different from the other filolials," Father commented.

"I don't disagree."

"It's her hair, right? Her hair color doesn't match her feathers or eyes."

"Did we do anything different with her?" I inquired.

"I mean, we have been feeding her the chimera meat, but we've all been eating it."

That shouldn't change anything. However, I couldn't help but recall that Filo-tan also had the same sort of difference in her filolial and angel forms. What could the cause be?

"Am I weird?" Luna asked.

"No, you're not weird," Father said. "You're just different."

Luna didn't seem like the conversational type. She never used sentences of more than a few words. Sakura also tended to be pretty short-winded, but she always responded to exactly what you asked her, and she liked to sing. No matter what you said to Luna, her responses were short. I figured that was just her personality.

"Different . . ." Luna muttered.

"Oink oink," Lazy Pig said.

"Are you copying Elena?" Father asked. "No need to do that."

"I'm not," Luna said.

So Luna was the cool, reserved type. She seemed to want to avoid attention. She had an atmosphere about her that almost reminded me of Fitoria-tan. Whenever we met monsters, Fitoria-tan always liked launching a single, powerful surprise attack.

"But still, why does she have a different hair color in her angel form?" Father asked. "I suppose Sakura's eye color is different from the other filolials in a similar way though."

Now that he mentioned it, Filo-tan really had a number of differences from other filolials too.

That night, Luna turned back into her filolial form and sat down. She patted her tummy and beckoned to Keel.

"Tweet . . . Keel, come sleep on me."

"On your stomach? Wow, looks warm!"

Keel went up to Luna and lay against her stomach. Luna looked down at Keel with gentle eyes.

"Man, this is crazy soft! Feels great!"

"You can come to me too!" Kou said and opened his mouth hungrily.

"I'm not going to go *inside*!" Keel barked. "Leave me alone!" Keel bared her teeth and growled.

"Luna, do you like being petted?" Father asked.

Luna nodded. "Keel's cute." And she gave Keel a tight hug with her feathers.

Kou liked Keel just as much, but for a different reason, I say. Luna was more like a little girl who loved her puppy.

"I ain't cute! I'm cool!" Keel growled.

"I . . . I wanna be like Keel," Luna said. "I wanna be small and say tweet tweet."

"Luna, you're plenty cute the way you are," Father said.

But Luna was just being sensitive. All filolials are positively adorable, I say!

"In your angel form, you're just as cute as Keel is," Father said.

"But I want to be . . . cuter," Luna said. "I wanna say tweet tweet."

Father sighed and turned to me. "They really all do have such different personalities. I feel like she'd get along with Lars."

Father was right. That panda also loved cute things, even though she didn't want to be dressed up. I think they would get along.

"I'm happy right here with Keel, tweet tweet," Luna said.

Father nodded. "Okay then. That's fine with me."

And Keel and Luna continued to snuggle, I say. I could tell that Luna really loved Keel.

"Okay, your feathers feel amazing, but man, I'm starting to get hot," Keel said, panting with her tongue out.

How could you possibly be *too* hot when wrapped in the loving feathers of a filolial?

"Luna, don't cuddle Keel for too long," Father said. "Sakura, same with you. You guys are so warm that we can't fall asleep like that."

"Okay," Luna said. "Then I'll cuddle Keel after he falls asleep."

"After I fall asleep?" Keel barked. "Just what do you want to do to me?"

All of a sudden, Luna's feathers sparkled and she started to shrink all the way down to a size that could fit into Keel's hands. She was turning into her chick form.

"Tweet!"

Father nodded. "Well, at that size, you can certainly sleep together without getting too hot."

"Tweet tweet!"

"I dunno what you're saying, Luna!" Keel said, holding Luna in her paws.

"Keel, I don't think she can speak in that form," Sakura said.

"She can't talk like this?"

"Oh, really?" Father asked.

"She can't. Naofumi, you didn't know?"

"I've never seen you or the other filolials go back into chick form," Father said.

Sakura tilted her head and thought about it. "Yeah, I guess so."

As quiet and calm as always, I say. And with that, we eventually went to sleep.

The filolials continued to pull our carriage full of bioplant fruit around Melromarc. We also stopped to sell medicine to the sick and elderly and heal them and continued to help the people of Melromarc in any way we could. We made several trips around Melromarc, but the food situation wasn't getting better in the southwest villages, so we did several rounds of donations.

Since our levels were already fairly high, we didn't need

to go to Siltvelt to hunt monsters. And now that Father had actually learned the portal skill, I didn't need to bring everyone there by myself anymore.

Father figured that the peddling was more important, so we gave it our undivided attention. And in his free time, Father studied magic and reading. He had already made it to first-class spells.

We did all that in the span of about a week after the wave of destruction.

We were in the middle of transporting the carriage between villages. Father was staring at his account book, groaning.

"Is something wrong, Father?"

He glanced up at me. "Oh, Motoyasu. Well, we're managing to sell, but . . ." He trailed off.

Father showed something or other to me in his account book. The day's sales, perhaps? We had done well yesterday, but only relative to the day before. It seemed like we were still meeting Father's sales objectives though.

"So what's the problem?" I asked.

"These are our total sales from both Elena and Keel. The problem is that one of them seems like they're doing almost all of the work."

"Well, it's obviously not Lazy Pig," I said.

Father rubbed his chin. "Actually, it's the other way around.

When Elena is doing the job, we sell much better."

What in the world! How could Lazy Pig actually be contributing to our sales? She had none of the essential qualities of a good salesman! All she did was sleep and be lazy. Every time I saw her, she was in a horizontal position, I say!

"Is that even possible?" I asked.

"It may have to do with the fact that we're in Melromarc," Father said. "Keel is a demi-human, so people might be prejudiced against buying from him."

Aha. People were afraid of the medicine and food when it was coming from a demi-human. Knowing Melromarc, it made sense.

"That is the only conceivable explanation," I said.

"I think it's the most likely explanation," Father agreed. "But actually, Elena does a good job of perking up and smiling when she sells to customers. She makes them like her."

Since pigs had deceived me so many times before, it wasn't inconceivable. But still, I found it hard to believe.

"Oink . . ."

As always, Lazy Pig was fast asleep.

"She's good at figuring out what to do when the customers are driving a hard bargain, and she knows just when to raise prices. Keel is good at attracting customers to buy, but Elena's much better at the deal itself."

Shocking. I figured that we would have to fire Lazy Pig

immediately, but it turned out that she was good at her job. And that was all I needed from her—to continue to help Father.

"Well, lately Luna's going out with Keel, and with Luna's charm, they've been able to sell a little bit more."

Right then, Luna was pulling the other cart with our supplies, and Keel was riding on her back. They seemed to be enjoying some idle chatting together. What a lovely scene!

"Naofumi, where are we going next?" Sakura asked.

"After we finish selling food in Elena's territory, we're going to east Melromarc," Father said.

That was pretty much how our days went. Thanks to all the filolials, we were able to easily transport all of our goods. It took us a few days to sell out of everything, even though we had productive days. We also started selling in Lazy Pig's territory. Everything was going smoothly.

Apparently, Lazy Pig was using the rumors about the saint of the bird god as a selling point, boosting our sales and starting whispers that she was a heavenly mother herself.

Father had just told me about some other peddler who we encountered along the way and had tried to get on the carriage, but Lazy Pig shut him down. Father had also gone out to politely turn him away.

"I just remembered something," I told Father. Back in the first go-around, Father had sold something else in addition to food and medicine. Filo-tan said something about it to me, but I couldn't recall the exact words.

"What is it?"

What did Filo-tan say back then?

"I remember that there was something else that you were selling," I told Father.

"Hmm. What could it be?"

"Oink," offered Lazy Pig.

"I could cook for people? I'm not a professional chef or anything."

At the word 'cook,' Keel and the others quickly rushed over.

"Big Bro! Can you make crepes for us? Please!"

Father glanced over at Lazy Pig. Perhaps that had convinced him that cooking might not be such a bad idea.

I, Motoyasu Kitamura, had the utmost confidence that any cooking of Father's would prove a bestseller in no time!

Father scratched his head. "Maybe, maybe that's it. Motoyasu says I sold something else, and besides food, I'm just not sure what that would be."

"Perhaps," I said.

In the first go-around, much later when I started following Father, I had simply obeyed whatever commands he issued to me. I wasn't aware of the bigger picture. I did remember one time when I went to visit Father in his room and saw some equipment in the corner. Maybe that was my clue?

"Elena, when we went peddling today, did anything else

happen? Any ideas for what to sell?"

"Oink oink." Elena was lying down in the hammock, eyes closed as she responded.

"That guy who tried to join us before was selling accessories? And is famous for it?"

"Oink oink."

"So in the first go-around, maybe I learned how to make accessories from him?"

"Oink oink oink."

"But he's supposedly a cheapskate? Still, it sounds possible that he may have helped me sell accessories in the first go-around . . ." Father trailed off.

Hmm, hmm indeed. I did recall that Filo-tan had a treasured jewel hairpin. Could Father have made that himself?

‖ Making Accessories ‖

While we were peddling, we met an accessory salesman who taught me how to make accessories. You can also use magic to imbue accessories with effects.

I think Keel also had a bone-shaped accessory of some sort.

"So how would we go about making accessories? Obviously we'd need metal, for one."

"Wouldn't it be easiest to have some made for us in Siltvelt?" I suggested.

"But we wouldn't be able to verify the authenticity or quality of those accessories," Father said.

It was a difficult dilemma. I knew that I had to be patient for the next wave, but I was starting to get bored.

"Oink oink," Lazy Pig suggested.

"You might be able to negotiate with your mom to get some accessories? That sounds good to me."

"Then that settles it," I declared.

"I still don't know anything about it, so I'm not sure if we should expect to make a ton of money out of it or anything," Father said. "For accessories, I feel like you'd have a better sense than me, Motoyasu."

I laughed. "Father, if you so command it, I shall make the best accessories this world has ever seen!"

"Let's do that," Father said. "To be honest, Motoyasu, all I've seen you doing nowadays is playing with Yuki in the carriage."

So Father had been paying attention to me, huh? I couldn't have him think I was slacking off, I say. I'd do whatever it took to please Father!

"So you'll make clothes and accessories for us to sell, then?" Father asked.

"Yes, I will!"

And that's how I started making accessories. We did have

thieves attack us from time to time, but Yuki and the filolials were always able to easily repel them. Father just had to chant Shooting Star Shield and we'd be safe instantly.

After that, I'd go and capture them. By the time I released the thieves, they always promised to amend their ways.

Chapter Thirteen: Tourist Attractions

We went back to Lazy Pig's territory, refilled our carriage with food, and headed to eastern Melromarc. We sold our food in a village crowded with adventurers. The village was flanked by a mountain range.

We took a break from business, put on comfortable clothes, and went to a local tavern.

"This place is lively," Father remarked.

"It's a flourishing village," I agreed.

The word of the saint of the bird god had even reached the ears of the villagers here, so they had already heard of Father.

"The Sword Hero slayed an evil dragon on the mountain here about a week ago," the bartender told us. "So a bunch of adventurers came by to take its treasure."

"Oh, really?" Father said.

So Ren had killed a dragon here? Maybe he stopped by on his way over to Zeltoble.

"Should we go check it out?" Father asked me.

"Is that really necessary?"

I didn't remember coming here in the first go-around.

"More and more adventurers are on their way," the bartender continued. "Didn't you know that the guild made a whole posting about it?"

"O-oh, yeah, I went to check and see for myself," Father said. "We're peddlers just passing through."

"Thanks to the saint of the bird god, our village is prospering more than ever before," the man said.

"That's great to hear," Father said, and the bartender left us to our meal.

When we went back outside, Father looked over at the mountain.

"I'd like to add some dragon drop items to my shield," Father said.

"Should we head over, then?" I inquired.

"I'm thinking about it."

"I despise dragons."

"I know that. Sakura doesn't react well to them either."

Yes, because filolials are dragons' mortal enemies, I say. And any enemy of a filolial is an enemy of mine!

Incidentally, I wasn't very impressed by this village either.

"So a dragon's treasure, huh . . ."

An adventurer standing nearby, who had looked like he had just gotten back from the mountain, overheard the conversation. His eyes sparkled as he immediately turned to his companions, then set out straight toward the mountain again.

"It's like an all-out war to get that treasure," Father said. "This town isn't lively. It's a war zone."

"For an ordinary adventurer, it might be a dangerous task to recover items from a dragon's corpse," I said.

"Yeah, you'd need to be strong to handle it. There are strong monsters in the mountains. But you can see a bunch of people bringing back monster corpses, regardless."

I nodded. Judging by what the adventurers were carrying, there appeared to be a wide variety of monster types up on the mountain.

"What type of creatures are dragons in this world, anyway?" Father asked.

"I haven't the slightest clue," I said. I knew that they were my mortal enemies, but besides that, they were nothing more than a good source for drop items and experience.

Back in Father's village, there were a few people who knew a lot about different monsters. I would ask them if I could, but I had no idea where they were in this go-around.

"I figured that in one chief dragon's territory, there were only other dragons, but I'm seeing people with all sorts of random monsters," Father said.

"Good point," I replied. There weren't only dragon-type monsters on the mountain. In fact, non-dragon types seemed to make up the vast majority. Some of them appeared to be crosses between dragons and other species of monsters. Something about it seemed to have captured Father's attention. Whatever could it be?

"So they say that Ren slayed the dragon here. But what kind of dragon was it? A boss class or something?"

"That very well may be the case."

"I played games where we worked together to beat boss-class dragons, but they were huge. Are all the adventurers just ignoring the main dragon corpse?"

"Why don't we go to the part of the mountain that is the most crowded?" I suggested. "We could probably find it there."

"Maybe. Look, all of the dragon-type monsters that the adventurers are carrying are super small, but some of them have those giant scales that they're showing off."

Now Father appeared to be glancing up toward the mountain in concern.

"Are you worried about something, Father?"

He nodded. "If no one is actually bringing back the dragon corpse itself, doesn't that inevitably mean that there's some problem or reason they can't? Maybe it's already rotten. I mean, so long as there's not an infectious disease or anything, that's fine, but it still concerns me."

"A disease, you say? A disease is driving people away from the dragon corpse?"

Unfortunately, I didn't know nearly enough about dragons to confirm or deny anything that Father was saying. I really wasn't interested.

"Exactly. I'm not sure how it would work in this world, but in works of fantasy, there are all these stories about how to dispose of a dragon's corpse. A strange amount. I think in some of them you have to use magic or even your own life force to get rid of it. I wonder how it works here."

"They're living creatures. Wouldn't they just rot?"

"Yeah, that's what you'd think on the surface. But we don't want a dragon zombie to rise or anything. They're a staple of a lot of RPGs, and they're even stronger than regular dragons."

"I do recall there being dragon zombies in *Emerald Online*," I said. "That's what I always used to play."

Father fell into deep thought.

But in *Emerald Online*, regular dragons didn't turn into dragon zombies—dragon zombies just spawned from a specific dungeon, kind of a mid-game boss.

"Hmm. Motoyasu, didn't you tell me before that relying on your game knowledge actually made a lot of things go wrong for you? Not saying that you're wrong about dragon zombies in particular."

"So why don't we just go to the mountain and crush all of your concerns?" I suggested.

"I guess so." Father frowned. "I'm not sure if we'll get much out of it, but if we can use materials from the dragon corpse in our weapons, then I guess it'll be worth it."

Father went back over to Keel and the others, who were waiting in the carriage.

"What's goin' on, Big Bro?" Keel called.

"There's a dragon corpse up in the mountain, so we were

thinking about going to pick up some materials there," Father said.

"Nice! Should we come too?"

The filolials stood up and came over to us. They seemed happy to do something new.

"I'm just worried about thieves and all of our food supply. Will one of you stay behind to watch the carriage?"

"Oink!"

Lazy Pig quickly and enthusiastically raised her hand.

"Elena, and . . ."

"So I can go, right?" Keel asked.

Father looked over at the filolials. Sakura, as always, must have wanted to accompany Father. And both Yuki and Kou looked like they had been bored out of their minds and happy to get some action. Keel had already mounted Luna.

Father pulled out a few tickets. "Let's do a lottery. Two of you will stay back with Elena."

Each of the four filolials took a ticket. I couldn't help but feel a little bloodlust coming from them.

Yuki and Kou drew the bad cards.

"That's a shame," Yuki said.

"Aw, man. Can I eat some of our food, at least?"

"Just a little," Father said.

"Yes!"

Kou looked overjoyed.

"Yuki and Kou, please take care of the carriage, I say!"

Yuki nodded earnestly. "Your command is giving me the enthusiasm to do it! At once!"

After we got back from our trip, I decided I would bring Yuki and Kou up the mountain afterward.

"All right, we're headed off," I said.

As we climbed the mountain, Father let out a sigh. "This is no different from a crowded tourist spot," he said.

The road that led into the heart of the mountain was full of villagers and adventurers. We slowly made our way up the mountain, and I started to think that Father was right. It was like we were on a school trip. They even collected a fee to let us enter the mountain.

"They've done a pretty shoddy job," Father said, surveying the area. The villagers had built a road, but everything looked like it had been constructed in a hurry. It made sense, given that Ren supposedly slayed the dragon just a week ago.

"I could not agree more," I said.

Every once in a while, dragon-like creatures leapt out of the brush to attack us, and the adventurers rushed to fight them. Since Father and I would end up revealing our identities if we fought back, we let Sakura, Luna, and Keel do the fighting.

"The church is saying that this is the legendary scene where the Sword Hero enacted his great battle against the dragon,"

Father said. "They're making it out to be a whole sightseeing spot."

"And charging a silver coin to see it," I said.

Father snorted. Sure, it was rare to see territory reclaimed from a dragon, but they certainly didn't need to be charging people to see it.

Ahead of us, we started to see the place where the dragon's corpse lay.

"They've made it a spectacle," Father said. "I wonder what Ren would think about all this."

Adventurers were lining up in front of the dragon corpse. I saw the villagers offering each of the adventurers a single scale of the dragon that the Sword Hero had slain.

"He must already be in Zeltoble," I said.

"I guess so. Do you get there by land or sea?"

"I'm guessing Ren would go by sea, although he can't swim at all."

Ren didn't know how to swim, but knowing him, I assumed he'd take the boat. That's what he did when we went to the Cal Mira islands.

We approached the dragon corpse and took a look. The horns, teeth, and eyeballs were already gone. It was as if the corpse had been attacked by a swarm of hungry vultures.

"Yikes," Father said. "They already took the heart. But besides that, all the organs are just sitting there."

"That's what it looks like."

"It stinks," Luna said.

"Yeah! Let's get out of here, Big Bro! It smells awful!"

Keel and the filolials were wrinkling their noses.

"It's been a week since he killed it, so it must be starting to rot," Father said. "We should be careful."

Father, keeping his cloak carefully covering him, approached the villagers. He had to hide his shield so they wouldn't recognize who he was.

"Excuse me," Father said. "About this dragon, here. I think it might be a good idea to dispose of the rest of the organs and the flesh. It's starting to rot, and what if it spreads a disease?"

"What the hell are you talking about?" a villager replied roughly. "If that happens, then the adventurers wouldn't come anymore."

"Yeah, but . . ." Father trailed off.

For some reason, the villagers were glaring at Father. Did they think he was trying to pick a fight or something?

Father talked to them for a while longer, trying to convince them, but eventually shrugged his shoulders and gave up.

"It's no use," he said. "They're too focused on making money from all the adventurers. Do they just not care about the health and safety of this? But if we dispose of it, they'll be furious with us."

I nodded and stepped forward. "Then I shall burn them all to the ground!"

"No, Motoyasu, you can't just do that!" Father shouted.

Huh? So should we just leave things the way they are?

Father did warn me that being reckless could come back to hurt us down the line, I supposed.

"Maybe we could at least warn the people back at the village." Father looked over at the droves of adventurers walking past us. "Where is everyone going?"

This group of adventurers seemed to be a bit stronger than average. They had classed up, at least, if I wasn't mistaken.

"Did they hear about the treasure at the tavern and came here looking for it?" Father asked.

"That must be it," I said.

"A dragon's treasure . . ." Father muttered to himself.

"Big Bro, didn't we find some before?"

"Yeah, with Lars that one time. There was so much money we couldn't even bring it back with us to Melromarc."

"Lars really goes crazy over some treasure! She's so cool!" Keel said.

Had Father been embarking on adventures without me? I supposed that you could find all kinds of dragons when out monster hunting, so it made sense that they would encounter dragons eventually.

"Are we gonna look for the treasure too?" Sakura asked.

"With so many adventurers, someone probably already found it," Keel said.

"Yeah, maybe," Father said. He examined the group of adventurers carefully. "Well, we may as well check it out. We already came all this way."

"I'm with ya, Big Bro! It's weird, but I'm all in!"

"Then let's follow them, I say."

We headed away from the dragon corpse, deeper into the mountains.

Not too far from the dragon corpse, we ran into a clash between the adventurers and other dragons, probably family of the one that Ren had slain, protecting their den.

So these were the sort of things you could find deep in the mountains. It was certainly an area that ordinary adventurers wouldn't go to.

We heard the grumbling of voices: "We've been fighting for days, and even with the boss gone we still can't break through to get the treasure."

If it were me or Father fighting, the dragons wouldn't be very strong. But the dragons did look considerably exhausted. The adventurers were starting to cut them down one by one.

Then, after a while, the adventurers finally took down the last remaining dragon.

"We did it! Now, everyone! The treasure lies ahead! Great riches await our village!"

The leader of the adventurers appeared to be a youth from

the nearby village. They were armed with swords and shields marked with a seal from their village, and by their shouts, I could tell that they had fought for the benefit of their village.

The adventurers let out a cheer and rushed toward the den. There were still a few dangerous monsters outside the den, but all of the adventurers quickly hurried away to the den. We followed after them.

There was one dragon left inside, struggling to protect the dragon eggs and the treasure within. But it wasn't as strong as the others outside, and the adventurers quickly exterminated it.

"Dragon eggs!" one shouted. "Those'll fetch a high price!"

"So they *were* guarding a treasure," another said, ogling the treasure. "I can't believe the Sword Hero didn't realize it."

Ren tended to miss things like that, I say.

"I don't like those guys," Keel said, rubbing up against Father and grabbing onto his cloak.

"They do seem like the slave hunters we encountered before," Father agreed. "Are you thinking about the lumo incident or when the soldiers attacked your village?"

Keel nodded.

"I understand," Father said. "They may be monsters, but the way they exterminated them . . . They weren't even the ones who took out the boss."

It made me sick to my stomach to watch those adventurers try to seize a prize they hadn't even earned. It was the sort of thing a pig would do, I say. The adventurers may have been men, but I was starting to see them as pigs instead. Some of them went to collect the treasure while others continued to slaughter the few remaining monsters.

"P-please, stop!"

A voice came out from the back of the den.

"Please, no more, I beg you!" The voice was wracked with grief. "Don't kill anyone else! Father . . . please save us . . ."

Keel's ears twitched and she immediately glanced over in the direction of the voice. She was clutching Father's cloak with a surprised look on her face.

"Hey, there's a kid in there!"

I saw ugly smiles light up the adventurers' faces as they turned in the direction of the voice. "Hah, they must've been raising a demi-human to rape! Let's capture and sell it."

More screams of dying monsters came out of the cave.

"I won't let them!" growled Keel. "I'll go fight 'em!"

"No, Keel!" Father said, trying to hold onto her.

Keel wriggled out of Father's grip and charged into the dragon den.

"All right, I guess we have no choice," Father said. "Motoyasu, you come too! And you too, Sakura and Luna!"

"Got it!"

"Okay."

"Keel!" Father hurried after Keel, while Sakura, Luna, and

I followed them into the dragon den.

"Hey! What's up with this dog?!"

Keel leapt barking and growling at the adventurers, already having rushed around them to protect something on the other side. Since their bodies were between us and Keel, I couldn't see exactly what it was, but it must have been the voice that we had heard before.

"Don't get any closer! Arf arf!"

"Uh . . . who are you?" It was the voice who had asked for help before.

"Get out of the way, stupid dog! Is it a therianthrope? What is a filthy demi-human doing here?"

"Hang on, that's a dog demi-human! We could make a huge profit selling something like that. Capture it!"

"I'm telling you to back down!" roared Keel, leaping forward, grabbing the extended arms of an adventurer by the teeth, and sending him flying. He landed in a heap in front of us.

"You," Father called to the man in a threatening voice.

The man straightened up and spun around to face us.

"What? Who are you? There's this weird dog in our way. If that's your dog, then I'm gonna—"

"The dog is mine," Father said. "I set him on you."

The adventurer glanced back into the den and then at Father again, who kept his cloak closed tight to conceal his shield.

"You're saying that you sent an evil hound against us?"

"Only because you've been committing actions that are obviously unjust," Father said.

"Unjust? How could capturing a filthy demi-human possibly be—"

As he glared at Father and then at me, he suddenly stopped, noticing Sakura and Luna in their filolial queen forms. By this point, the filolial queen forms were widely known to be the bird gods that had roamed around Melromarc helping people. We were known across the whole country. We had even sold medicine and food right here in the village before heading up the mountain.

"H-hang on!" called one of the adventurers. "Isn't that the dog that goes around with the saint of the bird god?"

"You're right!" Keel snarled. "And I won't forgive what you've done! Arf arf! Arf arf!"

I had never heard Keel get this angry before.

"I know that you're adventurers, so I didn't come here with the intention of stopping you from taking a dragon's treasure. But . . ." Father said with a glint in his eye as he stared down the adventurer and put a hand into his cloak. "You've given me no choice. If there's someone back there that's a part of that treasure, I will protect them. You want to sell a person? Then maybe I should never bring my medicine and food to this land ever again!"

"S-saint of the bird god!" cried the adventurer. "There must be a misunderstanding! We were going to protect it! It was held captive here by the dragons!"

Keel and the leader of the group of adventurers overheard Father speaking and stood aside to let him come forward. I finally saw what Keel was trying to protect.

What in the world? It was none other than Filo-tan's doctor's assistant!

She was still a young demi-human with dog ears and a tail, not too different from Keel. She had helped take care of Filo-tan and the other filolials . . . I had always wondered about her hair but realized now that it resembled a dragon's cut.

That was definitely her. I remember how she always pacified those dragons that Filo-tan despised so much.

"We were just going to return her to where she belongs," one of the adventurers started to say. But that was obviously just an excuse. By that did he mean a slave's tent? Perhaps she had been a slave at one point before, but she belonged here, in the dragon den. The assistant rushed over to protect the last surviving monster.

Keel and Father stared blankly at the scene and then glanced at each other.

"Unfortunately, I overheard everything that was said before," Father said. He looked farther into the dragon den. "The dragon eggs . . ."

"Those are ours!" one of the adventurers shouted, holding them tight.

Father let out a long sigh.

"Then let us handle the remaining monsters. They're ours."

"B-but!"

One of the adventurers started to protest, but Father gave him a glare that could be felt even from within his hood and cloak.

"If you're just going to protect them, then you shouldn't mind us doing the same job, should you? Or were you thinking about doing something else *besides* protecting them as soon as we got out of your way?"

"Fine, fine," the leader said. "But isn't it dangerous? That is a demi-human with the monsters, after all."

Father ignored the adventurers and went over to the assistant. The dragon creature she was holding growled as Father approached.

"It's okay. I won't hurt you."

Father gently extended his hands toward the assistant and the dragon, who stared back blankly.

Any living creature will come to like Father in no time, I say. But monsters are monsters, of course, and without a monster seal, you can't totally ignore the possibility that they might attack.

"Let's get you out of here," Father said. "Otherwise, more might come later. So I want you to come with us."

"Yeah!" Keel barked. "There are lots of bad guys out there! You're not safe here!"

Keel and Father both had their arms extended, but the assistant didn't move, holding on tightly to the dragon.

"I don't know . . ."

"But if you stay here . . ." Father trailed off.

"We're waiting for Father to come back," she replied. "If he comes back and we're not here, he'll be sad."

Who is the girl's father? Since this was the dragon den, did that mean it was the boss dragon?

What an unfortunate father to have, I say.

In the first go-around, the filolials in Father's village did tell me that this girl was really helpful though. If she had helped the filolials, then I shall accept her fully! Even if she was the child of a dragon, I had to repay her kindness!

"And your father is?" Father rubbed his face, unsure of what to say.

"Gar! Gar!" said a young dragon, standing up and taking a few tottering steps forward.

"Hey! Wait! Where are you going?"

"Gar! Gar!"

"But . . . but what about Father?"

"Gar!"

The young dragon turned to Father and pointed.

"O-okay . . . So it's really okay for us to go with him?"

"Gar!"

The dragon jumped onto the assistant's back and the girl walked toward Father.

"Okay," she said. "Please, can you help us just for a little?"

"No problem," Father said. "Let's get out of here. I'm going to take care of them," Father said to the adventurers. "Do whatever you want with the treasure. I'm off."

Glaring at the adventurers, Father took Keel and the assistant's hand and led the dragon back toward me and the filolials, and we left the den.

"Let's get out of here," Father said.

Sakura and Luna didn't look happy about having to help out dragons, but since Father was protecting them, they nodded and came with us as we left the dragon den behind.

Once we made our way about halfway down the mountain, we paused. Father scratched his head.

"Hm . . . what to do now."

Keel slowly approached the assistant and tried to cheer her up.

"Hey, can I ask you a question?"

"Uh, okay."

"What's your name?"

"I'm . . . I'm Wyndia."

"So Wyndia, is it?" Father said. "Well, what do you want to do now, Wyndia?"

"I want to find Father," Assistant responded at once.

I was pretty much sure by this point that Assistant's father was the boss dragon. Which meant that he was no longer in this world, I say.

"Before we look for him, there's something I want to ask you first. Is that okay?"

Assistant nodded.

"Would you rather live in a fantasy where you can still hold on to hope or face the harsh truth?"

She understood the meaning of Father's words at once, and burying her face in her hands, started to cry.

"Big Bro! That's so cruel!"

"I know it is, but it could've been way worse if we didn't get out of the dragon den. They need to move forward."

"But still!"

"But still, Wyndia needs to decide for herself what to do."

"Big Bro . . ." Keel trailed off.

Assistant continued to cry.

"Gar gar!" The little dragon tried to cheer her up.

She wiped the tears away. "Yes, I know. Thank you." She looked up at Father. "I want to see Father."

Father went pale and shook his head. "I . . . I don't know about that. I wish I could've protected him. I'm sorry I couldn't do anything else."

Assistant watched Father. The little dragon climbed back up onto her back.

Well, things turned out the way they did. We wouldn't be able to undo the death of the dragon or what happened to all the treasure. We also couldn't let anyone find out that the Shield Hero was the saint of the bird god, or all of our plans would go to waste.

If you left it all to me, I would've just killed everyone so we wouldn't have to deal with this situation in the first place.

"Father told us before," Assistant said, "that he might die someday—that we needed to focus on protecting ourselves before mourning him . . . I remember my little sister got so mad."

"Is that your little sister?" Father asked, gesturing to the dragon.

"Gar?"

"Yes, she's my little sister."

Assistant did her best to put on a smile and turned to Father and Keel.

"Thank you for helping us."

"No need for thanks," Father said. "We haven't taken you to see your Father yet."

"Yeah!" Keel agreed. "I'll keep you safe, Wyndia!"

"Keel, you need to be more careful," Father said. "There were so many enemies in there—you can't just rush into them."

Keel hung her head. "Got it, Father. I'll be more careful."

"I was surprised," Luna said.

"Me too!" agreed Sakura.

"Sakura and Luna, I know that these two may smell like dragons, but they're not your enemies," Father said.

"I understand," Luna said. "If I look closely, they look kinda cute. So I don't want to fight them."

"I get it," Sakura said. "They're our friends now."

Hearing the voices of the filolials was like a breath of fresh air for me. I had been starting to feel pent up and angry after seeing so many horrible sights.

"I can kill every last one of those adventurers single-handedly," I declared. "If they lay another hand on you, it'll be over for them. And then I can erase all the evidence of the deed!"

"M-Motoyasu! No, I'm begging you, no!"

I knew that Father wouldn't let me.

I wasn't exactly thrilled about having to work alongside people associated with despicable dragons. But I wasn't so uncouth to steal someone else's accomplishments either, I say! The easy thing to do would be to just go into another mountain and get some dragon's treasure yourself, after all.

We slowly descended the mountain with Assistant and the little dragon. I kept a close eye on the dragon. Looking closely, I realized it was a little different from a typical dragon. It seemed like it had blood from other monsters in it as well. I think I remember one of the filolials telling me in the first go-around that mixed dragons were actually quite common.

I don't like having it around, but I may as well give it a name. So I'll call it Monster. If it grew up into something more dragon-like, I'd just rename it.

Once we approached the cliff near the area where the dragon corpse was, Father paused and turned to Assistant.

"Wyndia, it's coming up."

She nodded without a word, and as we made our way around the crag, the sight of the dragon corpse appeared.

Assistant gasped. Large teardrops fell from her eyes.

Father gave her and the dragon a squeeze.

"No need to be brave. No need to hold back." Father nodded. "Cry into my cloak. And don't ever forget this feeling."

Assistant fell into Father's arms and sobbed her eyes out into his cloak so that her voice didn't leak out. Sakura and Luna also chanted a spell to summon a rush of wind that hid the sound of her voice.

She let out an anguished wail into Father's chest and didn't stop crying for a long time.

Chapter Fourteen:
The Assistant and the Dragon Girl

"Gar!"

Monster tried to cheer her up, and Assistant eventually stopped crying. Monster started to creep closer to the dragon corpse.

"Don't go any closer," Father said. "You might get hurt."

Assistant grabbed Monster by the tail and she stopped moving.

"Please—don't go."

Even though she had stopped crying, I could tell she hadn't overcome her sadness. She snuggled up close to Monster. They were sharing their immense pain.

"Were you friends with the other monsters on this mountain?" Father asked.

"Well, with the other monsters from Father's den," Assistant said.

Father nodded. "Too many people have invaded this place. As a demi-human, it might be hard for you to keep living in Melromarc."

Assistant didn't say anything.

"Do you want to come with us?"

"You want to look after us?" she asked.

"Well, I can't just say, 'Bye, good luck.'"

Assistant frowned, like she wasn't sure what to do. She certainly was immature to not know to simply accept the help of glorious Father, I say.

"But you should know," Father said. "I know someone who you have good reason to hate."

"Who?"

"One of the Four Holy Heroes, the Sword Hero, is the person who killed your father. I'm another one of those heroes, the Shield Hero, Naofumi Iwatani."

Assistant watched Father suspiciously.

"Father, is it okay to tell her that now?" I inquired.

"Better to tell her ahead of time than to pull her into our group, where she might be in danger," said Father.

"So cool, Big Bro!"

"Keel, don't interrupt. This is serious."

"Father told us that even if someone killed him, we shouldn't try to get revenge," Assistant said quietly. "And you're not the one who did it!" She looked angrily at the crowd of adventurers around the dragon corpse.

I understood how she felt. Things weren't easy for me either. People worshipped the heroes only when things went our way and turned against us when they didn't. Even if I killed every last person in this world, I knew that even that wouldn't satisfy my anger about the way I had been treated.

"I . . . we don't have anywhere else to go," Assistant said.

"Gar!"

Monster appeared to be saying something to her.

"Gar, gar gar!"

"Okay. Yeah. You're right." Assistant nodded.

So she was one of the rare people who could understand the language of monsters.

"What did she say to you?" Father asked.

"That she wants to get stronger," Assistant said. "So strong that she could even be a match for Father." Assistant took a breath. "I want to get stronger, too. So I won't ever lose anyone again."

"That's just how I feel, Wyndia!" barked Keel.

"That's great," Sakura said.

Father nodded. "There are a lot of ways to get stronger. Us heroes have the ability to level up monsters quickly. If you want, we can help you get stronger. What do you think?"

Assistant looked down at her hands and back up at Father.

"I . . . I want to do whatever it takes to get stronger. Even if I have to become a demon!"

"A demon? Well, I'm glad to have you. You're coming too, right?" Father asked the dragon.

"Gar!"

Monster held out a hand to Father.

"Nice to meet you. And your name?"

"Gar?"

"She doesn't have a name," Assistant said.

"No name?"

"Yes. And that's why . . ." Assistant took Monster's hand and closed her eyes, as if in prayer. "That's why I want to name her after Father. So that she'll grow up into a mighty dragon."

Monster looked at her for a second and then growled in agreement.

"That's right. From now on, you're Gaelion."

Monster howled enthusiastically.

"So your father's name was Gaelion?"

Father tried to officially register Assistant and Monster to our party.

"Why can't we register Gaelion?"

"The rules are different because she's a monster," Father explained. "We need a monster seal."

"We need to register her with a monster seal?"

"Normally, you don't have monsters join your party unless you hatch them from an egg," I said.

"I think the fastest way for you to get stronger, technically, would be for you to register temporarily as a slave, like Keel is doing," Father said. "But I wouldn't want you to have to do that."

"If that's the fastest way to get stronger, I'll do whatever it takes!" Assistant said.

"Gar!" Monster agreed.

I could sense their determination.

"All right then, so let's get out of here. We can either go back to the monster tent, or maybe Elena can hook us up with someone to take care of the registration," Father said.

"Nice to meet you," I reluctantly called to Assistant.

Father glanced over at me with a funny expression. *Did I do something weird?*

"Motoyasu, I noticed that you were being pretty quiet. Is there something wrong?"

"She reeks of dragon," I said. "I can't help but wonder why."

"Uh, why? Isn't it obvious?" Father shook his head. "Never mind. Did you meet Wyndia in the first go-around, by chance?"

"As a matter of fact, I did," I said. "She was Filo-tan's doctor's assistant. She took care of the other monsters in your village."

Assistant tilted her head in confusion. But that was just a ploy to attract Father's attention. She couldn't fool me, I say!

"And then she helped raise the dragon that you received, Father. She even gave it the same name, Gaelion."

"Do you know how we met each other in the first go-around?"

"I never heard the details."

"So what was her relationship with the Filo girl you keep talking about?"

"Just like I said. She was the assistant of Filo-tan's doctor, who was in charge of taking care of all of the monsters in your village. So she got along great with the filolials, and everyone liked her. And then—"

"What are you talking about?" Assistant interrupted.

"Uh, this is Motoyasu. He's also one of the Four Holy Heroes, the Spear Hero. But he came from a different timeline. And in that timeline, he's telling me about how we met."

She looked like she couldn't believe it. I mean, I wouldn't have expected the daughter of a dragon to understand anything complicated in the first place.

"Hey! Wait a second!" barked Keel. "Why can Motoyasu understand Wyndia when he couldn't understand me? Wyndia, are you a boy?"

"No, I'm a girl!"

"A girl, huh . . . So maybe he can only understand people who were close to Filo," Father said. "Anyway, Motoyasu, just what relationship did Assistant have with Filo?"

"She raised Filo-tan's greatest rival, I say! But Filo-tan will never lose!"

"Um . . ." Father shook his head. "So she's a dragon girl. She took care of the monsters, was Filo-tan's doctor's assistant, and raised Filo-tan's rival. That's a lot of roles. You must be a talented girl."

Assistant blushed and looked away. But I knew that she was

just feigning it. I knew how she looked down on Filo-tan for not being able to fly like Gaelion!

Oho? I started to remember a time when Filo-tan was flying. *Did that really happen?*

"I don't know what he's talking about," Assistant mumbled.

"Gar?"

"Yeah, don't worry too much about it," Father said. "Most of the time Motoyasu can't understand women for whatever reason, but he seems to be able to understand you, so that's fine."

"That doesn't make any sense."

Father chuckled and then let out a long sigh.

"Regardless, I've noticed for a while that you reek of dragon," I told her. "You should thoroughly wash yourself to remove the stench."

"What's wrong with smelling like dragon!" Assistant exclaimed. "You smell like filolial! So badly that I think my nose might fall off!"

"Bah!" I spat. "I should've expected that a dragon girl would never be able to comprehend the elegant scent of the filolial!"

Assistant's face went from an angry twitch to a broad grin. She was that happy about being called a dragon girl. What nonsense.

"Yes, because dragons are the strongest monsters!" she said.

"Filolials are the strongest, I say!"

"Filolials are just birds that can't fly!" shouted Assistant. "They're not any different from horses! Knight's dragons are a thousand times better!"

I narrowed my gaze.

"So it appears that you want to die young," I hissed.

Father would probably stop me anyway, so I might as well threaten her.

Knight's dragons? There was nothing remotely good about a knight's dragon! They could barely fly any better than a dragonfly—lowly creatures that couldn't even sniff the feet of a filolial!

Father was holding his head in his hands. Was this really that upsetting?

And our group became as noisy and lively as ever, I say.

Epilogue: To Filolials, I Sound My Cry of Passion

Once we got back to the village, Father warned a man who seemed to be a town representative about the rotting dragon corpse and recommended taking care of it as soon as possible. But the man didn't seem too pleased about the suggestion.

We then went to board the carriage. The filolials weren't happy about a dragon getting on with them, so we ended up having Gaelion fly by herself outside of the carriage.

We debated whether or not to stay at an inn in the village, but the swarm of tourists had jacked up the price of a place to stay for one. Plus, Assistant didn't seem to love the idea of staying in the town that killed so many of her family members, so we decided to leave the town behind.

A little while after we departed, the sun was about to set, so we stopped on the roadside and set up camp.

Up until then, Assistant and I had been clashing, to say the least. But in front of the campfire, everyone fell silent, watching the flickering flames.

Father was sitting next to her and gently patted her and Gaelion on the back.

Assistant looked exhausted. She leaned against Gaelion and fell asleep.

"Today was crazy, wasn't it, Wyndia?" Father muttered. "It must've been tough for you. Rest well."

Gaelion growled softly.

"B-big Bro!" called Keel. "What about us?!"

Sakura and Keel were getting ready for bed and couldn't get enough of Father. Father patted Gaelion once more, stood up, and walked over to them. After Sakura and Keel were fast asleep, Father called me over.

"So based on what you're saying, in the first go-around, the original Gaelion was killed. Assistant was sold into slavery and was treated horribly but somehow eventually came to my village. I guess it all worked out in the end."

There was no doubt that Assistant had gone through some rough times in the first go-around.

"I hope that girl Filo isn't going through anything like that," said Father.

I shuddered and nodded. "I hope so."

We hadn't managed to find her yet. It wasn't impossible that she had ended up with a cruel monster trainer. Which made it all the more important that I never give up my search for her.

If she had fallen into dangerous hands, I would rescue her at all costs. And take the lives of those who hurt her as a just punishment.

"Is it possible that we won't be able to meet Filo-tan because you've been helping me out in this timeline?" Father asked.

"I don't believe that in the slightest."

"I mean, I only met Filo-tan after going through terrible experiences, right?"

"That part is true," I said. "But even if you only met Filo-tan by undergoing traumatic experiences, that doesn't change that she is out there somewhere."

Keel was the perfect proof of that. Even if the place we encountered her was different, she had still been there all along.

"You're right. She's probably out there somewhere."

"Mmm . . . Naofumi . . ." Sakura was mumbling in her sleep. Father glanced over at her with a smile.

"It's not going to be easy to find her," he said.

"But I won't give up, I say! No matter what happens, no matter how many times the time loop resets, I will never give up! For Filo-tan, and for you, Father!"

Father sighed. "You're pretty incredible, Motoyasu. If I was going through the time loop, I'd want to give up sooner or later."

We were talking about Filo-tan here! Of course, I would never give up.

"But everything we've done has helped me get closer to her," I said. Even all of the foolish deeds I had done, even turning against Father when he was falsely accused—everything had led me to this day.

"When things go wrong, there is still the possibility that

those circumstances will allow me to reunite with my beloved Filo-tan," I said. "Because with each passing day, I can tell that we're getting closer. One step at a time!"

Even though she didn't hatch from the egg at the monster tent, I was sure that she wouldn't stay there for long. As beautiful as she was, someone was bound to buy her quickly. I would find her, even if it took my whole life!

Father looked surprised at first and then smiled at me.

"You sure are an optimist, Motoyasu."

"That I am!"

I had a vague memory of Father shouting at me that I was *too* much of an optimist in the first go-around, but maybe that was just my imagination.

"Oh, Filo-tan!" I cried. "How I long for your sweet embrace! But soon we shall be reunited, I swear it!"

With my resolution renewed, I lay down to go to sleep. Tomorrow, my search would begin.

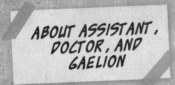

Wyndia is a dog demi-human who was raised by a dragon. Since she got along well with monsters, she took care of them in Motoyasu's village.

Doctor is an alchemist who was expelled from Faubrey, accused of heresy. Ratotille Anthreya. Ratotille, or Rat, focused on conducting magical research to create useful monsters to serve humans. Rat used magic to make monsters stronger, but Wyndia thought that the best way was to have them fight against each other and train. When Rat came to the village, the two discussed the best ways to strengthen the monsters in the village. That's how Rat became the doctor of Naofumi's village, and Wyndia the assistant.

Not long after, an egg from a wooden box hatched into Gaelion, a flying dragon. Gaelion is a Wyr dragon, extremely loyal and noble. Wyndia named her after the dragon that raised her, and Wyndia and Rat raised Gaelion.

Baby Gaelion at one point consumed a Dragon core and went berserk. But Wyndia was able to transfer Father Gaelion's soul to the young Gaelion. So Gaelion has two different souls in one body.

Gaelion

Flying dragon (Wyr)

Gaelion is a flying dragon hatched from an egg found in a wooden crate. He's named after Gaelion, the dragon that raised Wyndia. Filolials and dragons don't get along, like cats and dogs.

Wyndia

Naofumi's slave

Wyndia is a dog demi-human raised by the dragon that Ren slayed. Because dragons and monsters raised her from a young age, she gets along with monsters and helps take care of the monsters in Naofumi's village. She also took care of Gaelion after he hatched.

Ratotille

Alchemist

She was an alchemist in Faubrey, but she was banished after conducting illegal research. She's so devoted to her research that she wouldn't mind becoming a slave in order to continue it. Her main focus is research on monsters, and she wants to create monsters that can aid humans. She believes that monsters and humans are equal.

CHARACTER CHAT
THE END OF VOLUME 3

So I guess that's it for today. Motoyasu did a good job of not screwing anything up too much this time. At least by his standards.

It looks like it's going pretty smoothly to me!

I am honored to receive your praise, Father! I feel better than ever!

That's hardly praise. You're just not screwing anything up. So keep up the pace.

Still, I remember that our peddling got really tough at around this point . . .

A fun adventure alongside filolials, I say!

I only remember being stuck in the carriage all the time, but I think it all turned out fine in the end. Melromarc had already embraced me as the saint of the bird god.

You're right. It was fine in the end. I think Keel and the others are doing a really great job!

We undid the curse of the pig on her, at least temporarily.

I don't think Keel would be happy to know that you're still thinking that way.

She causes more trouble in her dog form too.

Our journey is just beginning, I say! Tune in again next time!

The Reprise of the Spear Hero Vol. 3
(YARI NO YUUSHA NO YARINAOSHI Vol.3)
© Aneko Yusagi 2018
First published in Japan in 2018 by KADOKAWA CORPORATION, Tokyo. English
translation rights arranged with KADOKAWA CORPORATION, Tokyo.

ISBN: 978-1-64273-106-4

Written by Aneko Yusagi
Character Design by Minami Seira
English Edition Published by One Peace Books 2021

Printed in Canada
1 2 3 4 5 6 7 8 9 10

One Peace Books
43-32 22nd Street STE 204 Long Island City New York 11101
www.onepeacebooks.com